Virgin Hall

Virgin Hall

Janet Taliaferro

Copyright © 2011 by Janet Taliaferro.

Janet Taliaferro
Leesburg, Virginia
janetmtaliaferro.com
author@janetmtaliaferro.com

ISBN 978-0-9844535-1-1

ACKNOWLEDGMENTS

First thanks must go to the girls on the third floor of Virginia Hall during my freshman year at SMU. There were many more than four of us, but my particular friends – Anne Lauhon, Bitsy Epstein, Jane DeBoyrie, Dana Sullivan, Uldene Longstreth and Margery Lucas – lent little parts of themselves, their names, and their backgrounds, thus enabling me to forge the characters to carry this wholly fictitious story. I have seen only two of them since that first year, but they live fondly in my memory.

The staffs of Fondren Library and the Loudoun County Public Libraries were a great help in searching the archives and refreshing my memory of years long past. I would be remiss not to mention three people who mentored me through my academic years at SMU: Dr. Gusta Barfield Nance, who believed in me, Father Curtis W. V. Junker, and Martis Michaelson, who challenged me intellectually and shared his Phillip Morris cigarettes with me while we sat on the metal fire escape steps of the library and talked.

Finally, my invaluable editors: Christine DeSmet of the University of Wisconsin, who tactfully steered me away from some unwise decisions about plot and character, and the ultimate professional, Arnie Friedman, who dealt swiftly with my problematic punctuation and whose humor brought me a new appreciation of a manuscript I had grown tired of amending. He, along with Molly B. Tinsley, made it a much stronger book than the first drafts. The delightful stories of San Angelo came to me courtesy of Elizabeth McGuinness and Lin Sanches. Jo Golden and Tracey Holinka of Chaos To Clarity were the instruments by which this book finally arrived in electronic print. Thanks also to my encouraging readers, Marilyn Walker, Sarah and Courtney Taliaferro, and Karetta Hubbard.

I also thank all the wonderful people I have gotten to know in working with various parts of Planned Parenthood Federation of America. A question by a young staff person, "What was it really like before Roe v. Wade?" was the catalyst for this story. Anonymous thanks, too, for my special friend who shared all of her story about an abortion in the fifties. I couldn't have written this without you.

Author's note: For plot purposes the author has changed details of sorority rush and she is also aware that Passover and Easter did not coincide in 1952.

CHAPTER ONE

Monday, April 29, 1985

A fine rain turned First Avenue to patent leather. I leaned my forehead against the windowpane and watched yellow taxis streak the scene with slashes of white light, a contrast to the quiet spots of watery color produced by the few neon signs in the Sutton Place neighborhood.

I thought about the odor of wet pavement and the tang of cold, dusty glass close enough to stir memory but not enough to summon images. "What's wrong with me?" Here I am in New York, which has always been home to me. I have a loving husband and an achieving daughter. "It must just be chemical," I said to myself. "I'm so damned depressed. Maybe it was just a hangover from a long cold winter."

The lights were off in the living room of the apartment. At last, I pushed away from the window with a thrust of my elbow and walked in darkness toward my daughter's room.

The "elegant rabbit warren" was the way I secretly referred to the apartment I shared with my husband, Hugh Cauthron, and daughter Elise.

Elise's fourteen-year-old presence was indicated in the April quiet by the faint but unmistakable sound of murmured conversation, Hugh's by the scratch of the dot matrix printer in the study. I was irritated by both sounds. Elise's telephone conversation with her friend Tiffany had long exceeded the parental time limit. It was time to assert authority.

In a way, I found the sound of the computer more disturbing than the telephone conversation. "Why couldn't I marry some normal man who just watches television all the time?" But then, Hugh was far more attentive than the man who had taken up too much of my life.

My footsteps slowed almost imperceptibly as I passed the study door, but instead of interrupting Hugh's concentration, I continued down the hall, aware that my irritation was mixed with the knowledge that I really wanted to be alone this evening.

"Elise," I said softly but firmly against the jamb of my daughter's closed door. No answer except for a "Yeah, uh-huh," obviously uttered into the phone.

"Elise!" Still no response.

Usually the girl was afforded the privacy due an adult by her parents, but this time I opened the door without knocking. Indignant slate blue eyes looked at me. Elise took the receiver from her ear and rested it on her shoulder, her other hand covering the mouthpiece. The headset of a Sony Walkman sat atop her small head, ridiculously askew, occupying the ear not engaged by the telephone. The other earpiece bunched up her dark curls in an unkempt cockscomb.

Nevertheless, the voice and the manner were imperial. "Yes, mother?"

"Elise, it's after ten. Tell Tiffany goodbye and get ready for bed."

"In a minute, mother." Elise was not pleased.

"*Now,* my dear," I said and stood my ground while the girl said a hasty farewell, her disgust with her mother patent in her voice.

"Tiff, Mom's hanging over me. Gotta run. Talk to you later. Yeah, bye." Elise hung up the phone and placed it on the round table by her bed. "Was that satisfactory?" Elise asked with a prim smile that contradicted the fire in her eyes. She had changed her tone. The question was phrased in her best prep school voice.

Weary, I closed the door without response. I could hear my daughter's feet hit the floor with a bad tempered slap. At least the process of getting to bed had begun.

I could hardly complain. Elise was an excellent student, a model of decorum at her expensive private school, and she seemed genuinely well liked by her friends and teachers.

It was just her mother she loathed, and I found the hate debilitating and bewildering even though friends assured me it was normal at her age.

I walked back to the living room through the length of the apartment, past the minute kitchen and formal dining room on my left opposite the master bedroom and bedroom cum Hugh's office. Elise's room had once been a servant's quarters in an earlier, and if not more affluent, at least more gracious day. Both child and parents found the isolation and privacy appropriate.

I was sure-footed in the dark, avoiding by habit and instinct the exquisite pieces of seventeenth and eighteenth century furniture Hugh and I had lovingly collected in the early years of our marriage—early years, but not necessarily young years.

I sat down in the wing chair by the empty black maw of the fireplace, stark against the white of the Adams mantel. I sighed and willed my muscles to relax. My eyes had just closed when the phone rang.

If that's Tiffany, I'll kill her, I thought, moving quickly to the block front lowboy and picking up the phone, anxious not to have the ring disturb Hugh in the den. "Hello?" My voice was as firmly efficient as it always was at my office.

"Miz Caughron? Miz Roberts here. The voice from the past." The unmistakable West Texas accent made the word come out something like "pay-ust."

"Well, for God's sake, E.A.! How are you and what brought about this unexpected pleasure?"

"Sort of a combination of nostalgia and pride, I guess," Eleanor Ann said, and then continued with a rush of words I remembered so well. "Now what would you think about coming out here to Texas in about four weeks? You owe me a visit anyway. It's been five years since Jim Ed and I were in the Big Apple and we had a visit."

E.A. had dated one Big Man on Campus after another until her senior year, when the red haired Aggie and cattle rancher I met at her home that first Thanksgiving began to show up at the Pi Phi House. It wasn't long before Jim Ed Roberts had cut her smoothly out of the herd without need for a horse.

"Oh, E.A., I couldn't possibly," I said, although I was aware that the thought of a trip to Texas had a strong, nostalgic pull for me, too.

"I'll tell you what started all this. It's my daughter, Edwina, named for Jim Ed, as you know, anyway, Sheila. You'll never guess. She's going to be valedictorian of the graduating class at SMU! Now, how's that for a couple of C students like Jim Ed and I? Anyway, I'm just so proud of her, and I want to show her off. Also, I got to thinking about the four of us our freshman year there and I just suddenly got a real yen to see y'all. Miriam and I've gotten together over the years and I asked her and she thought it would be a great idea. Can you come?"

As Eleanor Ann talked, I felt the muscles of my face relax into a broad smile. I had always been in awe of Eleanor Ann's ability to dominate a conversation without ever abandoning her drawl.

"God, E.A., you haven't changed a bit. You must set the record for the number of diphthongs uttered in a lifetime!"

"Huh?"

"Never mind. It's wonderful to hear your voice. But about coming down, I really can't say. I'm awfully busy. We're just at the end of our annual fund drive at the office. I have zillions of things I've let slide in the meantime, but it would be great to see everybody. Have you talked to Paula?"

"She's so hard to get ahold of. I'm letting Miriam do that. I said I'd call you and if you could come, we'd work on Paula."

"What's she doing? I completely lost track of her after that year."

"She's a nurse—in Calcutta somewhere."

"Calcutta?"

"I think she works with that Saint Teresa outfit …"

"Mother Teresa," I corrected absently.

"Whatever; anyway, it's some sort of missionary work. She's been there for about ten years now, but Miriam and her husband managed to hook up with her when they were in Singapore and they made that trip at least seven or eight years ago. Paula came over on a vacation and met them at the Raffles."

"Miriam would look Paula up, bless her. I still get a holiday card from her every year, even though I quit sending Christmas cards years ago, even to you, old dear. I apologize for being such a bad correspondent."

"Forget it. Who has time? But I am going to be disappointed if you don't come down. We've just got to have our own reunion. The four of us haven't laid eyes on each other since 1952. You know that's been thirty-three years? You suppose they would let us go to the class stuff even if we didn't graduate?"

"I don't know that I'd want to. What I really want is to see all of you."

"Then you'll come, right?"

"E.A., I can't commit myself, but I really want to. Write me the details." I gave Eleanor Ann my office address, and was aware that Hugh was standing at the door of the study. Light from the room made a bright rectangle on the parquet floor, his distorted shadow a freeform blot in it center.

Eleanor Ann was saying, "Now you come. Hear?"

"I'll try. I'll really try. And it's so good to hear from you." I could hear the vibrancy in my own voice. Eleanor Ann's enthusiasm had struck a spark.

"Let me know soon. I'm countin' on it."

"I will, I promise."

We said our good-byes and I turned toward my husband. His face was completely in shadow, but the light outlined his blue shirt in silver.

"What was that all about?" His voice was amused.

"That was my old college roommate at SMU. Do you remember me telling you about Eleanor Ann Cabel? I had lunch with her and her husband a few years ago when they were in New York."

"The busty blonde?"

"Blonde, but I don't remember ever saying busty."

"I'll bet she was, though," he said.

"How do you know?"

"It just goes with the Kilgore Rangerette description you always gave of her." Hugh moved toward me, pulling me lightly against him.

"She wants me to come down to a sort of reunion with the other two girls who were our suitemates."

"Why don't you go? You've earned it after a dynamite campaign."

"Go where?" Elise stood in a long cotton nightgown. Fuzzy slippers muffled her step.

"Texas," I said.

"What for?" the girl asked, a decided sneer in her voice.

"My old roommates from college are getting together."

"I thought you went to Columbia?"

"I graduated from there, but I went to Southern Methodist University my first year, remember?"

Elise shrugged, dismissing the subject.

"I told your mother she ought to go. She's earned a vacation, and getting together with old friends is always a treat," Hugh said.

"I can't imagine it would be very interesting," Elise said. She hugged her father goodnight and gave me a cool peck on the cheek.

Hugh went back to the computer he alternately adored and swore at. I started for the living room and something made me walk back toward Elise's room. At the door, I distinctly heard her giggle and then whisper.

In a rage, I yanked open the door.

"Off the phone, young lady!"

Startled, she hung the phone up hurriedly.

"Was that Tiffany again?"

My anger was met with a smoldering look. "Yes, and you wouldn't like what we were talking about."

"Then you'd better not tell me what it was. But since you're awake, get up and hang up your uniform. I've told you a hundred times not to leave it on the chair."

Reluctantly, she dragged out of bed and I thought I heard her say under her breath, "You're not my mother and I don't have to do what you say."

"I am your mother and you do have to do what I say."

"No you're not. You told me my mother and father were dead and I was adopted, just like you were when Aunt Grace and Uncle Howard adopted you."

"What are you talking about?"

"My mother's dead. You said so."

"I never said that. I said your father was dead."

"You're a liar. Daddy said so, too."

I was aware that Hugh had come up behind me, drawn by the wrangling.

"Isn't that right," Daddy? "Didn't you tell me when I was little that I was adopted? And didn't you say my parents died in an accident like Mom's?"

Hugh walked past me and put his arm around his now trembling daughter. Her eyes, so like her biological father's, had filled with tears of real pain. I wanted to take her in my arms, too, but knew this was not the time.

"Sit down, Elise." Hugh pulled her onto the edge of the bed and wrapped his other arm around her. "We haven't talked about it in a long time, and you haven't asked, so we both thought you knew exactly what the story was." He nodded at me and I nodded back in corroboration. "Sheila, why don't you go on while I clear this up with Elise?"

I gave him a warning look, but I was sure Hugh was only going to stick to the facts of how he became her father and not tell her the whole story. One day I would tell her—when she was older. Perhaps.

I walked to Hugh's den and sat on the couch, my head in my hands. The printer abruptly stopped its scratching. How had all this happened in the space of thirty minutes? First the reminders of all the events of my year in Texas and then Elise going to the heart of everything that was a result of that period in my life.

Hugh came in and sat next to me. I let him enfold me the way he had comforted his daughter. "Damn." He said it as softly as he said almost everything. "I'm so sorry. Somehow when we told her as a little girl, she got what happened to you mixed up with my adopting her."

"There's not much similarity. I was ten years old when my parents died. She was two when we married."

"I know. But still, she just didn't get it straight. Since she almost never mentions it, I thought she knew. It seems this all came out because Tiffany has been prying information out of her father about what the legal rights are on adoption records. She had some fantasy about finding out who her real parents are."

"What did you tell her about her father?"

"I said you would tell her all about it when she was old enough, but that he was a man with some fine qualities."

"And a few that weren't so great and one really bad habit."

"Speaking of old times, I think you ought to make the trip to Texas."

"Why?"

"I don't know. I've always felt you were avoiding something."

"I've told you absolutely all that happened that year."

"No unfinished business?" I just shrugged and he held me tighter. "You said you didn't tell E.A. about Elise. Does that bother you?"

"Not really. I would tell her everything if the subject ever came up." We sat silent for a moment. "I do sometimes think I should have told his parents but he was so adamant about denying his paternity and swearing me to secrecy."

"Okay. All the drama aside, you need a break. Leave the hormonal teenager to me for a few days, anyway."

"She's obviously not going to miss me." Her earlier dismissive attitude and her cutting words brought out a flash of rebellion in me. I had to smile, "God, I sound just like her."

Hugh laughed. "I guess that's where she gets it. Anyway, I'm glad to see you smile. Maybe a little Texas sunshine will bring back my wife with the serene disposition."

"I don't know about that, but I think I might really like to go and see everybody. I'll see what happens at the office tomorrow and then decide."

"Bedtime," said Hugh. I kissed his neck.

We walked down the hall with our arms around each other. I hesitated at the door to our bedroom, realizing I already had begun to plan what to pack to go to Dallas when a chill replaced excitement. Suddenly, I was standing in the door of my bedroom in Brooklyn, looking at the suitcases packed for college. That September flight to Dallas had certainly changed my life. I left Brooklyn a schoolgirl, returned at Christmas a woman in love, and left for the second semester of college totally changed.

It all seemed so long ago. More importantly, Hugh was right. A lot had happened since the end of that freshman year that I had not shared with my friends. But then, there was no reason to discuss it with them even now. After all, this was going to be a fun girlie weekend.

CHAPTER TWO

My job with the World Children's Fund sometimes took me out of New York but usually to Chicago and Los Angeles. Most of my work as development officer for the Fund was done at my desk, on the telephone, or over lunch with wealthy East Coast donors who made up the majority of the Fund's large givers. My job was mostly to oversee an enormous direct mail campaign, which was the backbone of the Fund.

By coincidence, Gerald Chinn, the director of World Children, had wanted for years to make contact with a wealthy Dallas businessman, so when I had asked for vacation time to go to Dallas, Gerald had offered to pay my way, provided I would try to get an interview with the man.

On impulse, I called the Dallas office of Theodore Behneke for an appointment. I was put on hold, the phone clicked several times, and once I heard a snatch of conversation. Then a male voice came on the line. "What?" The voice dimmed as though the speaker had turned away from the instrument. "Lilah, have I done this right? Which one of these damned buttons ... I'll never learn this new system."

I took a chance. "Mr. Behneke?"

"What? Yes? Who is it?"

"Mr. Behenke, this is Sheila Cauthron and I'm with the World Children's Fund in New York. I'm going to be in Dallas the end of May and I wondered if I could make an appointment with you?" Without a breath, I continued to hold Ted Behneke's attention until I had persuaded him that it would be a breach of etiquette to not spend fifteen minutes with this charming woman who toiled for a just cause. I got my appointment.

The serendipity of all this made me giddy with anticipation. I felt there was destiny in this trip. Everything seemed to be falling into place: the prospect of seeing old friends and a free trip in the bargain.

The mood continued as I deplaned at DFW. The Hartman carryall, which accompanied me everywhere, was heavy. I stopped at the edge of the red carpet and shifted it to the other shoulder, then continued toward the baggage claim area, heels clicking on the hard floor. As I passed one of the vendor stalls on the concourse, the odor of baking sugar cones stopped me.

Why not? The taste of two scoops of rocky road in a sugar cone carried me happily through the trauma of retrieving my suitcase and getting a taxi.

The long drive from the airport to downtown provided a view foreign to the Dallas I remembered.This trip on an eight-lane interstate highway passed miles of antiseptic looking suburbs and clumps of multistoried buildings. There was the air of a fevered rush as though the building would never stop. Cranes stood in clusters on the landscape, looking like the water birds for which they were named. On my first trip to Dallas, the old drive from Love Field to the campus was tree lined and had the feel of a suburb. Suddenly I was back to that September day.

Dallas, Texas
Sunday, September 16, 1951

I sat on the bed farthest from the windows, feet on the floor, back straight, hands in my lap, like the good little Catholic school girl I was taught to be, and waited for my roommate. My pink chambray dress looked fairly unwrinkled after the long flight from LaGuardia to Dallas, but I kept my elbows clenched against my hipbones to hide the damp half moons under my arms. My stomach shivered. I was aware I wanted to run, but there was no thought of any possible destination. If I had known then how the events of this single year would infinitely change my life, I would have run blindly as a deer. But then, had I done so, I would have missed the blessings of knowledge dearly gained and the support of good friends.

I stared at my feet. The black Pappagallo shoes, with their tiny string bows, looked like a ballet dancer's, but instead of positioned in any of the school figures, my ankles were pressed together. To me, the tension was a sure sign that I would rather be anyplace else but here. Part of me knew that was just the result of the drastic change from home to college, from the East Coast to Texas, waiting for this unknown girl with whom I would share the next year and this room. And I also knew why I had come so far from home to go to college. It was exactly that—far from home, far from memories of my parents. My Aunt Grace urged me to apply because she thought it would be a good place for a convent-educated girl to see something of the world without it being too "wild."

The job of helping daughters move into Virginia Hall, the freshman dormitory, seemed, at least here, to be the province of fathers. I managed by myself to transport the two suitcases and one box from the curb where the taxi left me to this bedroom on the third floor of the dormitory. I may have been anxious but I also felt proud and independent.

My thoughts were interrupted by a shrill, almost mature feminine voice echoing down the hall. "Man on third. Man on third."

I heard the door open and jumped up, partly in fright, partly in anticipation.

"Hi," the tall girl said in a loud voice. "I'm Eleanor Ann Cabel and you must be Sheila from New York. I'm your roommate." Her smile was outlined in pink lipstick that looked as though it were made of crushed pearls.

A man who must be Eleanor Ann's father followed the girl into the room. Here was the quintessential Texan, tall, rawboned, wearing jeans, cowboy boots, a blue shirt and a ten-gallon hat. He carried a suitcase almost the size of a steamer trunk.

"Over there by the window, Daddy. Set it on over there on the floor and I'll do the rest. Sheila, this is my Daddy."

"How do you do, Mr. Cabel," I said

"Glad to meet ya', m'am," Mr. Cabel answered, removing the Stetson. There was a tan line across his forehead. The rest of the face was seamed and chiseled

I offered my hand and he took it shyly, but the handshake ended with a firm grip. I noticed the palm was rough and callused.

Pushing long blonde hair from her eyes, Eleanor Ann kept up a steady flow of instructions and comments as her father placed the suitcase under the windows. "Now, Daddy, I think if I go back to the car with you, we can get everything else in one load. Wouldn't you know," she said shaking her head at me, "we'd end up on the third floor and, of course, no elevator. Well, at least we'll catch the breeze up here."

The couple left as quickly as they came. I sat back down on the bed and laughed to myself. I certainly had drawn an authentic Texan for a roommate.

The dormitory room was clean, but unadorned. Two small desks and two three-drawer dressers were lined up military style along one wall. On the opposite side of the room was a serviceable table flanked by twin iron bedsteads, their blue and white ticking-covered mattresses looking at once precise and well-used.

The half-open windows at the end of the room were covered only in plain buff roll shades, as impersonal as the cream colored walls, dark woodwork and brown asbestos tile floor. The hot September breeze pushed at me in insistent little nudges. The air had a faint but pervasive dusty smell.

Although the room was plain, our windows opened onto a view of the entire quadrangle of the main campus. Dallas Hall, the oldest building, stood on a prominence known as "the hill." The Rotunda, with its white columns, set the Georgian theme of the other buildings at the University. Red brick and white trim was repeated in the two newest buildings, Fondren Library and the Science Building, with its small gold, cupola. The grass, crisscrossed by white cement walks, was so green it almost looked artificial. The fountain in the center of the quad sparkled, but I was too far away to hear the fall of water.

When Eleanor Ann and her father returned, they were both laden with bags and boxes. "Put the record player and the radio on the desk by the window, Daddy. I guess, Sheila, you want the bed you're sittin' on? You sure you don't want the one over here by the window? Be glad to let you have it."

"No, this is fine. Really."

"OK. Daddy, I guess that's it. You can tell Mama I arrived safe and sound and got everything into the room." She eyed the dresser. "Now puttin' it away is another story, but you don't have to tell her that." She gave her father an affectionate kiss on the cheek.

"Now, you be a good girl, hear?" Mr. Cabel gave his daughter a tight, awkward hug and backed out of the door, hat in hand. I thought he looked as though he were escaping.

"Have you unpacked?" Eleanor Ann asked.

"No, I was waiting for you so we could decide where to put what."

"That's so sweet. Well, I've landed on this bed so I'll take the dresser and desk closest to it and the closet on the right of the door. How's that? That gives you the desk and dresser and the closet on your side." She seemed to finalize the arrangement by putting what looked like a pint bottle of Shalimar perfume on top of her dresser.

"Fine with me," I said, hauling my white Samsonite suitcases on top of the bed. I opened the larger one and began to take the plain cotton underwear from the top of the neat pile inside. It was what I was used to wearing under my school uniform, but these were all new, and I loved the feel of the fine thread. The dresser drawer, empty and clean, held only a slight acrid smell of varnish and old wood. I transferred the underwear, several lace-trimmed nylon tricot slips, and three pairs of pajamas, one cotton, one flannel and one nylon, into the drawer. There was just enough room for a satin pouch that held stockings, a garter belt and a small Vasarette girdle my aunt had insisted that I bring. I tucked two pairs of white cotton gloves in the drawer behind the stocking case and glanced over at Eleanor Ann's side of the room.

The girl opened the enormous trunk and pulled a stunning array of skirts, sweater sets, cotton shirts and silk blouses from its depths. It reminded me of the old circus trick of clowns emerging from a small car. Eleanor Ann dumped all the garments on the bed and then began, one by one, to hang the skirts in the closet, rummaging first through a smaller case to find safety pins, and to my surprise, a pile of padded hangers.

"If you need them, you can have whatever hangers are in my closet. Mama sent these. She thinks they're easier on clothes."

"That's beautiful luggage," I remarked. The three matching leather cases were a soft, butter yellow.

"It's unborn calf."

"Ugh," I said before I could stop myself.

"Oh, I know. Doesn't that sound awful? I don't want to know any more about it that that. I'm going to get the handyman from downstairs to take it to storage. Do you want to send yours with it?"

"I think mine will go under the bed."

"Now, Sheila," she continued, "tomorrow we've gotta get this place shaped up. Let's go to Sears and buy some curtains and bedspreads for this place."

"What do we do for sheets?"

"Oh, they're in a closet down the hall. The dorm supplies those. We just have to worry about decorating the place."

I wondered how Eleanor Ann had known about the sheets, and for that matter, how she had known her roommate's name. Was there an instruction book somewhere I failed to receive? And how would we get to Sears anyway? I voiced the second question.

"Oh, I have a car. It's not new; I've had it since I was sixteen," Eleanor Ann added with a wave of her hand.

"So," I wondered, "did you and your Dad both drive here?"

"Heavens, yes. It took my car and his pickup to carry all my stuff.

I began to unpack my own clothes. I hung them methodically in the closet the way I did at home, coats at one end, then jackets, skirts and blouses. Eleanor Ann's closet was jammed full of colorful garments, pastels, jewel tones and brilliant reds. I looked at my own clothes. My Aunt Grace and I had gone to Macy's for the glorious adventure of buying everything new and nothing that resembled the navy plaid skirts and blue sweaters I had worn through high school. But now, looking at the clothes, brown, beige and gray, I felt as though my belongings were fading into the colorlessness of the room. The one green skirt and my old blue blazer stood out like beacons in the closet. It couldn't be changed now. I shrugged and began to unpack cosmetics from my traveling case.

"Now, honey, everybody at home calls me E.A. for short. Don't feel you have to call me by my full name. So, what made you come all the way down here to school?"

I hesitated a moment, fascinated with the way the words emerged from Eleanor Ann's generous pink mouth. They seemed to roll from her tongue like round single pearls as lustrous as the lipstick.

"It was my aunt, she's Irish ..."

"I should have known, since your name's O'Connor and you've got that wonderful black hair and blue eyes, kind of like Elizabeth Taylor. I've always wanted black hair and violet-blue eyes."

I thought, *wouldn't you know. I've always wanted blonde hair and brown eyes.* Aloud, she said, "Well, anyway, my aunt's Irish, like I said, and she's always loved stories about the South and especially Texas, because she says the rebels remind her of the IRA. Then, for about ten years, she lived here in Highland Park when my uncle worked in the legal department of Mobil Oil Company, and she loved the SMU campus. She said she wanted me to broaden my education by seeing something of the country—the United States. She helped me get my clothes and things ready for school."

I panted a little to regain my breath after getting out so much information at one time, but I was proud of myself for staking claim to that much verbal space after Eleanor Ann's domination of the conversation.

"I'm almost scared to ask, but what about your Mama and Daddy?"

"They were killed in a car accident when I was ten. I went to live with my aunt and uncle."

"Oh, I'm *so* sorry."

I was used to the murmers of standard sympathy from adults but the obvious distress in E.A.'s voice made me look up in surprise. The brown eyes were huge velvet pools of concern. The girl was really horrified at the thought of not having a mother and father.

"It's okay. Well, not okay, but it's what it is," I said, pushing away the pain and quoting Aunt Grace, but I was terrified I might cry.

"Well, I just think you're so brave to come all the way down here. It was all I could do to go two hundred and sixty miles from the ranch."

"I gathered from the way your Dad was dressed that he owned a ranch."

"Oh, yes, he's a real cattleman. Works every day right alongside the hands. I tease him he's got a name for every head of cattle and knows each one by sight. I bet you've never been on a ranch."

"I haven't"

"Well, you've got to come visit me and Mama and Daddy soon. Right now, though, let's see who we can rustle up right here. Have you met the girls across the hall? Let's see who's over there, and if they are any fun, let's go get a hamburger or something at the drag."

"The drag?"

"Yeah, the drag. You know the street alongside the campus. There are all kinds of shops and places to eat and the cleaners and everything."

The girls across the hall were Miriam Saperstein, from Fort Worth, gorgeous and petite, with black hair and eyes the color of unsweetened chocolate, and Paula Hendricks from, of all places, Guatemala, where her father was in the Foreign Service. I didn't feel quite such an outlander. Paula, while not fat, was what my uncle would describe rather inelegantly as "built like a fireplug." She also looked as though she might be an athlete. She was plainly dressed, her naturally curly sandy hair cut without much style, and she wore no eye makeup on candid blue eyes.

After perfunctory introductions, the four of us put a nickel each into the Coca-Cola machine at the end of the hall, opened the bottles and settled comfortably into the smoker, to begin the process of getting acquainted.

Although the girls were allowed to smoke in their own rooms, there was an austere little room down the hall set aside as a smoker. It was furnished only with several couches and chairs the same brown as the woodwork. They were well worn but serviceable, and the windows had the same panoramic view of the campus as our room.

After perfunctory introductions, the four of us put a nickel each into the Coca-Cola machine at the end of the hall, opened the bottles and settled comfortably into the smoker, to begin the process of getting acquainted.

Paula and Eleanor Ann lit cigarettes.

"Don't you smoke?" Eleanor Ann asked Miriam.

The girl shook her head and Eleanor Ann pressed on. "Don't Jewish people smoke? Is it against your religion or something?"

"Of course not. I just don't care for it."

"Is it against your religion?" Eleanor Ann asked me.

"No, but the nuns at school wouldn't let us, so I never started," I said, hearing the slightly apologetic tone in my voice.

"You're a Cath'lick. I just knew it. Is it true they tell you French kissing is a mortal sin?" asked E.A.

Three pairs of curious eyes stared at me. I was beginning to feel defensive. "Yes, they do say that."

"Well, of course, all churches say fucking is a sin, but French kissing?" Eleanor Ann laughed and rolled her eyes.

Paula giggled and Miriam began a spirited discussion on the position of feminine morality in the decade of the 1950s.

I was stunned. Eleanor Ann had said that word. Out loud. She hadn't even whispered it the way my friend Rose Marie Carmody had when we were discussing what Kathleen Kearny and Joseph Gilpatrick were surely doing in the balcony of the Odeon.

"Well," Eleanor Ann was saying to Miriam, "this may be Virginia Hall to the University, but all the boys call it Virgin Hall. You and Sheila ought to fit right in." She turned around sideways in her chair and hung her feet over the arm, taking a deep and decided drag on her cigarette.

I had an overwhelming urge to escape the smoky little room. How was I going to stand feeling like Ruth among the alien corn for an entire year, or even a semester? These three women seemed to live in some sort of parallel universe.

There was E.A., slouched in the chair, and Miriam leaning forward from the couch. The two were absolutely vibrant, one dark, one blonde, still engaged in a spirited but friendly argument over what constituted petting and how far was it safe to go in the back seat of an automobile. Paula sat fiddling with her cigarette, watching with the curious beady-eyed look of a bird.

I began to relax. My innate sense of curiosity was aroused. I had no idea what I was afraid of, but I was as fascinated as if I was watching a snake and a mongoose. The discussion about sex ended predictably enough in a consensus that "bad girls did and good girls didn't." The only controversy was that Miriam thought the main reason good girls didn't was because they were sure they would get pregnant.

"I know that would be just my luck," said Miriam.

"Well, you may be right. But you can have a lot of fun in the backseat of a car without going all the way."

Paula wrinkled her nose in what seemed like disgust.

I wondered what had happened to the morality the nuns talked about.

CHAPTER THREE

"Rush is going to be such a lot of fun," Eleanor Ann was saying. "Think of all the girls we'll meet."

"But it's so barbaric and mean," said Miriam.

"It's not. It's just college."

I had lost the thread of the conversation. Finally, I had courage enough to interrupt. "What are you talking about?"

"Rush," said E.A.

"Rush what?"

"Rush Week," Paula said. "All the Greek sororities on campus have parties this week during orientation and before classes start. If you want to join one, you sign up to do what they call 'Go through rush.'"

"I never heard of it," I said.

"Well, you don't have to do it. Only if you want to," said Paula.

"Now that's just nonsense," E.A. said. She lit another cigarette. "Of course you want to. Everyone does it except the girls who are real drips. That's the way you make friends on the campus and meet boys and go to all the fun parties."

"Everyone doesn't do it, either," objected Paula.

"Oh, gosh." E.A. suddenly looked both horrified and embarrassed. "I'm sorry, Paula. Have you decided not to go through rush? If you have, that's certainly your decision."

Miriam rolled her eyes and opened her mouth, perhaps to defend Paula, but Paula just laughed and pulled her legs up onto the couch into a lotus position.

"Yes, E.A., I'm going through rush. My mother would kill me if I didn't, but I must say I'm sort of like Miriam. I'm not as thrilled with the idea as you are, especially since I have to be dressed up all week."

E.A. sat up in the chair and turned her attention to me. "Honey, you really never heard of any of this?"

I shook my head, all the earlier tense feelings again showing themselves. Here was my next encounter with the new and unknown.

E.A turned again to the other two. "Do all of you have your recs in?"

They all nodded. "Such as they are," said Miriam with a hint of some hidden meaning.

I was again mystified. "Recs?"

"Recommendations." E.A. uncrossed her legs and sat up straight in the chair, looking like a sixth grade schoolteacher. "That's a letter from somebody who belonged to the sorority in college. Some older woman. They write and say what a wonderful member you would make and a lot of garbage like that. I hear they go over the stuff, but it's really the impression you make at the parties that counts."

"Oh, it is not," said Miriam. "Lots of times it's who your family is and who you know, and even how much money your Dad has!"

I flinched.

Miriam noticed and immediately changed her tone of voice. "Sheila, do you think it's anything you would be interested in?"

"I don't know."

"Of course she would. So, c'mon, y'all. Let's get busy and see that our cute friend from up East has a good time. I'm callin' my Aunt Mamie this very evening," E.A. said this with finality and a quick nod of her head, as though everyone in the room knew exactly who her Aunt Mamie was and what was needed in this circumstance.

"And?" queried Paula.

"Well, for recs, of course. She knows just about everybody in Dallas and she'll take my word for Sheila's good character … especially," E.A. said, laughing, "when I tell her what a demure creature Miss O'Connor from Brooklyn is."

"Why not?" I said, surprising myself.

Miriam opened her mouth, perhaps to protest, but Paula cut her off. "Sheila, I'll be glad to call my mom and get her to send a Delta Gamma recommendation."

"Oh," said E.A., giving her full attention to Paula for the first time. "So you're a DG legacy?"

"Yes."

"What's a legacy?" I thought it sounded like something itemized in a will.

"A legacy is when your mother, or your sister, or even an aunt belongs to a sorority. They give you a little extra special lookin' over and they say legacies have preference when it comes to getting a bid, but I think it depends a lot on the girl."

E.A.'s explanation raised as many questions in my mind as it answered. I frowned.

"Enough," said Miriam. "I'm starved to death. It's way past lunchtime and I want to go to the drag and get a hamburger. Anybody else want to go?"

All four of us rose as though by a military command. E.A said, "Just let me put some lipstick on and get my purse."

I followed her to our room and dutifully refreshed my lipstick, too. For the first time since I left New York, I was more excited than frightened. This was going to be fun, I told myself.

The drag turned out to look to me not much different from the blocks of storefront businesses I was used to in Brooklyn, except here they were only one story. There was a hair salon, a clothing shop that catered to students, a drug store, a cleaners, and other assorted businesses. In the next block there was a small white bank building standing solidly on the corner. The name Hillcrest Bank in block letters advertised that it was named for the street we called "the drag." The sandwich shop we went into was long and narrow, like the ones at home, with a Formica-topped counter and short stools covered in yellow leatherette lined up in front of the counter from the back of the store to the front. Four more stools marked the end of the L-shaped serving area. The girls and I took these. A waitress in a pink and white uniform bustled up to us. Her name tag said "Frances" and she had striking, overly made up turquoise eyes

"What do you girls want to drink?"

We all ordered Cokes.

"I bet you're freshmen," said the waitress.

We nodded.

"Virginia Hall?"

"Yes, but do we really look that green?" asked E.A.

The waitress took a step backward, crossed her arms and took a good look at the group.

"Well, sure, but a right good lookin' bunch at that. You'll settle in soon enough."

"So, got any tips for us?" E.A. asked.

I was astounded at this. The thought of doing more than placing an order in a restaurant in New York was unthinkable, unless, of course, it was a neighborhood place you frequented, and got to know the proprietor and employees. But E.A. was talking to this woman as though they had known each other for years. I stole a look at the other girls. They only seemed genuinely interested in what the woman would say.

"I'm Frances," she said.

"Hi! I'm Eleanor Ann, this is Miriam, that's Paula and over there is Sheila. She's from New York."

"No kidding? Now, you'll love it here. Texans are just that friendly." Frances turned her huge eyes on me. I felt like a butterfly pinned to an exhibit, but couldn't help but smile. All of this was said with honesty and humor, and with a broad Texas accent. Best of all was Frances' statement that I surely would love Texas.

We ate in hurried bites between ongoing speculation about what classes would be like, the coming football season, boys, and dates, then finally Rush Week again.

"OK, Paula. Let's get to plannin'." E.A. attacked the subject again. "We have some phone calls to make this afternoon to get Miss Sheila taken care of."

I couldn't help smiling at the impression I had that E.A. was reveling in this predicament and approaching it somewhat as though she were rescuing an abandoned and forelorn puppy. *So,* I thought, *I'll be a puppy.* For the first time, the prospect of the daunting ritual of rush almost sounded appealing.

E.A. turned to Paula. "What time is the Dean supposed to talk to us?"

"Seven. Downstairs in the cafeteria."

I had until the meeting to make up my mind whether to be a part of this rush thing or just an observer. I couldn't decide.

The process seemed straightforward enough as the Dean explained it, quite devoid of all the mysteries the girls had talked about concerning legacies and recommendations, but I heard an almost imperceptible snort from Miriam.

Several assistants helped the Dean hand out packets to each girl. We filled in the forms, turned them in and then went back upstairs. We gathered in the smoker.

"Now, that wasn't so painful, was it?"

"It seems like a very logical process," I said.

Paula laughed and Miriam didn't answer.

I had the good sense not to pursue the subject and finally the girls' chatter was punctuated by yawns. Miriam excused herself to get ready for bed.

Later, as I passed her room, she called "Sweet dreams!" She was standing in front of the mirror in a pink chenille bathrobe, rolling her hair in large rollers.

I wondered briefly how she could sleep with the bulky things on her head, but I also had other things on my mind.

I leaned against the door to Miriam's room. I didn't know how to put my worry into words without sounding either stupid or cowardly. I knew I was frowning.

"What? Are you worried about all the rush business?"

"I guess I am. Are you?"

Miriam laughed and looked like she wanted to give me a hug.

"Not really. It's just different for me."

"Like how?"

"Like there is only one sorority for me, not the theoretical eleven you have to choose from."

"Why?"

"Because I'm Jewish. There's only one Jewish sorority on campus, and if they don't want me, there's no place else for me to go."

"You mean the others don't take Jewish girls?"

"Most of the sororities have rules against it although a couple of them could if they wanted to. They just don't want to."

"Oh." I was astounded. The thought of such segregation had never occurred to me. Certainly, I had known Jewish families in Brooklyn, but not well, I realized. They went to other schools, had other activities, and went to Temple instead of church. I knew all of this, but for the first time wondered how voluntary all that segregation was, including my own. What was really behind the desire of my uncle and my aunt to send me to parochial school?

Miriam smiled at me, and I knew I must be standing there gaping like an idiot. The smile lit Miriam's dark eyes with something akin to mischief. The beautiful oval face came alive. When she was not smiling, I thought, Miriam looked like the statue of the Madonna at home in St. Leo's Church. I smiled back, wondering if the Madonna, that nice Jewish girl, ever looked like this in real life. How could anyone not want to be a friend of this woman, I wondered? I turned to go to my own room.

"Sheila."

"Yes?"

"If you feel like this is all so new and you have a lot to learn, the rest of us do, too."

"Even E.A.?"

"I'm sure."

"Goodnight."

"Goodnight."

It had been a long and full day. I felt stifled. Instead of going to my room, I walked down the stairs and into the dim light of the quadrangle across from the dorm. It was lit by only a few tall lampposts with opalescent globes covering the lights. It gave the impression of moonlight, although only stars, almost as bright as I remembered them from summers in Vermont, spangled the prairie sky. The air had lost all its heat and taken on the odor of recently cut grass.

Perhaps a walk would settle my nerves. I walked halfway to Dallas Hall and sat on the edge of the fountain. The water whispered behind me like voices in another room.

I sat for about twenty minutes, trying to concentrate on the falling water instead of the million questions that poked uncomfortably at the edges of my mind. The occasional student on the way to the dormitories would pass me without notice. I was surprised to look up and see the outline of a tall and well built young man looking at me.

"Freshman, I bet," he said with no other introduction.

Stunned, I just nodded like an idiot.

"Virgin Hall?"

"Yes."

"Do you happen to know Miriam Sapperstein? Probably not, since you just got here."

"Oh, but I do. She's across the hall from me." I was delighted to have found my voice and have something to say that connected me with this attractive person.

"I'm Josh. Tell her I'll give her a call tomorrow."

"Be glad to."

He was already walking away. I hurried back to the dorm, suddenly afraid I had stayed beyond the ten p.m. closing time. The door still stood wide open behind the screen door, emitting light and letting in the evening breeze.

I got to the room, undressed and climbed into bed. E.A. was already fast asleep. I lay awake, watching the lights of the occasional automobile reflect across the ceiling. I really should have called home. Also, I probably should have called Aunt Grace to talk to her about this sorority thing before I committed myself. *Oh well, in for a dime, in for a dollar, as Aunt Grace would say,* I thought. I had made the choice. I just wasn't sure I had made the right one.

CHAPTER FOUR

The next morning, my body still on Eastern Standard Time, I awakened at six. Pale light seeped in around the edges of the paper shades. E.A. was only a lump under a baby blue blanket, one tuft of blonde hair sticking out above the self-imposed cocoon. A soft soughing emanated from somewhere near the top of the blue heap.

I thought about calling home, but decided to dress first. I slipped my feet into terry cloth slippers, took my towel, washcloth, and toiletry kit and walked down the hall to the communal bathroom. The room was stark white with a gray asbestos tiled floor, clean and warm, and at this hour, nearly unoccupied. There was the sound of water from only one of the shower stalls. The pair of scuffed moccasins by a white painted bench looked like the ones Paula liked to wear in the dorm.

"Good morning," I said. "Paula?"

"Sheila? Hi."

After I showered, I peered around the shower curtain. Paula stood in front of one of the lavatories in bra and panties, a hand dryer aimed at her short, damp curls. The dark color lightened slightly as each brushful dried in the rushing air. *How nice to have naturally curly hair,* I thought.

The water dripped down my legs as I stood on one foot and then the other. I had never quite gotten over the shyness of an only child. I kept my back to Paula, partly in modesty and partly because I did not want to know if she even glanced at me. *Dumb,* I thought, *these girls never give nudity a thought.*

"There's still no breakfast in the dorm today. Want to join me at the drug store for a cup of coffee?" asked Paula.

"Sure. Just let me get dressed and get some of this water out of my hair. And I ought to make a phone call."

"You have plenty of time. They don't open until seven."

Fifteen minutes later, dressed in a summer skirt, sandals, and a peasant blouse, my still damp hair pulled back in a barrette, I walked down the hall to the pay phone booth with a quarter in my hand. The brown booth with its folding glass doors stood in the center of the hall across from the bathrooms and showers.

I pushed the door closed and the light automatically went on. A tattered phone book with doodles marking most of its cover lay on the shelf under the phone. I took down the receiver, put a quarter in the slot and dialed zero. The operator answered and I gave her the number in Brooklyn, "Collect, please," I said, and gave her my name.

The operator's voice, with its distinct Southwestern accent, negotiated with the more familiar male voice on the other end of the phone. My uncle said yes, he would accept the call. The quarter clinked loudly in the metal coin return bin.

"Sheila?"

"Hello, Uncle Howard."

"I guess you got there all right, Princess."

I hated the epithet. "Yes. The flight was fine and I didn't have any trouble getting a taxi."

"I thought you might call as soon as you got in."

"I was pretty busy getting settled."

"Still, I thought you might give your old uncle and aunt a call." He was using the gruff tone of voice he thought jocular and I just found offensive.

"I meant to."

There was a long silence. I felt a pang of guilt knowing I had put the call off as long as possible. I found myself staring at a split image of the door across the hall. The bevel in the glass made the door appear broken. The air in the booth was close and stuffy.

"You have plenty of money?"

"So far all I've spent was for the taxi. It was about five dollars with tip. Oh, and food. The cafeteria isn't serving until Tuesday. That was a couple more dollars. But I did want to talk to you about money. There's a bank across the street from the dorm, and I thought I'd open an account there. Is that okay?"

"Why would you want to do that? They'll just charge you a lot of fees for not very much business."

"Well, I thought maybe I would need to write some checks for books and things so I wouldn't have to carry around so much cash. And I also thought you could just deposit money directly there for me. Wouldn't that be easier?" I fished the quarter out of the return bin and nervously tapped the edge of it on the phone book cover.

"Not for me. I'm going to send you a money order for two hundred dollars the first of each month. You do with it what you please." The finality in his tone let me know it was futile to argue.

"Well, I just wanted you to know I was here. Is Aunt Grace around?"

My Aunt had made me promise to call collect anytime I wanted to talk. From now on. I would try to call when I thought Uncle Howard was away.

Unlike the conversation with him, Grace wanted to know every detail about E.A. and the other girls I had met. To my relief, she was enthusiastic about my going through Rush Week. Grace admitted she knew little about sororities, having attended a women's college, but it seemed the thing to do on the coeducational campus.

I hung up the phone and came out of the booth smiling with relief. Paula was standing in the hall waiting for me. Miriam came out of the room and joined us in the hall. "Let's get something to eat. Slug-a-bed can fend for herself,"

"Before I forget, I took a walk to the fountain last night and some guy asked me if I knew you. He said his name was Josh and to tell you he'd call." Fast work, honey, I wanted to add. I was awed to think she already knew someone on campus who looked to me like a real catch. She just rolled her eyes.

"I thought he looked kind of cute."

"Handsome, really, Sheila, and does he know it. We practically grew up together. He's like a brother and irritates me sometimes as much as my own. Anyway, I'm glad to have somebody around to take me places if I need an escort."

I wondered if she was as blasé about this young man as she pretended.

Awkward schoolgirl chatter served as conversation until we were at the drug store counter. I breathed in the fragrance of coffee, bacon, and fried onions. The diner was almost full, but we found three stools together near the grill.

Frances was the waitress again this morning, eye makeup firmly in place. As Paula and Frances chatted about movies they had seen recently, I absently traced the pattern on the yellow Formica with my fingernail. The pattern looked to me like tiny overlapping outlines of Australian boomerangs.

Between the chatter, we ordered coffee and toast.

I thought Paula had been the least communicative of the four of us, but then again, maybe I appeared quiet and standoffish. I was never terribly good at small talk and I hadn't seen any of the movies the women were discussing. However, I was determined to get to know all three of the women who would be a large part of my year. Evidently so was Miriam. We plied Paula with questions about what it was like to grow up outside the United States.

At first she was hesitant, but then told us in detail what it was like to move all the time when she was growing up.

"What I found was the real pitfall in that kind of life," she said, "was that I found I could move on before anything got too serious; I could leave any conflict, any difference of opinion, put it out of my mind and move on since I was going to have to do that anyway."

"Haven't you kept up with any of your old school friends?" asked Miriam.

"Not really. There's one girl I still write to sometimes, at least at Christmas.

She lives in Washington, where Dad was posted when I was in junior high. But there's no one in Guatemala." She hesitated a moment. "Except the children I help."

"What do you do for children?" Having never been around young children, I was in awe of anyone who could minister to them, even teachers.

"It's for the church. They have a sort of day nursery thing for working mothers. It's really just babysitting."

"I never did babysit," I said.

"Actually, I like taking care of kids. I even like taking care of them when they're sick. I think that's what gave me the idea to be a nurse. I wanted to go right on to nursing school, but Mom and Dad insisted I get a college degree first."

"That makes a lot of years of school. You might as well be a doctor," said Miriam.

Paula changed the subject. "I saw you in the phone booth. Did you call home?"

I nodded. "What do you do about calling overseas? Have you called home yet?"

"Yes, I called Mom yesterday and, by the way, she said she'd be glad to call an old friend here who she was sure would get in a Delta Gamma recommendation for you, even at this late date."

"Oh, thanks, Paula. That's an awful lot of trouble. And it must cost you and your mother a lot to call back and forth." I was embarrassed by all the fuss my decision to go through rush had caused.

"It's no problem, at least for me. I just call collect."

"But then your Mom had to call back up here."

"Forget it. She was pleased to do it. Besides, Mom said I could call anytime, but not too often, whatever that means."

Paula laughed and drank the last of her coffee. "Maybe we ought to go back and be sure E.A. is up."

"She said something about going shopping this morning. Open houses don't start until one, so if we get back by noon to dress, we should be okay," said Miriam.

We paid Frances, each leaving her a 15-cent tip, and started for the door. As we stepped outside, Paula stopped at a *Dallas Morning News* distribution box beside the door.

"Got to buy a paper," she said as she put a coin in the slot. She looked a little apologetic. "I always check the war news. My brother's over there."

Paula tucked the newspaper under her arm and we crossed with the light toward the dormitory.

CHAPTER FIVE

E.A. was one of the few freshman girls to have an automobile. Her sixteenth birthday present turned out to be a pale blue and white Oldsmobile hardtop convertible, the metal top painted white. The two-door sedan had white sidewall tires and white leather seats.

"Miriam," E.A. said. "After we go to Sears, can I drop you and Paula at North Park? You can shop at Neiman's. We'd come with you, but I promised Aunt Mamie I'd run Sheila by for a cup of tea."

"That's great," Miriam answered.

The visit was news to me, but Miriam didn't seem at all surprised.

At Sears, we went directly to the linen department, where we looked at every conceivable color of Cannon cotton bedspread.

While Paula and Miriam tried to decide between dark red or navy blue spreads, I whispered to E.A. "I didn't know we were going by your aunt's."

"I forgot to tell you. I talked to her about writing a rec for you and she said great, but she'd like to meet you, and Miriam and I thought we'd have plenty of time this morning."

I had the same feeling I had in parochial school. Someone else was in control of my life. I was miffed, but then thought better of it in this situation. I still had only a vague idea of the protocols of rush.

"If you'd told me, I would have worn something different." There was an edge to my voice.

"Oh, honey. I'm sorry. I should have said something. And you look just fine. A little lipstick and you're perfect. Aunt Mamie will love you. Now what do you think we should get, the forest green or this great pink?"

"The green. I don't much like the pink."

The decided statement made me feel in control again, but I was apprehensive about the coming interview with E.A.'s aunt. I reasoned to myself that the poor woman could hardly be expected to recommend someone she had never met.

The four of us went with our choices to the drapery department and I found chintz panels, bright enough to put some sparkle in our rooms. We stowed all the purchases in the trunk of E.A.'s car.

After leaving the two other girls at the door of Neiman-Marcus's Preston

Center store, E.A. steered the car through Highland Park. I stared out the windows at the immaculate lawns and fine houses. Used to the precision and similarity of Brooklyn row houses with their minuscule plots of ground in front and constricted gardens behind, the idea of generous lawns and the suggestion of equally generous backyards was a revelation.

"The houses and yards are beautiful."

"Mama says there's so little to look at in Texas, especially out in our part, that people spend a lot of money on their houses and yards. Anything for a little beauty. Dallas is great, though, because it's got some hills, a few creeks and the river. We just have horse tanks."

Aunt Mamie's house turned out to be a combination of styles with a 1920s feeling, stone, painted an off-white, with a shake shingle roof, shutters in blue, antiqued to look as though they were weathered, with a matching round topped front door. The house was bordered with azaleas that would be a vivid red in the spring.

"It's beautiful," I said.

E.A. opened the door of her aunt's house and walked in. I was amazed the door was not locked. "Aunt Mamie?"

"Come in, girls," said a voice from the back of the house.

We walked toward the sound of the voice, through a foyer from which a broad staircase rose to the second floor. Beyond the foyer was a more informal and sunny room that faced the backyard. As I had suspected, the yard was deep and completely landscaped. There was a small kidney shaped pool at its center, surrounded by stone walks.

Aunt Mamie, slender and stylish in cerise silk pants and a silk print shirt, held out her hand, "You must be Sheila. I'm Lenore Hamilton. Call me Aunt Mamie like E.A. does. Have a seat, girls, while I get us something to drink."

I sat down in one of the cane-backed chairs around a permanent card table while E.A. flopped on a couch facing the window.

Mrs. Hamilton, as I really wanted to call her, brought iced tea and cookies from the kitchen and put the tray on the card table next to a small glass bowl of still fragrant fall roses.

"I should have made some sandwiches. Goodness, it's almost lunch."

"We'll grab a bite on the way back to the dorm, Aunt Mamie. We have to be dressed and at the houses by one."

"Then we'd better get acquainted fast," she said, turning to me with a warm smile.

The interview went better than I expected. I felt quite comfortable answering questions about what my father had done for a living (attorney), where I had gone to school (Saint Catherine's Catholic Academy for Girls) and later in the interview the fact that my aunt had once lived in Highland Park.

"Really? What was her name?" asked Mrs. Hamilton.

"Grace Finnerty."

"Grace! Well, for heaven's sake. We used to play bridge when she lived here. We've lost touch, but you've got to give me her phone number."

"I told you," said E.A. "Everyone in Dallas knows everyone else."

I suspected it was more like everyone in Highland Park knew everyone else in Highland Park.

"And your uncle. Was it Howard? Is he still … around?"

I mentally filled in her hesitation. *Yes, and he's still drinking*, I thought, but I let the inflection in my voice carry the message. "Oh, yes."

After an exchange of addresses, phone numbers and profuse thanks, we started for the door. As I passed through the foyer, I realized what seemed so different to me. It wasn't just that everything in the house was coordinated, color, pattern and size, it was that everything was new. There was none of the family hand-me-down feeling I was used to in houses on the East Coast.

"Goodbye, Mrs. Hamilton," I said as I walked down the steps. I couldn't help but call her that. I didn't think I would ever be able to manage the "Aunt Mamie" thing.

E.A. drove faster than I thought necessary back to Nieman-Marcus. We picked up our dorm mates, four "pig" sandwiches and drinks at a drive-in. E.A. insisted on introducing me to Dr. Pepper.

"This is what we all drink in Texas," she said. "You'll love it, and Mama says it's made partly with prune juice, so it's better for you than Coke." Nevertheless, both Miriam and Paula ordered Cokes.

Despite the hot weather lingering into the Texas September, we put on our best fall suits.

I took my brown gabardine suit and a white cotton blouse with a notched collar out of the closet. No girdle for me today. It was hot enough as it was. I put on the garter belt and struggled into a pair of new nylons, hooking them to the snaps on the belt. The part of my outfit I liked the best was the pair of stylish brown leather shoes with a contrasting darker brown heel and toe, like a spectator pump. I would probably rue the height of those heels before the day was out.

E.A. was standing in front of her own mirror, a black suit on its hanger in her left hand and a bright red one in her right.

"What do you think? Shall I be chic or racy?"

"From what you tell me, chic might make a better first impression."

"The black one it is, then. But, God, what did I do with my hat? Oh, shit, it's under that pile of sweaters, smushed!" E.A. began to reshape the crown of a smart black velvet derby.

Once again, I shook my head at E.A.'s language. This was all very strange. She was obviously well-bred and brought up. But to use a word like "shit?" Was this a product of being raised on a ranch?

I finished dressing first, not forgetting to put on my pearl earrings and dig a pair of white gloves out of the drawer. For the first time, I looked at myself critically in the mirror. What I saw I thought was passable, but only that. I looked clean and well groomed, and, I had to admit, dull.

I clutched my brown cloche hat in my hand and walked across the hall to see what the other girls were wearing.

Miriam stood before the mirror in her room and applied the last touch of makeup. The large dark eyes needed no mascara. Her blue-black hair curled away from the oval face in what was called an "Italian Boy" haircut, the coiffure created by the huge curlers. Her small but perfect bust line was clothed only in a white nylon brassiere. Below the tiny waist, the skirt of a purple wool suit with a shadow gray stripe hid the undergarments. A half slip smoothed telltale lines. Her pumps were black leather.

"Great color. And great on you," I said.

Miriam turned and smiled at me as she slipped on the fitted jacket. "Mother insists on calling it aubergine, but I love any color of purple."

She finished the outfit with a small velour hat of two shades of purple and the ubiquitous white gloves. As a final touch, she attached a gold circle pin to the notched lapel, gave herself a final nod in the mirror and joined me in the hallway.

I noticed Miriam's eyes subtly taking in the details of the brown suit and its accessories. I wondered if "dull" was also Miriam's appraisal of the outfit. Maybe I was just suffering a fit of nerves.

"Ready?" was all Miriam said.

"Ready as I'll ever be." The trite phrase did nothing to relieve my anxiety.

E.A., after wrecking her side of the room, was dressed in just the right silk print blouse and accessories, gloves, hat and jewelry. The stark black suit had a scalloped standup collar, set off by a striking pin made of silver with a huge stone resembling an aquamarine. The matching earrings were a simple square-cut stone. Her eyes were as bright as her jewelry, and on the blonde hair sat the rakish derby hat.

Paula appeared at the same time, simply clad in a gray glen plaid suit and bright red silk blouse that fit her body and her personality perfectly. Her small hat was an almost nonexistent band of black velvet.

"My, your aunt sure loves brown," E.A. commented. "My grandmother says brown may be smart, but it's never pretty." She laughed and then quickly added, "But it's a great color on you, Sheila."

All of my vague concerns about appearance congealed into one knot of tension in my stomach.

Miriam, fiddling with the buttons on the coat of her purple suit, seemed to cringe at the insensitive remark, but her expression was a plain indication that the import of what E.A. had said was just as clear to her.

"So," said E.A. brightly, exchanging a look with Miriam. "Here we are, all ready to go. Sheila, honey, I love the suit, but let's see if we can spice it up a little. Would that be okay?"

I had no idea what to do next. My experience with clothes was limited to school uniforms and Aunt Grace's shopping tours. I caught Miriam's encouraging nod.

"What should I do?" I asked and looked directly at Miriam.

"Well, first, how about a different blouse, or at least a scarf?" offered Miriam.

"I don't have any," I said.

"Come on in here." E.A. took command like a general, with Miriam acting as aide de camp. For the next ten minutes, I was totally shut out of the conversation. Paula watched from the door.

Miriam and E.A. pawed through the clothes tossed on E.A.'s bed until a royal blue silk blouse with a jewel neckline surfaced and Miriam retrieved a plain gold necklace and button earrings from her own stash of jewelry. Once I had changed into the blouse and put on the necklace and earrings, the two girls stood back.

"Now the hat," said E.A. "What have you got?"

I shyly produced the brown felt cloche. E.A. grabbed the hat, turning the item in her hands with an expression of utmost concentration. Finally, she flipped up only the right side of the brim. From her jewelry box, she took out a huge pin with a fake lapis lazuli stone, pinning it half on the brim and half on the crown of the hat. "Sit down," she commanded. She pulled my mane of heavy dark hair back and fastened it with a rubber band and stuck the hat on my head, tilting it slightly. The brim of the hat just covered the rubber band.

I stared at myself in the mirror. The transformation was startling. The color of the blouse brought out the blue of my eyes and the entire impression was changed from dull to distinctly charming.

"Now you look like somebody comin' out of Bergdorf's instead of Macy's," said E.A. triumphantly.

"Come on, ladies," said the always practical Paula, "or we're going to be late."

"Let's take my car," said E.A., "I'll find somewhere to park closer to the houses. Miriam, are you coming with us?"

"No. The girls are picking me up out front in thirty minutes."

On the way down the stairs, I asked what that was all about.

"She's goin' over to the Phi Sigma Sigma apartment," E.A. explained. "They use one of the apartments right off the campus as a chapter house. That's where they have their own rush."

"Oh," I said, only half understanding. I wondered if the Jewish girls and the single Jewish sorority were included in the calculations of Pan-Hellenic when it came to assigning places to each house that they could fill with new pledges. I speculated briefly about whether that changed the odds of receiving a bid to one of the sororities.

At the bottom of the stairs was a fragile looking girl with pale hair and eyes. She looked lovely in a robin's egg blue suit and straw hat. "Hi," she said, looking at Paula.

"Hi, Susan." Paula introduced her to us as Susan Simpson from Houston. She nodded shyly to everyone, and I realized she looked terrified. I wondered if she knew anyone on campus other than her roommate, who obviously had abandoned her and Paula. E.A. must have sensed the same thing."

"Hey, Susan," she said, "Want a ride with us to the houses. I'm takin' the girls in my car." The look of profound relief on the girl's face was enough of a yes.

The three of us and Susan climbed into E.A.'s Oldsmobile and she was lucky enough to find a parking place down the block from the Chi Omega house.

The afternoon was exhausting. Each girl was assigned to a group that trotted from one sorority house to the next on increasingly uncomfortable high heels. The smiles on our faces became stiff and fixed, our eyes glazed with the effort to be polite, always aware of the impression we were making, or hoped we were making.

In each house, the rushees were seated in chairs and on the sofas, and the sorority members sat on the floor in groups, chatting with each of us individually and sometimes all together.

I was aware that some hidden routine was ordering the visit to each house. The questions were the same, the smiles were bright, the hospitality gracious, and no one stopped to talk to me very long.

Paula and Susan happened to be in my group, and when we reached the Delta Gamma House, the three of us made a point to sit next to each other on the piano stool. The girls who came to introduce themselves and talk to us stayed for most of the twenty minutes allotted each house. The only other place I had a lengthy conversation with anyone was at the Zeta Tau Alpha House.

Most of the time there I spent talking to a senior from Queens named Natalie, who was not only from the familiar New York City environs, but appeared to be almost as shy as I felt.

I wondered if this attention I received at the last two houses was a reflection of the all important recs provided by E.A.'s Aunt Mamie and Mrs. Hendricks. Then, perhaps I was just getting used to the routine. Surely it was too early for the paperwork to have reached the houses. I looked around the Zeta House and thought how nice it would be to belong, to be one of the members instead of a rushee.

It was nearly six-thirty when I left the Zeta house with my group of young women. It was a long walk back to the dormitory for these rushees, after the final open house, but here was this group of some thirty young women, flushed, bright eyed, sharing the minutest detail of each conversation, their impression of their reception at each house and their feeling about the women they met. Some of them were walking in stocking feet on the warm pavement, their high heeled shoes in their hand. But nothing so minor as being footsore could take the edge from a genuine and finely honed enthusiasm.

As Paula, Susan and I left them to walk down Daniels Avenue to E.A.'s car, I suddenly appreciated how involved these young women were with the process. I could see clearly that all of them wanted to be "taken" as some imprimatur to affirm your womanhood, your femininity and perhaps even your eligibility to enter into the hallowed precincts of wife and mother. Surrounding these thoughts were all the feelings of belonging, of being accepted, a chance finally to dispel all the uncertain adolescent fears of being different, if not an outcast. I realized that I, too, had come to want desperately to belong.

At the dorm, we changed into more comfortable clothes.

"I'm not sure my feet are going to make it through," said Paula.

"Oh, tush," said E.A. "This was hard because we had to walk around all afternoon in heels. The rest of it will be a breeze. You're going to have a great time."

The other three of us said nothing. Miriam was caught up in her own thoughts. Paula finally voiced what I was too afraid to say. "What if we don't get asked back anywhere?"

"You will. People always do." E.A.'s optimism was met with a guarded silence. "Besides, you're a legacy."

"I'm not sure how far that takes you," Paula said. "Actually I don't care much. I liked the girls at the DG house and if they ask me, I'll join. If they don't, I've got other things to do."

"Like what?" asked E.A.

"Like study, try to get into nursing school, and maybe," said Paula rolling her eyes dramatically, "a little social life."

They all laughed and my tension began to ebb.

"Well," said Miriam, "you and I seem to be in the same place since all I'm interested in is Phi Sigma Sigma. Time will tell. All of this'll be over by Thursday and we can get on with the business of school and everything else."

"How did it go?" E.A. turned to Miriam.

"Really fine," Miriam said and seemed to fight to contain the smile that pushed at the muscles of her face. Her mouth finally relaxed into a broad grin of relief.

"Ooooh, look at the sparkle in those eyes," E.A. teased.

"Tell us. Tell us." Paula and I begged, playing the chorus.

"Well, things are a little different with the Jewish sorority rush, since there is only one on campus. But what I *think* they were trying to let me know was they wanted me."

I could see how important this was to Miriam, who I thought had viewed the entire process with equanimity and at times even a bit of cynicism.

"Come on, y'all," said E.A., "It's almost seven and time to go to the cafeteria to see who has asked us back."

I followed the other three, a fuzzy ball of terror sitting on top of the sandwich I had eaten.

CHAPTER SIX

If the mood in the cafeteria was subdued excitement the evening before, tonight it was nervous anticipation. Susan joined the four of us at the table in the back of the room. It reminded me uncomfortably of the sort of repetitive behavior some athletes indulged in before a big game. I had not bitten my fingernails since I was six, but tonight I caught myself chewing on a hangnail. I looked around and thought perhaps there were not quite as many women in the room as there had been yesterday. There was a small pile of very short sharpened pencils in the middle of each table.

The meeting was presided over by the president of Pan-Hellenic, which was made up of two members of each sorority. A table was set up at the front of the room. Five long boxes with letters printed on their ends sat in front of five young women. The boxes were marked with segments of the alphabet. The next to the last box, N–S, was presided over by a young woman I recognized as one of the Zetas.

Miriam, Paula, E.A. and I watched in silence as one group of young women after another went to the table and retrieved their envelopes. The suspense built and whispers began to rise from the girls who already had gotten their envelopes.

"Please don't talk among yourselves," said the president. "This is your decision and yours alone."

At last, I followed Miriam to the boxes marked N–S. Miriam did not look at me as she turned to go back to her seat. I gave my name to the Zeta, who smiled and handed me an envelope.

I fingered it carefully. At least it seemed to have something in it, and even something that seemed like more than one slip of paper.

I sat back down at the table and held my breath as I opened the flap. Inside were three long pieces of cardboard; they looked to me like theater tickets.

Two of them said Delta Gamma and Zeta Tau Alpha, where I knew I had recommendations. To my surprise, there was one from Delta Delta Delta. I had enjoyed the visit in the Tri Delt house, but was sure I didn't have one of the precious recommendations for that sorority. The pleasant surprise made up for the fact that there were only three invitations in my envelope.

Paula, Miriam and I marked our preferences and put the invitations back in our envelopes and returned them to the girls with the boxes. E.A. was still fussing with her invitations.

The three of us waited for E.A. in the hall outside the door to the cafeteria.

Paula said, "So, Miriam, it looks like you're asked back."

"Whew," said Miriam and grinned.

"And you?" Paula looked at me.

I named the sororities that had invited me back. "How about you?"

Paula said she had put DG first. I was relieved not to be going all by myself to the second round of parties. "What's taking E.A. so long?

"It looked to me like she got asked back to every house," said Paula.

"Nice to have influence," said Susan.

"She's probably trying to make up her mind where to go for the first three dates," said Miriam. "You know she'll go to Pi Phi, Kappa and Theta first."

"How do you know that?" I asked.

"Because she thinks they're the best ones on campus," said Paula.

"Are they?"

"Some people think so," said Paula. "Personally, I like the houses that liked me. They're less stuck up."

"Oh." I was disconcerted by all the ranking and judgment, on top of the fact that Miriam wasn't even welcome in the houses that expressed an interest in Paula and me. Still, I was happy to have been invited back at all.

E.A. joined us and we made our way up the three flights to our rooms.

We went over the information again for E.A. and, to my relief, nothing more was said about sororities that night. We spent most of the time in Paula and Miriam's room, listening to Paula's collection of Peggy Lee 45 rpm records and doing our fingernails. Paula put only clear polish on her nails, Miriam chose a pale pink, and E.A. replaced the bubble-gum pink on hers with a coral lacquer. I rarely wore any sort of colored polish, but tonight I chose a brilliant red called Fire and Ice from E.A.'s stash of Revlon polishes. It fit my mood. I spread my hands to look at my shiny fingertips and thought, *I'm on fire to get this rush stuff over with and cold with terror I'll make a fool of myself.*

CHAPTER SEVEN

The next morning, it was E.A. who was dressed, up and gone by the time I awakened. There was a note on her dresser written in a round, girlish hand, the dots for the 'i's a small circle.

"Hi, sleepyhead! I'm off to Aunt Mamie's to pick up my formals. Mama sent them there instead of here. She was afraid they would get lost. Be back in time for parties this aft. What time is orientation tomorrow? I can't find my packet. Love—E.A."

The mention of the formals brought the thought of what I would wear to the rest of the parties, if I was lucky enough to be invited back to any of the houses. I shook off the chill that came with the thought I might not get an invitation.

This time I took a long and critical look at the contents of my closet. I pulled out a camel colored skirt and took a matching sweater set of the same color from the drawer. These, with the brown penny loafers and the white sox everyone wore, would be fine to wear to this afternoon's parties. The only long dress I had was, of course, brown, but it was a wonderful combination of chocolate and honey woven into stiff, changeable taffeta. It was plain but quite pretty. I thought about what the girls had done to my brown suit the day before. To my now more discerning eye, both outfits needed something added.

I dressed quickly and went to the cafeteria for a cup of coffee and toast. Then I retrieved my purse from the room and started for Delman's, the dress shop across the street from the dorm. I was a little relieved that neither Miriam nor Paula was in their room as I passed. I needed to do this errand myself.

The dress shop was long and narrow, like the sandwich shop in the same complex, but the white walls and cabinets made it seem larger.

"May I help you?" An older woman stood by a circular counter in the middle of the store, marking merchandise.

"No, thank you. I'll just look around a little."

"Let me know if there is anything I can do."

On the scarf rack I quickly found just what I wanted, a silk square with a burnt orange border. The middle was filled with a print of red, orange and yellow zinnias. It would look lovely against the camel sweaters. Now all I needed was something to help the brown taffeta dress.

I picked over the trays of costume jewelry. Everything seemed too large, too fancy, too garish. I tried on a pair of turquoise and rhinestone earrings and made a face at myself in the mirror.

The sales woman appeared at my elbow.

"Are you sure you wouldn't like some help?"

"Thank you, I would," I said and explained my mission to the store. "I really like the scarf, but I can't find anything I like to go with a brown taffeta formal."

"What about another scarf? A stole, really." The woman pulled out a long scarf of chocolate brown sari silk, lavishly embroidered in gold and draped it around my shoulders. It looked awful with my summer printed cotton blouse and skirt, but I could see it would be a lustrous accessory to the taffeta dress.

"And now," the lady said, "let's find some jewelry." She picked out a pair of gold earrings with topaz-colored stones and a bracelet of similar design.

"What do you think about this?"

"It's perfect. Thank you so much."

I paid for my purchases which made a decided hole in what was left of the two hundred dollars cash in the wallet, my monthly allowance. I would have to be careful for the rest of the month, but then, there were only ten days left in September.

I thanked the saleswoman and walked out into the sunshine, carrying the package and checking to see if I had put the wallet back in my purse. It made me nervous to carry around so much cash. Perhaps tomorrow I would open a checking account at the Hillcrest Bank just down the street. I didn't care what my uncle thought.

I walked back to the dorm and stopped long enough in the front hall to say good morning to the house mother, Mrs. Jackson. There was a small apartment near the front door for the house mother. She usually sat in a comfortable chair placed strategically against the wall of her tiny sitting room, so that she could see the front door and look out her window at the porch without moving her head. She had a reputation for being decidedly cool to young men who came to call and were loud, boisterous or drunk. She often asked ones who were all three to leave the premises. She was known as the dragon of Virgin Hall.

To the girls, she was pleasant enough, and I thought she made a special effort to be accommodating to those of us from out of the state.

I said hello and then mounted the two flights of stairs to my room.

As I walked down the hall, I could see Paula sitting cross-legged at the head of her bed, a copy of *The Dallas Morning News* spread out in front of her. Paula called out, "Hey Sheila! What have you got there? Been shopping?"

Instead of going on to my own room, I happily went into Paula and Miriam's room to show off my new finery. I took my purchases out of the bag and began to model them, standing as I had seen the women in *Vogue* pose in their beautiful clothes.

"Isn't this ghastly with this skirt?" I made an exaggerated arc with my right arm, flinging the stole across my shoulder. "But it's going to look great with my formal."

After the new finery was examined and approved, making me feel the morning's adventure had been a success, I sat down in one of the desk chairs. "What are you looking at?"

Miriam was sitting against the head of her bed with a booklet and papers on her thighs, her knees bent at a ninety-degree angle.

"We're talking about what courses we're going to take," said Miriam. Any discussion of what courses to take was interrupted by footsteps in the hall.

"There's E.A.," I said.

Eleanor Ann clutched a huge cardboard box to her chest. She leaned against the door frame, panting in an exaggerated way. "Those two flights of stairs are going to make me old fast. At least maybe it will keep me from gaining weight."

"Have you been shopping, too?" asked Paula.

"No," answered E.A. "Just been to my Aunt's to pick up my formals Mama sent." She went across the hall and tossed the big box on her bed and then came back to join us. A breeze was blowing in the south windows of the room. They looked out on Peyton Hall, the much newer women's dormitory, reserved mostly for upper classmen. E.A. lifted her long hair so that the wind would cool the back of her neck.

"Yuk. It's hot today. Thank goodness it was cooler yesterday when we had to wear those wool suits. What are y'all doing?"

"Looking over the catalogue and trying to decide what to take this semester," said Miriam.

"I think I will take the Greek so I won't have to take math," I said, picking up the conversation after the interruption. "I'm pretty good at languages and lousy at Algebra."

"Oh, Jesus, Sheila. That sounds like a horrible idea," was E.A.'s reaction. She added, "I'm only going to take twelve hours. I want some time to play this year, but I am going to take Religion and get it out of the way, since it's a requirement." She looked at Miriam, "Are you going to take Religion?" E.A. asked Miriam. "Are you allowed to?"

Miriam laughed. "It's required, remember? And beside that, the first semester ought to be a snap for me. It's Old Testament."

"Oh, so it is. Then I'm depending on you to pull me though the course," said E.A. "What time is freshman orientation tomorrow?" asked Paula.

"Ten o'clock," said Miriam, "We probably won't get out until noon."

The newspaper rattled as Paula turned a page.

"Anything in the paper?" I asked.

"They're still fighting at someplace called Heartbreak Ridge. I think the real heartbreak is to have to search around close to the sports page to find any war news. More than two thousand men dead, twice as many wounded and God knows how many captured by the Red Chinese and nobody wants to talk about it."

"I'd like to read the paper when you're through," I said.

"Sure."

"After me, though," said Miriam. "I've got a cousin with a low draft number. He's just waiting to be called up."

"Heard from your brother, Paula?" I asked.

"Just what Mom said in her last letter. He's behind the lines in something called a MASH unit. He says he's fine and about to go to Japan on R and R."

"One of my mother's best friend's sons was killed over there. He was a fighter pilot," I said, remembering for the first time that I had any connection with the far-off war.

E.A., who had not seemed to be paying attention to anything except the course catalogue said, "You know, my brother Sam is at Texas A&M. He graduates next year. I hope the fighting's all over by then." She looked up and since I was beginning to be familiar with the many expressions of my roommate's mobile face, I could see the real concern in the brown eyes.

"If he's an Aggie, he has to go in for four years anyway," observed Miriam. "At least he'll be an officer if they're still fighting."

"I don't like to think about it." E.A. said. "Daddy was an Aggie, too, so he served as an officer in the war. That didn't keep him from seeing a lot of action, even though he was older. Mama had to run the ranch all by herself. I was in the sixth grade by the time he got back from Germany. I was always scared to death he'd get shot."

Paula said, "When I think about it, I can't believe it's only been five years since the war, and here we are at it again."

"I would have thought your dad could have gotten out of serving since he was a rancher," Miriam commented to E.A.

"He could have. He just thought he ought to go. I think he would have gone to Korea, too. He's a colonel now, but Mama would have killed him first. She's scared enough about Sam having to go when he graduates."

"My friend Manny has a low draft number. He's just hoping to graduate before he gets called up." It was the first time I ever saw serene Miriam with a look of real distress on her face.

"My friend?" teased E.A. "Could that possibly be the young man in the picture over there?"

A blush replaced the concern. "Yes. He's a senior at the University of Chicago."

E.A. picked up the picture. "Cute, but not as cute as Sheila says your other buddy is."

I could have killed E.A. I didn't realize I had talked that much about the guy. I didn't even know his last name.

"Josh? You'll never catch him in uniform. He'll find some way to charm his way out of it or get posted to *The New York Times*, or something," Miriam said.

"You really don't like him, do you?"

"Oh, E.A., I do, I just know him too well. Whatever Josh wants, Josh gets. He's managed to work his parents every way possible. But I also admire him. He's really a talented writer. You'll see his stuff in the *Campus* newspaper."

Paula began to unwind from the bed, cutting off the conversation. "Let's get some lunch, ladies. We have to be at the sorority houses again by one."

The informal second round of parties was more enjoyable for me than the earlier ones. We sat on the floor with the other rushees. It may have been the more comfortable skirts and sweaters, or maybe I was just getting used to the routine of Rush Week, but I felt my natural shyness abate. The tried and true questions, "What are you majoring in?" and "Where are you from?" were replaced with talk about books and movies. I was able to throw in a little movie-star gossip gleaned from E.A.'s stash of movie magazines.

The walk back to the dormitory in loafers instead of high heels was not the solitary affair I had anticipated. There were several young women like myself who only attended three of the last round of four parties. We shared our afternoon and evening's experience and giggled a lot on the way, and I found I was truly looking forward to the rest of Rush Week.

By the time I got to the third floor, Miriam was already there and had changed into a pair of Bermuda shorts.

Instead of going through the motions of attending the parties of the other sororities, Miriam again spent the afternoon at the apartment the Phi Sigs used as a chapter house.

"How did it go?" asked Sheila.

"Just great. I had a wonderful time, and they officially asked me to pledge. They're having a dinner Thursday night and I'll get my pledge ribbons then."

"I'm so glad, Miriam. I know you really wanted this."

"I did, I have to admit. How was your afternoon?"

"Fun. And I enjoyed myself more than I thought I would."

"You'd like to have a Zeta bid, wouldn't you?"

"Yes, I would."

For the first time I admitted to myself as well as to Miriam how much I wanted to join the sorority.

The routine in the cafeteria was repeated for two more nights.

When the time came, I was relieved to be asked back to both the Delta Gamma and the Zeta house for final parties. I began to breathe more easily over the ordeal of Rush Week. Tomorrow at this time, it would all be over except for the final giving out of the bids Friday morning.

CHAPTER EIGHT

Behind the new Science Building was a row of World War II Quonset huts, long, barracks-like portable buildings that remained as extra classrooms to accommodate the overflow of GIs who attended college on the GI Bill of Rights enacted after the war. Six years later, they were still in use.

On the other side of the quadrangle was McFarlin Auditorium, the primary venue for all campus activities that required extensive seating.

E.A., Miriam, Paula and I crossed the quad to the auditorium and spent most of the day there on Thursday, being lectured and admonished and finally provided with a red hat, called a freshman beanie.

"We have to wear this thing?" I whispered to E.A. "Tell me we don't."

"You have to unless you want to be thrown in the fountain. Besides, it's kind of cute."

"It's awful!"

"Well you only have to wear it until we win the homecoming football game. Then you're free to toss it in the trash."

The silliness of the entire exercise irritated me. Here I was, sitting in freshman orientation and they were talking about stupid little red hats. I realized that all my time since arriving in Dallas was taken up with anything and everything except education: sororities, clothes and inane school traditions. I hoped that when classes started the following Monday I could get back to the business of getting an education. Wasn't that why I had come down here in the first place? Well, it was true that Aunt Grace kept emphasizing that I need a broader exposure to the United States, and I suppose the lessons learned about relationships with people other than one's family was possibly as valuable as what one learned in school. Ruefully, I realized my conversation with myself sounded stiff-necked and Eastern, just what E.A. had teased me about. Unconsciously, I shrugged my shoulders. E.A. looked around curiously. I just shook my head at her and smiled, in spite of myself.

"You're gonna look gorgeous in that little red hat, Mimmi." The voice was the same lyrical one I remembered from the fountain, but as we looked around, the laughing remark had been meant for Miriam. She made a face at him as he turned toward the stage. As one of the presenters for the freshman class, I learned the voice and the handsome profile belonged to Josh, whose last name was Cooper. The long orientation session afforded me all the leisure I wanted to admire the broad shouldered frame, still a little boney from adolescence. His smile was electric. It creased the square jaw, not into dimples, but into parallel lines that stretched from cheekbone to chin. I thought he looked like the actor Jeff Chandler, with dark hair. His demeanor was relaxed and confident. Now I really had a crush.

The final parties were in the evening. All of us were ready and dressed by five-thirty. Eleanor Ann was in a confection of strapless pink tulle worn over hoops and petticoats; her sandals were gold and she carried a small gold purse. Paula had on a red silk skirt and black top with sequined trim. Miriam wore only a strikingly simple black cocktail dress. She was waiting for her new "big sister" from Phi Sigma Sigma to pick her up for the dinner the sorority was having for their new pledges. I was quite satisfied with my brown taffeta, worn over a petticoat that rustled against the fabric of the dress. The shawl-like stole of sari cloth made me feel as though I stepped out of one of the illustrations in the Jane Austen books I loved. Still, I envied Miriam, who already knew the outcome of all this activity and anxiety.

Paula, E.A. and I descended the stairs, skirts lifted high so as not to step on hems or petticoats. Our strappy little evening sandals clicked on the treads like castanets.

At E.A.'s car, Paula and I sat in the back, each on the edge of the seat so as not to crush our skirts. E.A. pulled her acre of tulle up almost to her waist and sat forward as far as she could and still steer the automobile. I thought she looked as though she was drowning in a frothy pink sea. She drove slowly—for her—and with her usual unerring luck found a parking place across the street from the Pi Phi house.

"Are we supposed to park here?" I asked.

"It's a public street," said E.A. "Besides that, if I'm lucky I'll be parking here a lot." This was the first time E.A. had indicated what her real preference was.

To me, this last party was the only part of Rush Week that lived up to its name. Before I knew it, it was nine-thirty and time to meet Paula and E.A. at the car.

I had thoroughly enjoyed myself and went to bed happy. We would pick up our bids the following morning. I said a small prayer before I fell asleep, asking that the Zetas would give me a bid. Immediately, I wondered if God would find this an appropriate petition.

Everyone but Miriam was edgy the next morning. This was the last of the anticipation and at last it was time to pick up the bids. Paula, E.A. and I made the familiar trek to the cafeteria. When we received our envelopes, each of them had only one slip of paper in it. Paula smiled at hers. E.A. let out a breath of relief, and I gasped. All mine said was "Please report to the Office of the Dean of Women at 11:00 o'clock."

It took a moment for me to realize I had not received a bid from either sorority that had asked me to the final parties. I was unprepared for the impact. I felt the way I did when my aunt and uncle took me into the library at home and told me that mother and father were dead. I couldn't breathe. Blindly, I pushed back the chair and ran for the stairs. By the time I reached the third floor, I was gasping more with sobs than with exertion. I flung myself into the room, slammed the door and sat on the edge of the bed. Then the sobs really began.

I didn't hear E.A. come into the room, but I could smell the cloud of Shalimar perfume that always accompanied her. E.A. sat down beside me, put her arms around me and pulled my head against her breast.

"Oh, honey, honey. I'm so sorry."

I continued to cry, but was comforted by this motherly gesture. In fact, it was exactly what I imagined my own mother would do if she were there.

"But I swear, it's going to be okay. You'll see."

How could it be okay? I'd been rejected!

E.A. waited until there were only a few sniffles left. Then she began.

"Now, first we have to get you cleaned up. Go to the bathroom and wash your face with cold water."

"I don't want anybody to see me."

"Who cares? You're going to come out of this smelling like a rose."

"Oh, sure."

"Go on, now!"

I meekly did as I was told, taking along a washcloth to the bathroom to sponge cold water over red eyes and swollen nose.

I looked marginally better when I returned to the room.

"Are you going to wear that?"

I just shrugged.

"If you'd gotten a bid, would you wear what you've got on to the house this afternoon?" E.A. was a model of patience.

"No. I was going to wear my navy blazer."

"Put it on."

E.A. waited while I changed clothes. With the motions of an automaton, I began to put makeup on a still red and shiny nose. While all this was taking place, E.A. hummed along with the radio and Kaye Starr. The song was, appropriately enough, "Wheel of Fortune."

"Now, are you ready?"

"For what?"

"To go to the Dean's office and sign up for open rush, of course."

"I don't think I want to."

"Sheila, don't throw in the towel now."

By eleven, I was standing in Dallas Hall in the Dean of Women's office with a group of about a dozen other young women. We all wore the same rather hangdog expression. I squared my shoulders.

The Dean went through the formal procedure of enrolling us in open rush. She explained that many of the sororities still had places for girls, if we wanted to take the chance. For me, the moment had passed. I was sick at heart not to be going through the ritual of pledging this afternoon when I knew my friends would be leaving for their respective houses. Then I thought of Miriam. It was nice that she had been asked, but she was perfectly prepared to make a life on campus without pledging. I could do that, too. I thanked the Dean and walked to Snider Plaza to the movies. I didn't want to face the girls right now. I don't remember what I saw, but when I got back to the dorm, it was so quiet the faint sounds of movement I could hear in the hall reminded me of mice scurrying in the attic of the cabin in Vermont.

I sat on the bed and opened up a novel, not really seeing the words on the page, when the telephone began to ring. By the fourth ring, I couldn't stand it and sprinted to the phone.

"Hello?"

"Is Miriam Saperstein around?" The voice was Josh Cooper's.

"No. I think she's at her sorority's apartment."

"Who's this? The blonde, the jock or the cute one?"

"This is Sheila O'Conner. I room across the hall from Miriam."

"That's what I thought. The cute one. And I think you're the girl I asked about Mimmi when you were sitting on the fountain."

"That's me." Whatever heartsickness I felt earlier in the day was rapidly disappearing.

"Are you wearing your red beanie?"

"Of course not. It's dreadful."

"If I see you on campus, it's into the fountain with you."

"I'll be careful to avoid you, then."

He laughed. "You didn't go through rush?"

"I didn't pledge."

"I knew you were a smart girl."

"Don't you belong to a fraternity?"

"Sort of. Mostly for free beer. But seriously, I view the whole thing as decidedly injurious to campus life, undermining any real sense of equality in this place."

I couldn't tell if he was teasing or not, so I mumbled something.

"Okay, tell the brat I called, and I'll be watching to see if your wearing that hat."

He hung up and I just stared at the phone. What a miracle, I thought, that I wasn't at the sorority house.

CHAPTER NINE

My experience of being fixed up for a blind date was limited to Rose Marie Carmody pairing me up with a drip of a cousin from New Jersey. It was not a wonderful evening.

Since I had not pledged, I thought I was going to avoid being subjected to the ritual of blind dates the sororities and fraternities used to introduce their freshmen members to each other. What I didn't know was that Dallas was about halfway between the University of Texas and the University of Oklahoma, as well as driving distance from Fort Sill, Oklahoma, and Parrin Air Force base in North Texas, and hordes of young men regularly invaded the campus, cajoling some good natured girl into lining up dates for them. In a moment of weakness, Susan and I signed our names to one of those lists.

I stood with my nose almost touching the mirror above my dresser and briefly hoped the phrase "blind date" would refer literally to the guy picking me up tonight. Close inspection didn't help a thing. My eyes were red and watery; my nose looked twice its normal size in the middle of a distinctly blotchy face. Somewhere during that first week of school I had acquired all my textbooks, a sweatshirt with a red, running mustang on it, a knowledge of where my classrooms were, a new swishy black dress from the cheap floor at Neiman's, and a nasty cold. I didn't want to go out at all tonight, especially to some fancy place with someone I had never met. Maybe without the cold it would have been bearable, even exciting, but now all I wanted to do was put on my pajamas and get into bed.

"Aaaaak."

"Honey, I'm so sorry," said E.A.

"The nose does nothing for the dress."

"Put some powder on it. Nobody'll notice. But here ..." E.A. went to her top drawer and pulled out a bottle of nose spray. Put that in your purse. You sound like somebody put a clothespin on your nose. And take plenty of Kleenex. God," she added, "I sound like my mother."

E.A., dressed in lacy black bra and half slip, sat back down, leaning against the head of her bed, and watched me in the mirror.

I stepped back and took a long look. The black dress was simple, cut to a low 'V' neck in the front, fitted to the waist and than flared in a series of broad pleats. Luckily, one of the things I had brought with me was a flounced crinoline petticoat. I bought some black strap sandals to go with the dress and I liked just my simple pearl necklace and earrings with it. My hair was up in a French roll, so the jewelry showed nicely, but there was still the runny nose and red eyes.

I found this whole ritual of matching dates up merely by heights absurd. I was just thankful I was tall enough that my dates at least wouldn't be shrimps. But what if, by some quirk of fate, this date tonight turned out to be just the one for me? Maybe the black dress would carry me through. Maybe the deep neckline would keep his eyes off my red nose.

"Who's your date tonight?'

"Some guy from UT. I think his name is Harvey. We're going to some fancy club."

"What kind of club? A country club?"

"I don't think so. It's called Poppa's or something?"

"Pappy's Showland? Jesus!"

"What?"

"It's a strip club."

"A what?"

"A place that they have these little tables and it's dark and smoky, everybody drinks a loot of booze, and then there's this stage lit up like the circus where the strippers take their clothes off."

My heart toppled. Now I really didn't want to go. "And I got all dressed up to sit in the dark in some smoky hole where nobody can see me?"

"Believe me, nobody will pay any attention unless you take your clothes off, too." E.A. rolled on the bed in laughter at the thought. I was appalled.

"Do they take them all off?"

"Down to something called a G-string, a lot smaller than your panties, and a couple of sequined things pasted over their nipples."

The image her description created revolted me. "I don't want to watch some woman take her clothes off. It's so embarrassing."

"It's really dark, Sheila. Nobody'll see you blush."

She got up from the bed and reached for the perfume bottle on her dresser with its rooftop-shaped stopper. She dabbed perfume from the bottle on the side of her neck and the top of her breasts. I knew the odor was elegant but I couldn't smell a thing.

"Here, put some of this on."

Hesitant about how much to use, I dabbed some behind my ears.

"Put some between your boobs."

I stared at her in the glass like a different kind of boob.

"Put some between your boobs. When you get hot or a little excited, it really smells then. Besides, you never know when somebody's nose will be down there."

"E.A.!"

"You never know."

"I've never met this guy."

She just shrugged. I thought of something else. "And how can they serve alcohol to us in a place like that. We're all under twenty-one." I had visions of being hauled off to the Dallas County Jail, black dress and all.

"You don't have to drink it, of course. Order a Coke or something. Soda water. But the boys all have fake IDs and they don't ask the girls unless you look ten, which you don't in that dress."

I was supposed to be picked up at a quarter of eight, so I sat down carefully on the bed to wait. "Who's your date tonight?" E.A.'s brown eyes sparkled and she lifted the long blonde hair off her neck with both hands. She was clearly pleased about something.

"I'm double-dating with my big sister in Pi Phi. She goes with Gary Stewart, the football player. Anyway, I have a date with a freshman footballer from Lubbock. He's okay, I guess. I met him the other day when she introduced us in the Union. I mean, he's nice and all, but what I'm really excited about is I think Chuck Bolton and his date are going to meet us there."

"Chuck Bolton's one of the backs, isn't he? Is that what they're called?" My knowledge of football had increased exponentially from a base number of approximately 1 to somewhere around 15 on a scale of 1 to 100 in my first week at SMU. Football, I found, was the second religion at the University, with surely more members than the plethora of Protestant, Catholic and Jewish clubs on campus combined. Even the wearing of the hated red freshman beanies was tied to winning the homecoming game.

E.A. just smiled and I could see the wheels turning. I wondered briefly what it would be like to be the sort of pretty girl the boys turned to look at as we walked across campus. I didn't think I was ugly; I just knew I wasn't the attraction when even some scholarly appearing guy with fourteen books surreptitiously took a good look at us from the corner of his horn-rimmed glasses.

"Where are you going? The movies?"

"No, we're going to O'Tooles. I haven't been there, but it's just over east near the Central Expressway. It's a beer bar. I guess the guys want to unwind a little from the game this afternoon. Especially since we lost again. Anyway, they have live music on Saturday, and there's some new Negro gal that they say plays wonderful rhythm and blues."

E.A. pronounced the word "Nigra," which at first I thought was just an appropriate Latin ending for a female. I had asked her about it once, and she told me that's the way her mother preferred to pronounce the word. It didn't sound as harsh as Negro and was distinct from the word "nigger," which Mrs. Cabel considered to be low class. Along with a knowledge of football, I had picked up this little bit of folklore during the week, chatting with the four girls in the smoker. The word came up when Miriam observed that for the first time there were students of color on the campus. Two men had been admitted to Perkins Theological Seminary.

The admission of a few students of African ancestry had been a matter of course at St. Catherine's and I had given it no thought. Now for the first time, I realized there were no such students in any of my classes or evident on campus.

The full impact of what were known as Jim Crow laws would become clearer to me as I spent that winter in Texas. Negroes simply were not in evidence, except in menial jobs. I would experience being careful to use the "white" bathrooms, drink from "white only" water fountains and wait in "white only" waiting rooms. All of this in public places. Anywhere else, it was as though Negroes did not exist.

The loudspeaker in the hall called my name and I suddenly realized it was time for my date. I grabbed a small black purse with Kleenex, lipstick and E.A.'s bottle of nose spray and started out the door to this new adventure, Pappy's Showland.

"Have fun," E.A. called after me.

"You, too."

At the bottom of the stairs, I stopped, took a deep breath and headed for the foyer, where boys called for their dates. Halfway down the hall, I met Susan.

"Are you going to Pappy's with the guys from UT?" she asked.

"Yes. Are you?"

"Yes, I'm so glad to be going with someone I know."

I wondered if I looked as terrified as she did. But, like her, I was considerably relieved to be double-dating with someone I knew, although it didn't make my runny nose any better. I could see two young men, dressed in blue blazers and gray flannel slacks, wearing shirts, ties and black tassel loafers. I briefly wondered if it was some sort of fraternity uniform. One was tall and thin enough to be called skinny. The other was shorter and baby-faced. They looked as nervous as we were.

"Sheila?" the baby-faced one said, hesitant but accurately addressing me.

"I'm Sheila."

"Hi. I'm Harvey Patterson."

Harvey wasn't much taller than I. I wondered if maybe someone got the height chart mixed up.

The taller boy introduced himself to Susan as Jim Herring. Each of them took us by the elbow and began to usher us out of the door.

At that moment, Josh Cooper opened the screen door. We were face to face.

"Uh-oh. No beanie. The fountains not going to do a thing for that black dress."

"Beanies are not to be worn with black cocktail dresses. It's a rule."

"Never heard that."

I stopped long enough to introduce him to my date, stumbling over his name. The men shook hands. So, I thought, the black dress had not gone unnoticed and I hoped the red nose was camouflaged by my blushes.

The men steered us down the steps and toward a snappy looking Chevrolet Bel Air coupe, dark blue and white.

Susan and Jim clambered into the narrow back seat. The car was obviously Harvey's and I was glad to see that his driving was considerably more careful than E.A.'s. We seemed to drive forever but finally pulled up in front of a rather nondescript building with no windows, but an enormous sign identifying it as our destination.

The boys did whatever they needed to do to pay our entrance fee, and we walked into a huge room. The lighting was low, and as E.A. had said, full of cigarette smoke. I was grateful, for once, for my cold. I couldn't smell it.

There were two low tiers with banquettes and small tables around the periphery of the room surrounding what in a ballroom would be an enormous dance floor. This floor was made of cement and jammed with tiny tables with too many chairs around them for their size. The black painted walls and ceiling looked tawdry with the lights on, but I was sure it would fade into a deep velvet background for the show once the lights went down. I felt as though the walls were poised to close in on me with suffocating pressure. A rather narrow stage spanned the far wall of the room hung with a curtain that looked like silver lame. In front of the stage was a bandstand that accommodated a small band. It already was playing a rather thin version of Big Band numbers. The rendition of "String of Pearls" didn't sound either real or cultured, but like a string of clinking glass beads. The sound echoed around the hard floors and bare walls.

A waiter showed us to a small table, halfway back on the main floor. We were slightly off to one side, but I noticed every table had a good view of the raised stage.

The waiter asked us what we wanted to drink.

"I'll have a Coke," I said.

"No bourbon or rum in it?" asked Harvey.

"No, thank you."

He just shrugged.

Susan hesitated and then ordered a rum and Coke. The boys each ordered scotch and soda, and the waiter asked for their identification. Each boy reached for his wallet, pulled out a card and tossed it on the waiter's tray. Then Jim ordered a couple of extra shots of rum. The waiter gave him a rather sharp look, but said nothing. He examined the cards carefully and handed them back, turning without a word.

None of us seemed to think of anything to say. I couldn't even remember reading any gossip or scandal in the paper to mention. The thought of any story connected with sex in this atmosphere made me ill. Any reference to the war would hardly be welcomed by two draft-age males. It would be safer to begin with the standard getting-to-know-you questions.

While I was dithering over all this social intercourse, the waiter was back with the drinks and a bowl of peanuts, all of which he thumped down on the table with more vigor than I thought necessary.

"So you're from New York City?" Harvey got in the first question.

"Brooklyn, actually." Everyone in this part of the country seemed to think New York City was made up of only one borough, with tiny satellites, when in reality my hometown was a large city, even more populous than Manhattan.

"I don't know anything about Brooklyn except the Dodgers are there and it has a tree." He laughed at his own joke and Jim joined in.

Harvey did not endear himself to me with his threadbare joke, referring to the popular novel and film, *A Tree Grows in Brooklyn*. The book was about conditions fifty years ago in the poorer section of the city. I lived in quite upscale Brooklyn Heights.

Before I could say anything, the waiter brought a second round of drinks the boys had ordered. As he set them down, the lights began to dim and the decibels of the band rose one hundred percent. Six trumpets squealed into the darkness. The only lights were spots in the back of the auditorium that created swirling gray cones as the light cut through the smoke and converged at the center of the stage in front of a curtain. Into that spot stepped a blonde woman, rather short, as I could judge from my vantage point. She was wrapped in some sort of trailing costume. She strutted around the stage for a few minutes to the rhythm of the band, its bass drum keeping up a steadily paced boom.

The audience, or at least the men in the audience, participated with occasional whistles, but I looked around at our two male companions and they were simply catatonic, staring at the stage. Harvey's mouth was slightly agape and I thought he might drool on himself.

"Yeah," he whispered to himself, as the woman on stage took off the outer garment, a long, marabou edged cape that looked to me like a cross between a cape and a negligee. She tossed it toward the curtain, where it immediately disappeared by the sleight of hand of some assistant backstage.

The stripper had a compact body with large and, I had to admit, shapely breasts, good legs and a narrow waist. The costume underneath was some sort of concoction made to look something like a cocktail dress.

I was reminded of the first time my father took me to the circus. I couldn't believe that the costumes weren't real silk, that the paste wasn't diamonds. I stared at the chandelier earrings and the elaborate necklace. Surely nothing but diamonds could glitter like that. I had to smile at the make-believe world that captivates all of us. Harvey happened to glance at me at that moment and gave me a huge, knowing grin. Damn, I thought, he thinks I'm eating this up. At the same time, I noticed Jim pouring a second shot of rum into Susan's glass while she was staring at the stage.

Harvey turned back to the stage with a satisfied smile as the woman began the long process of taking off her costume bit by bit. With each divestiture, the band, with its bass drum, became more insistent. Finally, with a roar of approval from the crowd, she was left with the costume E.A. had described, a narrow sequined belt that reminded me only of the equipment we all wore to hold sanitary pads, and two glittering patches over her nipples. I hoped that would be the end of the routine. It wasn't.

The strutting she had done while taking off her costume now changed into an athletic performance, designed to insinuate what she would do if she were really in the midst of a sex act. The routine ended with a spectacular back bend, her thighs spread toward the audience. The men went wild with applause. She took a bow, and the lights came up.

"Would you like to go to the Ladies?" Susan asked, reaching for her purse. I didn't, but mostly I did not want to be left with the two guys while she went. I picked up my purse and followed her toward the back of the building. The two boys did rise politely, as we left the table.

It didn't take us long to find the door marked "Women." There was a considerable line.

"No more rum in the Coke for me," said Susan. "I'm beginning to feel woozy."

"Susan, I thought I saw Jim spiking your drink?"

"Really? I'll watch it."

"I've been holding my glass of soda, just in case Harvey got ideas. I guess he'll be sober enough to drive after all this."

"Oh, he'll be sober enough. I'm just worried about where he's going to want to drive after all the bumping and grinding on the stage. They'll probably want to head straight for White Rock Lake."

"And?"

"You know. To park."

By now, we had reached the front of the line. A stall door opened and Susan went in. I did some quick calculations as I took my turn. We had come to the early show that began at eight o'clock. It was now a little after eight-thirty and we had to be back in Virginia Hall before eleven o'clock when the doors slammed shut like a prison, with Mrs. Jackson standing guard. There were two more acts for us to sit through, which meant we would be out of here by about ten-fifteen. Depending on how far White Rock, or wherever we went, was from campus, there was about thirty minutes of dead time in there, or, as the boys probably viewed it, a window of opportunity. I joined Susan at the washbasin and we went back to the table just in time to see the lights dim again.

The second act was a comedian. About half of his material was really funny and the other half simply suggestive. I laughed about half the time.

Out of the corner of my eye, I caught Jim put extra rum in Susan's drink again. At the break between the second and third acts, Susan wanted to head for the bathroom again. I followed like a dumb lamb, not knowing what else to do.

"Gee," said Jim as we left the table, "you girls sure have a bad case of TB."

"Tiny bladder," explained Harvey as though we didn't know, and both of them laughed at the tired joke.

"Just order me a plain Coke this time, Jim," Susan said.

"C'mon!"

"No, really."

As we stood in line, I looked at Susan. She was a little pale. "Are you okay?"

"I don't feel very well."

"But you're not going to be sick, are you?" I whispered.

"I don't think so. I just wanted to walk around a little and get out of the smoke."

We finished, went back to the table, and once more the lights dimmed.

Harvey leaned over to me and whispered, "This is the headliner. She's famous in New Orleans; named April May, not her real name," he chucked. "But all the rest of her is real."

Harvey did not have a future as a comedian, I thought, and turned to the stage. The girl who entered was clad like the first one in an elaborate cape-like gown. There was something different about her, though. Instead of strutting, she moved with grace, and she was extraordinarily beautiful.

The routine and the band making indifferent music was the same as the first act, but I found myself mesmerized by the dancer. She glided from one end of the stage to the other, playing to every part of the huge room, her face impassive as a porcelain doll. As she began to disrobe, one lovely piece of costume after another, each with a subtle suggestiveness, looking at the audience with an expression both arch and aloof, I began to feel the erotic pull of the performance.

I was surprised at myself. Most of the first two acts, while enjoyed by the two young men, had left me at first cold, and then slightly repelled. Not this act. As the girl and the stage got to the final orgasmic bumps and grinds, I was definitely aroused. I ruefully thought about the Shalimar daubed somewhere in the vicinity of my breastbone and hoped I wasn't reeking.

The lights went up, and the sustained applause lost some of its momentum. The boys rose to hold our chairs and we made our way to the exit. One look at Harvey's pasty face in the white glare of the ceiling lights and I knew that aroused as I may be, I did not want to go to White Rock Lake with this guy.

But that's what we did. Harvey steered his car straight to a lake surrounded, from what I could see in the dark, by broad lawns with a hint of huge homes beyond.

"You smell nice, Sheila."

Oh, damn, I thought. There goes any hope he has a phobia about germs. My cold wasn't going to keep him at arm's length.

"Excuse me a minute, Harvey," I said. I pulled the squeeze bottle of nose spray from my purse. I really did need it to breathe, but I also was playing for time and hoping he would be repulsed. I snorted and blew on one of the many tissues in the little purse.

"I don't know where I got this awful cold," I said.

None of this dissuaded him. I found myself being kissed with a copious amount of tongue, his left hand reaching somewhere close to the Shalimar scented area in the 'V' of my dress. I started to push him away when Susan saved the day.

It had been quiet in the back seat and I had wondered if they were simply watching our contortions in the front one or engaged in their own struggle.

"Stop! I'm going to be sick." It was Susan.

Luckily, Harvey had all the windows open in the little car. Susan flung herself halfway over the front seat, her head out of the window, and vomited copiously.

"Jesus Christ," Harvey said. He reached beyond me with the hand no longer occupied with seeking my breasts and opened the door next to me. "Get out, Sheila. Jeez, did she get any of that on the car?"

I found myself standing in the grass, trying to keep my heels from sinking in the soft ground. I was glad I was on that side of the car. I must admit to considerable squeamishness when someone throws up. But Susan needed my help. She was still hanging halfway out the car window, crying and retching.

"Jim, get out and let me back there," I said. The car light illuminated a considerably relieved young face. The boy had been trying to comfort Susan as well as possible by patting her on the back.

He clambered out of the back and I got in.

"Susan," I said, "Here, I have some tissues. Do you think you got it all up?" I wasn't sure where all this motherly concern came from. But I was glad to be out of the front seat.

The boys were discussing the state of the automobile, not the girl.

"Well, thank God, most of it hit the ground, but there's a bunch on the door," said Harvey.

"Any inside?"

"Probably."

I coaxed Susan back from the window. She sat next to me and took the tissues from me, blowing her nose on them and then tossing them out the open door on my side. She even tried wiping her tongue on one, then gave up and put her head on my shoulder.

"Feel any better?"

"A little."

Harvey had turned his attention for a moment from the car to his friend.

"Damn it, Jim, I told you not to keep ordering all that rum and Coke. She was feeling no pain halfway through the evening."

I don't know if Jim felt he had any part of the blame or not, but he was clearly angry. He turned around and got into the right front seat, slammed the door and said, "Let's get the girls back to the dorm."

At Virginia Hall, the two ushered us up the steps as far as the front door. There we parted with murmurs of "Thank you," "Nice time," "Hope you feel better," and "See you sometime."

We stepped inside the door and I was too preoccupied with Susan to notice all the people standing around. I hoped to get her to her room without much notice.

"Sheila, is everything okay?"

I looked up to see everyone I knew standing around. Paula had asked the question. E.A. was standing next to one of her sorority pledge sisters and two distinctly athletic looking young men stood nearby. And there was Miriam, with Josh Cooper. I wanted to disintegrate.

"We're fine," I said, just as Susan began to crumple in my arms.

The two football players seemed rooted to the carpet, both with a look of horror on their faces. Josh was different. He moved quickly from Miriam's side and before I knew it had bodily picked up Susan.

"Where's her room?"

"I'll show you." As we walked down the hall of the dorm, I announced the obligatory, "Man on first."

I pushed open the door to Susan's room and flipped on the light. "This is her bed," I said and indicated the one next to the door. Thank heaven her roommate wasn't there, sitting half dressed on the other bed.

He put Susan on her bed and she moaned, conscious enough to sit upright.

"Little too much happy juice?" he asked.

Susan moaned again and I nodded.

I couldn't help but grin at him.

"Can you handle it from here?"

"I think so. She got rid of most of it out the window of the car."

"Serves those tea sippers right. I'll bet they pushed the booze so they could push a hidden agenda."

"How did you know that?"

"More than just a good guess, honey. I'd better get back to the entry hall before the Dragon Lady out there thinks I'm tarrying in here with some nefarious purpose of my own."

I said something incoherent as he backed out of the room and felt like a fool. Now why couldn't I have ended up at Pappy's Showland with him and gone on to White Rock? Somehow, I couldn't picture anyone who would use the word "nefarious" as casually as he did being interested in Pappy's. I fervently hoped I might get the chance at the lake thing, though.

I turned and helped Susan unzip the taffeta dress she was wearing which, thank goodness, had avoided the contents of her stomach, I caught sight of myself in the mirror. My hair straggled from the French knot, I had dark circles under my eyes and no lipstick—none.

"Oh shit!" I said.

CHAPTER TEN

Since I had never spent a summer in Texas, I could not appreciate the gift of green grass that filled the space in the quadrangle between white walks with emerald when I first arrived on campus. The natives of the city remarked that summer had been unusually cool and rainy with none of the hundred-degree weather Dallas residents were used to enduring. But as October ended, the Bermuda grass took on a dun-colored tone. In contrast, the elms and sycamores turned glorious shades of gold, the elms new-minted and the sycamores the color of old coins, their dinner plate-sized leaves stiff as paper. Driven by the wind, their edges scratched along the concrete walks like fingernails, as though the leaves were still resisting their displacement from high branches.

On Sundays, Paula and I, sometimes with E.A., would cross the campus to Daniels Avenue for church services at Canterbury House, the Episcopal chapel on campus. From the street, it looked like an ordinary suburban clapboard house, and in fact it was—the dining room converted to an office and the living room serving as a parish hall.

The chapel built behind the house was small but an architectural jewel: contemporary, built of stacked stone, with a glass wall to the right opening onto a lovely garden. The service was familiar, since I was used to translating the Latin Mass in my head and the Elizabethan English of the Book of Common Prayer was nearly the same. The service litany was somewhat different, and I hesitated before taking communion at the rail, but did anyway, wondering if my own priest would consider this a sin.

After the service, we gathered in the living room of the house for coffee. I learned a little more about the place. The priest was a burly ex-Marine chaplain who had survived the battle of Okinawa. His name was Heinz Froelich and he lived on the second story of Canterbury House with his mother. Other than the Canon and Mama, it was completely run by and for students.

I told Father Heinz I was a Catholic and he assured me that since I was confirmed, from the Episcopal Church's view, I was welcome to take communion there.

"Do you have a good relationship with your parish priest?" he asked.

"No. But there was a nun at school I really loved."

"I'm always here if you need a little spiritual counseling, and I promise not to try too hard to steal you from the RCs."

I couldn't imagine needing any such counseling, but I decided this could be a convenient place for any religious observance I wanted during the school year.

The Sunday after my disastrous date, Paula and I arrived back at the dorm. We joined Miriam and E.A. in Paula's room. They had the record player on again, this time playing mostly Perry Como records. The window was open but the air was filled with smoke from E.A.'s cigarette and I noticed she had brought her own huge ashtray from across the hall. Paula pulled her package of smokes from her jacket pocket.

"Hi," said Miriam. "E.A. has been filling me in on your eventful date last night."

"It was awful. But I want to hear about your date. And E.A, I never gave you a chance to talk last night, either."

"Oh, mine was fine," said Miriam. "Josh took me somewhere down off Greenville Avenue to a theater that shows foreign films. We saw Jean Cocteau's *Les Enfants Terribles*. It was just great."

E.A. made a face and Miriam laughed. "Too highbrow for you, E.A.? What was your date like?"

"My date was okay. Nice, really. He's a jock. We didn't do anything highbrow, but we didn't park, either." She gave me a mischievous smile. "We went to O'Toole's Lounge over by the Expressway and listened to this great Negra gal play R&B. That's all we did, have a couple of beers and talked."

"E.A.," I said. "Somehow that sparkle in your eye tells me there's more to the story."

"Looks like it to me, too, Sheila. Come on," said Miriam. "Let's have it."

"Well, we were with these two other couples, see? One of them was Chuck Bolton and his date. I just think he's dreamy."

Her eyes did take on a faraway look. I had always thought the current term, "dreamy," to be insipid at best. But E.A.'s expression expanded on the concept.

"He's got these great blue eyes. He's not really blond, but has that color skin that makes him look like a blond. And he has a great build, naturally."

"Naturally," said Miriam. "Does he talk, also?"

"Oh, come off it, Miriam. Yes, he talks, and he even makes sense when he talks."

"About something other than sports?"

"Yes. As a matter of fact, we had a quite a long discussion of movies and things. We talked about that silly Jeanne Crain movie, *Take Care of My Little Girl*. It was so fakey, nothing like sororities really are. Chuck said casting Jeanne Crain in that part made as much sense as Jane Russell playing Camille."

I didn't want to puncture E.A.'s rosy picture by pointing out that the remark was really a quote from the editor of the *Campus* newspaper in a column on the movie. Evidently, Miriam had similar thoughts. She pursed her lips as if to bite back a comment.

Paula asked the pertinent question. "Did he think you were cute?'

"Well, he did talk to me a lot."

E.A. closed the conversation at this point, but I reopened it later in our room when we were alone.

"Is Chuck going steady with his date?"

"No. At least I didn't get that impression."

"Do you think he'll ask you out?"

"He will if I have anything to do with it."

"So, what are you going to do?"

E.A. laid out a plan to make herself as available as she could to Chuck Bolton. She knew where his classes were, when he was likely to go to the Union for coffee, and what the football practice schedule was. I was astounded that she had done that much research already and wondered if she had even manipulated the occasion of the triple date last night.

"Hmmmm," I said to myself.

"Thinking of that dreamy Josh?"

"Maybe, since Miriam really isn't interested in him."

"She says he puts on a great front, but is really a spoiled brat. Never has been able to think of anyone but himself."

The criticism rankled. "Well, he's been perfectly nice every time I've been around him," I said defensively.

E.A. just shrugged. "Miriam ought to know. She's known him since they were born. And "perfect" isn't a word I attach to the men I know. But, it's worth a try, Sheila."

I looked for Josh Cooper around every corner.

I saw him most often when he came to pick up Miriam to go to a movie or the library. I didn't know which since all of us signed out for the "Library" no matter where we were going, to a movie, to O'Toole's to drink beer, to the "drag" or occasionally even to the library to study. Josh was always friendly and usually asked me about living in New York. He hoped to go to Columbia for graduate work the following year, if he was accepted. Miriam said he was obsessive about studying for the GREs.

By chance, I discovered Josh tended the John Leddy Jones Library in the afternoons. It was a special section of the huge Fondren Library dedicated to books concerning Comparative Literature. Josh was a favorite of Dr. Harrison, the head of the department, and so he was one of the students who got the plummy assignment.

The Jones Library was relegated to a far corner of the Fondren, accessed most easily by a flight of stairs like a fire escape. The Comp Lit students loved it, partly because it was furnished with a number of old, overstuffed couches, much more comfortable than huddling in one of the carrels assigned to graduate students, or sitting in one of the hard library chairs.

Since students were only allowed to take Freshman English their first year and not Comp Lit, the Jones Library usually was reserved for sophomores and above. I consciously picked an assignment for an essay that would require me to look for materials in that special section. I hoped, of course, to see Josh. As it happened, the very first time I went to the library, there he was sitting at the top of the steps, smoking a cigarette. The smell filled the stairwell and I thought it rather pleasant.

"Hi," he said.

"Hi. I need to look up some things on the Lake Poets and Dr. Redford said I could look here," I said, rushing through the well-rehearsed sentence.

"Sure. I'll help you, but wait until I've finished my smoke."

"I'm surprised you can smoke in here."

"This is the only place. It's pretty fireproof. Hate the thought of book burning and it would be terrible to see this place go up in flames. Cigarette?"

He held a package of Phillip Morris cigarettes out to me.

"No thanks, I don't smoke," I said. The words sounded prissy to my ears. I stared at the package. It was the awful brown color of the tobacco juice my Great Uncle Michael used to spit, much to the consternation of my family.

Josh grinned at me. "So what does that frown mean? Curiosity? Disgust? Maybe a little of both?"

"I don't know," I stammered, not wanting to talk about Uncle Mike's filthy habit. "Why?" I countered.

He shrugged. "Writers spend their lives wondering what goes on in other people's heads, and making up stories to fill in the gaps they can't know. Now I think there is maybe a little curiosity there. I hate to lead an innocent astray and it's a terrible habit, but you're welcome to try one."

I was obviously hesitating.

"Sit down," he said.

I sat down on the step beside him. "Okay. I'll try one; tell me what to do?"

Josh smiled at me with something like triumph. He pulled one of the white tubes from the package. "Put it between your fingers like this." He demonstrated holding the cigarette between the middle and first finger of his right hand, balanced between the first and second knuckles. I was fascinated, not so much by the lesson in cigarette deportment but by the long, beautiful fingers of his large hands. "Don't hold it like this, ever." He grasped the object between his thumb and first two fingers. "That's okay for guys, but it makes girls look cheap. And don't wave it around all the time. Some people seem to think it's a part of the conversation. Now, you take it."

I held the cigarette as he had instructed.

"If you want to, you can tamp down the tobacco on the end against your thumbnail or the table or something. It keeps it from coming loose and sticking to your lips. Like this." He took the cigarette from me and tapped it on his thumbnail. I could see that the little tube of paper did firm up on the end.

"You try."

I copied his movements and then put the cigarette in my mouth. The paper was dry and stuck to my lips. He held out a Zippo lighter and flipped the steel wheel against the flint with a practiced motion. I breathed in as he touched the fire to the tobacco. The next thing I knew, I was bent over coughing the acrid taste of smoke in my mouth.

He was laughing as hard as I was coughing. He rescued the burning cigarette from my hand before I burned a hole in my green wool skirt. I had tears in my eyes and for one awful moment was afraid I was going to be as sick here on the stairs as Susan was that night in the car. In a moment, I felt better and sat up and looked at him. Was he doing this to tease me? I didn't know whether to be angry or simply bask in the complete attention he was affording me.

He handed the cigarette back to me. "I promise. When you get used to it, you'll love it. Then when you love it, I'll show you how to smoke dope."

"Oh, sure," I said, laughing. My only introduction to marijuana had been Uncle Howard telling me in detail about "reefer madness." At the time I thought he was exaggerating to make it somehow different from the quantities of scotch he drank.

Josh was right about the tobacco. At first, I only smoked his cigarettes, but within two weeks I was buying my own and I was joining E.A. and Paula in the smoker for a cigarette. Only Miriam continued not to smoke. She did comment, however, that I liked Phillip Morris cigarettes, just like Josh.

My stomach turned over when Miriam made the comment. I felt almost guilty, as though my times with Josh in the stairwell were some sort of love affair I was hiding.

Since I couldn't check books out from the Jones collection, I went there to read what I needed for the assignment. After my paper was done and turned in, I continued to visit Josh, to talk on the stairs and bum cigarettes.

If it was anything more to him than friendly chatter about books and movies and current events, he gave no indication. For me, each visit made me feel closer to him. Even though we never touched, I could sit beside him on the stairway and imagine feeling a magnetic pull. I could feel the warmth of his body even through winter sweaters.

I thought I was being very clever and discreet until one day near the first of November, E.A. sat on the bed and watched me tug at my hair with a critical look on my face.

"So who's the guy?"

"What?"

"Come on. Fess up to your old roomie. You've been going around for the last two weeks with the moony look of a girl in love. You've bought two new sweater sets at Delman's and now you're thinking about restyling your hair."

"How did you know?"

"About the guy or about the hair?"

I laughed and sat down on the bed. "Both," I said, deciding it was time I shared the secret. Especially since I was about to burst to tell it, anyway.

"Well, it's Josh Cooper."

"Surprise. Surprise," she said never changing expression.

I told her briefly about my trips to the library. She tossed her package of cigarettes to me. "Here, have a real cigarette."

We lit up, sitting cross-legged on our beds, leaning toward each other like a couple of conspirators.

"And how's your campaign for Chuck going?"

"Not bad," she said with a triumphant grin. "We meet for coffee in the Union on Wednesdays. There are a bunch of us, but he's started paying more attention to me, and ..." E.A. paused for effect, putting her arms up like a victorious boxer. "We're going to the movies Sunday afternoon after the team gets back from South Bend."

I hopped off the bed to give her a hug, nearly spilling her ashtray on the floor.

"Now, about your hair," she said. "You really should cut it. Mama says if a woman wants to change her life, the first thing she should do is change her hair."

I wondered why E.A. wore hers in the long schoolgirl bob, but said, "I'd love to have it cut like Miriam's."

She shook her head. "You don't have enough curl. Just get it cut in a shingle, with some side bangs. It'll look great."

She recommended the man who owned the beauty shop on the drag. He was used to styling coeds' hair. He cut my hair very short, with slightly longer pointed wisps in front of my ears, drawing attention to my earrings, and springy bangs on either side of my natural part. I wondered if Josh would notice.

On Wednesday, I caught sight of him standing by the balustrade of the rotunda on the second floor of Dallas Hall. I knew he had a class with Dr. Harrington at ten, so I deliberately walked that way from my nine o'clock English class.

"Hey, cute haircut. Did you take a look at the *Campus* today?"

So much for bowling him over with a new hairdo, I thought. But I laughed at myself while giving him a bright smile.

"No. What's in it?"

"I was going to ask you. I haven't had time to pick up a copy. You know the editor, Jim Soderberg, is a friend of mine and we were having coffee the other day and he was in a fit of rage over a new book by the head of the history department. Jim's threatening to write an editorial about it and I wondered if he had."

"What's the book about?"

"The man's a bit of nut, in my opinion. He has this theory that our participation in the war was a mistake and we only got involved because Justice Brandeis convinced Woodrow Wilson to help out the Jews in Eastern Europe after World War I and bled the continent economically so that Germany was forced into doing something about it."

"That's crazy." I suddenly had a flash of memory; the grainy black and white wire photos of the death camps in the newspapers the spring of 1945. The pictures of the emaciated prisoners had shocked me more than all the battles.

"He believes it, and I understand his book has sold rather well in certain circles. Anyway, my friend the editor thought that since I was Jewish, I would think it was awful for Harvey to publish the book. We got into a row over the First Amendment and I think Harvey has a perfect right to publish whatever he can get a publisher to print, even if I think its garbage. I told Jim I thought he was on safer ground to keep on publishing stories about movies, reforming rush and freshman beanies. Something tells me he's not going to take my advice."

"I didn't see much on the front page except the Notre Dame game. It's kind of like your experience with your friend, the editor. I've had three people ask me if I was going to cheer for Notre Dame since I'm a Catholic. My Dad went to Fordham and we never cared much for Notre Dame at our house."

Josh laughed. "That reminds me. Would you like to go to a listening party on Saturday? Some friends and I are getting together at an apartment over on Airline."

"Sure. I'd love to."

The bell was about to ring for class, so he said over his shoulder, "I'll call you."

I didn't care if I got to class or not. The marble floor of the rotunda turned into clouds for me.

My interest in football had increased in the past month. I had gone with some of the girls from the dorm on a chartered bus to the Cotton Bowl to watch SMU defeat Missouri. I wasn't particularly interested, but wanted to see for myself what all the fuss was about. I came home an enthusiast.

There was something about the noise and color that caught my imagination. The game was played at night and the lights made the colors appear as vivid as a Technicolor movie. I felt as though I had stepped into a scene from *The Wizard of Oz*.

We wore white blouses and the unattractive red beanies because we sat in the card section. My only disappointment was that I couldn't enjoy the display, only dutifully hold up one of my yard-square pieces of cardboard, obeying the instruction as to which color at the command of the cheerleader on the field with a megaphone. The music made me want to march around with the band, but my written instructions for the card section specifically said, "Pay Attention!"

I did manage to pay attention while keeping one eye on the field where the band was performing spectacular maneuvers, spelling words or making images all while playing a tribute to the State of Missouri. I thought the musical tribute was a nice gesture, since we were beating them badly. "Flingin' Freddy Benners," the quarterback with a talent for throwing a football in a long graceful arc down the field to its intended recipient, was in fine form.

The girls told me it was too bad I had come to school one year too late to see the great Doak Walker play, but no one suggested Benners was a second fiddle.

The ride home on the bus was fun, with some of the guys standing in the middle of the aisle telling rather off-color jokes. There was a lot of laughter and good humor and I couldn't wait to go to another game. I could only dream of going to one with Josh Cooper.

Listening on the radio might not have been as exciting as the color and sound of brass instruments and drums, but my heart was enough of a drumbeat when Josh came by the dorm to get me on Saturday.

I sat alone in my room, wearing a new powder blue sweater set with a little white Peter Pan collar at the neck. The collar, called a dickey, was not attached to a blouse, but to a wide yoke hidden by the neck of the sweater. I was almost as nervous as I had been the first day at university. E.A. had gone to the Pi Phi house to listen to the game with her big sister in the sorority and Paula and Susan had gone to the DG house. Miriam was home in Fort Worth for the weekend for some family occasion after assuring me that she thought it was wonderful I had a date with Josh

When I was paged, I ran to the bathroom for one last time. The mirror in the bright room confirmed that I looked the way I wanted to: rather chic but still collegiate. The blue cashmere sweater set was the color of my eyes and went well with the gray skirt. I looked at my calm face, which belied the butterflies that had taken up housekeeping in my abdomen.

I took a deep breath and went downstairs. Josh greeted me with a smile and even put his arm around my shoulders to guide me out the door. He was wearing khakis and a blue dress shirt, and carried a navy jacket over his right arm. The shirt was open at the collar and rolled up around nicely muscled forearms. I thought about Michelangelo's David. That's who he reminded me of, with his crisply curling hair, broad shoulders and long body. I briefly wondered about the other anatomical details.

We walked north across the campus, mostly in an easy silence. This time, the warmth of his body I had only imagined was pressed against my side. The day was cloudy, but so far without rain, and the persistent Texas wind was absent. Josh filled me in briefly on who would be there. The listening party was given by a couple of Dallas boys, former Sigma Alpha Mu members from the University of Oklahoma who transferred to SMU and preferred to live near campus instead of at home.

"This ought to be a fairly tame party," he observed. "They had one last week for the OU–Texas game and I thought it was going to end in a riot. This week, at least everyone is on the same side."

The one-bedroom apartment had a small kitchenette and the space was filled with young people sitting on couches, the floor and even the beds in the bedroom. The couples who chose the bedroom seemed on slightly more intimate terms than the ones in the living room. Josh introduced me and I struggled to remember as many names as I could. I felt a little like I had at the rush parties in a room crowded with people I didn't know, and realized I was as eager to impress these people as I had been with the women in the sorority houses.

I was grateful when the conversation ceased and we began listening to the pregame commentary on the radio. My face was beginning to ache from the effort to appear bright and relaxed.

For the next three hours, we munched popcorn, drank Cokes, and listened to the news flowing from the black plastic radio set on the coffee table in the living room. There also was plenty of beer. At halftime, the hosts circulated with brown paper garbage bags, picking up the amber beer bottles and the clear soft drink ones that filled every level space. There was a steady stream of people to the bathroom beyond the bedroom, where a second radio echoed the proceedings in South Bend.

Josh and I sat with our backs against the wall, his legs, considerably longer than mine, stretched out in front of him. I stared at the difference in size between my feet in their black Papagallos and his in brown cordovan tassel loafers. I could hardly believe I was here and that this was a real date.

Josh and the other men became more excited as the news proved all our hopes to be well-founded. Fred Benners, the super passer, lived up to his reputation, and we beat the Irish 27 to 20, the final gun accompanied by an eruption of cheers and backslaps in the tiny apartment. I got a long hug, which thrilled me.

After the party, people began to leave, but Josh and I stayed and chatted with some of those who stayed on. The girls were friendly and were especially so when they discovered that Miriam and I were friends. There was no one in the bedroom when I excused myself to use the bathroom, but I could hear voices from behind the closed bathroom door.

"Cute girl Josh has a date with."

"Yeah, but she isn't Jewish, is she?"

"I don't think so, but she's a friend of Miriam's. That's how they met."

"Even so, can't you imagine Mrs. Cooper? She and Mrs. Saperstein have had Josh and Miriam engaged since they were born. She'd have a cow if she knew Josh was dating somebody besides Miriam and a goy at that!"

I didn't want to hear any more, so I went back to the living room. I could wait until we got back to the dorm for the bathroom.

Instead, six of us walked to Snyder Plaza and ate at a hamburger joint. It was pleasant enough and everyone made me feel quite at home, but a pall hung over my happiness of most of the afternoon.

I had always been a dutiful child, and I just assumed Josh probably would accede to all that family and community pressure.

Yet, he kept his arm around me as we walked back to the dorm in the dark and even gave me a friendly kiss on the mouth when we reached the door.

"See you," he said. But I wondered. He seemed detatched, as though I was just a nice change of "sister" from Miriam.

CHAPTER ELEVEN

Midterms came and went. My only disappointment was a B in Western Civ. I had hoped for straight As. When I called my uncle, he was noncommittal about the grades, but told me to keep up the good work. Aunt Grace was more encouraging. She thought it was wonderful I had made such a good start on an academic career.

October's mild weather continued. The highlight of the month, even for me, who cared little about football, was our team's victory over Notre Dame. It was the one animated conversation I had with my uncle. A Fordham graduate, like my father, he always thought Notre Dame's reputation was overblown and this time he even called me first to congratulate us on knocking his old rival out of the top twenty ranked football teams.

We also won the homecoming game, so the hated red beanie was retired to the wastebasket. Homecoming weekend dominated everything, including academics. I went to watch the traditional tug-of-war that was performed in the middle of the quad, the rope stretched across the fountain. Paula and Susan were active participants, but their side lost and they were close enough to the front to get a thorough dousing in the water.

That evening, I bundled up to go to the bonfire in the vacant lot across from the Pi Phi House. Josh hadn't asked me to go to the game, but he did offhandedly suggest I meet him at the bonfire. We stood together watching the flames and cheering at the direction of the cheerleaders. The six of them were all men, dressed in the white slacks and shoes reminiscent of the 20s. Tonight, they had bulky cable knit sweaters pulled over their shirts for warmth. The red MG they drove was parked next to the bonfire.

Josh kept his arm around me and it wasn't so much the warmth I appreciated as the feeling of intimacy, the dark night and the companionable smell of wood smoke. I was perfectly content.

E.A. was making progress with Chuck Bolton. I could see her animated face lit by the firelight in the circle across from us. I thought he looked a little too bright-eyed and perhaps just a bit drunk. This was not a good thing the night before the game, but E.A. looked completely taken with him. He was trading quips with the cheerleaders and she was looking up at him adoringly.

Josh walked me back to the dorm, but tonight there wasn't even a friendly kiss.

From the look of E.A.'s makeup and the distinct redness around her chin, she evidently had better luck than I did. I wanted to pout, but smiled instead, "How was it?"

"Great," she sighed. "And he asked me to go out to O'Toole's after the game, win or lose." A fleeting look of concern crossed her face, but was quickly replaced by a dreamy look.

"What?"

"Huh?"

"Why the worried look a minute ago."

"Nothing."

I sat and stared at her.

She suddenly grinned, "But he sure likes to French kiss!"

"I can tell by the whisker burn."

She didn't answer but just grinned.

"Does he go at it a little hard?" I couldn't help but ask the question although I knew it was none of my business.

"Not really," she said, but the same look flitted across her face.

By November, the weather blew in raw and cold. I pulled out my long, camel colored coat to wear to class. E.A. produced a three-quarter length brown sheared beaver coat from the depths of her closet. When Josh saw me on campus, he teased me about looking like an Eastern preppy. I still preferred it to looking like a teddy bear, which I thought the fur coat did to even the slender E.A.

I gave him a casual wave and headed for class, pondering the fact that clothes and football had begun to dominate even my thinking. Other than the remark about the coat, Josh and I had spent the last few minutes discussing the deplorable incident of one of the Baylor players kicking a member of our team in the game the previous weekend. The incident was bad enough that Baylor University made a formal apology to SMU.

On Saturday, I really paid attention to what I was going to wear, and to the football game. I was going to the game against Texas A&M with Miriam as my "date" but I wanted to be prepared to look great if we ran into Josh.

My choice of clothes probably had nothing to do with anything, but we sat three rows behind Josh and his fraternity brother Steve.

Our mood swung from elation to depression as the game seesawed back and forth between our Mustangs and the Aggies. The game was on our turf this year, and I could see acres of khaki uniforms across the field. The truth was I thought all the guys looked wonderful in their uniforms with their high spit-and-polish riding boots and Sam Brown belts. Whenever SMU made a touchdown, Steve and Josh would turn around to wave victorious fists in the air, sharing their obvious pleasure with us. But the game ended in a disappointing tie. After the game, they asked us to go out for a beer.

Steve had a car and suggested O'Toole's since it had live music. Miriam and I had ridden in with Paula and Susan in her car. They didn't seem disappointed when we said we wouldn't ride back with them.

Steve and Miriam sat in the front and Josh and I in the back seat of his green Ford.

O'Toole's was crowded and we were lucky to find an empty table. It looked like it was made for two, but had four chairs. The boys ordered a pitcher of Lone Star and four glasses. I didn't really like beer, but tonight the bubbles and the tang of hops tasted just right.

The subject of Thanksgiving holiday came up and Steve was anxious to go to Houston to see a girlfriend. Miriam and Josh were looking forward to the long weekend with their families in Fort Worth and I hadn't given much thought to being alone on the holiday. I knew that one of the dorms stayed open for orphans like me, so I just assumed I would hook up with the other girls who lived too far away from school to go home for the holiday. I felt forlorn. The Negro pianist playing and singing St. John's Infirmary in the smoky bar added to my depression.

"I guess I'll see what Paula's doing and maybe we can stay together during Thanksgiving."

Miriam looked confused. "Paula's going to take the train to Houston with Susan," she said.

"Oh," was all I could say. Now I truly felt abandoned. I concentrated on making little overlapping circles with the bottom of my sweaty beer glass. There was a rather long silence while Josh and Miriam exchanged looks.

"I thought you were going to San Angelo with E.A.?" Josh finally asked. "I thought we were all going to drive down in her car, Miriam and me to Fort Worth and the two of you going on to her Dad's ranch."

"She never said anything about it," I said. "Well, she did mention my going home with her early in the semester, but I didn't know anything about Thanksgiving."

"Well, she talked to me," said Miriam, "and Josh was standing right there. I thought that was a plan."

"She's been a little distracted," I said dryly, and the other three laughed.

"Concentrating on school," said Steve.

"It's a sudden interest in football," said Josh, and the conversation turned to the perennial subject in the Southwestern United States. The men began to dissect the game we had just seen, play by play. Josh only interrupted the discussion of sports to occasionally light a cigarette for me.

Miriam and I ignored them and gossiped first about clothes and movie stars, then about friends and campus social activities. Miriam talked about the holiday party the Phi Sigma Sigmas were planning. I couldn't help but feel left out of everything.

As though my sudden wave of depression had infected the atmosphere at the table, Josh changed the subject and said with a frown, "Did any of you see the *Dallas Morning News* this morning?"

"I did," Steve said.

"Did you see where Ridgway confirmed that fifty-five hundred POWs had been massacred in those North Korean prisons?"

"I can't believe it, fifty-five hundred of our men." The two young men stared at each other for a moment. Steve continued, "I hear Stan Meyerson got his draft notice."

Josh nodded, "Yeah."

"What's your status?"

"High number and just lucky so far. Hope I get in at least a year of graduate school, but my number's bound to come up sooner or later and it doesn't look like things are much better over there."

"Are you going to ask for a deferment?"

Josh shook his head. "Almost everyone else I know has put in his time."

Steve continued with an observation that it also looked like the French were losing the war in Viet Nam.

I didn't pay much attention and couldn't have identified Viet Nam on a map other than it was somewhere in Indochina, but the thought of Josh going off to the mountains and snows of Korea where young men were getting blown up or shot in prison camps horrified me.

It was a subdued group of four students who headed back to the dorm. Josh and Steve occupied the front seat on the way back, and Miriam and I sat silently in the back. They dropped us off with a friendly but hardly intimate good-bye.

"Thanks for the beer, guys," Miriam said, and added under her breath as we turned away, "and you're both a barrel of laughs."

As we headed up the stairs, she said, "Let's find E.A. and straighten out this holiday thing."

As it happened, E.A. was already in the room. Later, she told me that she came home early because Chuck wasn't feeling well. I wondered if he'd had too much to drink, perhaps drowning his disappointment over the tie with the Aggies.

Miriam wasn't shy about broaching the subject of Thanksgiving. "E.A.," Miriam said, "didn't we decide Josh and I would catch a ride to Fort Worth with you and then you and Sheila would go on to the ranch?"

E.A. looked nonplussed for a moment and I was distinctly uncomfortable. I didn't want to push myself on the Cabels for a long weekend if they didn't want me.

"Yes," E.A. finally said.

"Well, Sheila doesn't know anything about going to San Angelo."

"I know." E.A. looked at me with those melted chocolate eyes. "I'm so sorry, honey, to be so long in talkin' to you about it, but it's Mama. She wanted to write and invite you formally before I went off and made a lot of fuss over it. I picked up the mail on the way up and you have a note from her. I'm sure that's the invitation."

I glanced at my dresser and on the edge was a monarch-size envelope of heavy cream paper addressed to me in a round feminine hand, not unlike E.A.'s.

It was the invitation, and Mrs. Cabel sounded on paper as enthusiastic about life as E.A. was in reality.

We all squealed and hugged each other in a way of teenage girls, an action I have since come to regard as singularly silly, but for me on that November evening, there was a real feeling of excitement and belonging.

The trip to San Angelo was through the sort of country I had never seen. The rolling grasslands that bordered the Trinity River valley on its way south and west of Fort Worth held the promise of spring lushness even in the dead grasp of winter.

Along the creeks leading to the Trinity, a few leaves still were clinging to the cottonwoods, their bright golden color now deepened to the patina of antique gold jewelry. On the hillsides, there was an occasional copse of stunted looking trees. I inquired about the gnarled trees and commented that they did not seem to have lost any of their desiccated leaves. Josh explained that jack oaks didn't lose their leaves until the old ones were pushed off the limbs by the new spring growth. To me, the writhing branches looked like Michelangelo's slaves trying to escape the stone. I found myself fascinated by the tangles of branches every time we passed a patch of the black-barked trees.

"I've never seen any trees in New England that look like these," I commented to no one in particular.

"Have you been up there when the trees turned? I'd love to go see the colors," Miriam commented.

"Once, but usually I was there either at Christmas or in the summer for camp."

"Camp," said Josh. "Ah, camp. Miriam always loved camp."

"I did not. You're the one who loved camp. You couldn't even wait to go back as a counselor. You're probably going back even this summer."

"Well, I've certainly thought about it."

"I'll bet you have. It's a lot different being stuck in a cabin with ten stinky kids when you are a counselor and can sneak out to see the girls at Agawak and drink beer."

"Squawk? Is that the name of your camp?" asked E.A.

"Agawak. That's a backwards spelling of Kawaga, which was the boy's camp named for the lake it is on. They're in northern Wisconsin. Gorgeous country. What was your camp like, Sheila?"

"Brownledge. It's in upper New York State, in the Adirondacks. It gets its name from a huge limestone cliff. I loved camp." The memory of those summers, a wonderful respite from school and home, flooded back on me. In some ways, going far away to Texas to go to college was like this; away from Brooklyn, but surrounded by friends and fun. Like camp, there was a routine at the university: institutional requirements and, it suddenly occurred to me, a beginning and an end.

"Was it on a lake?"

"Oh, yes. We had all the boating and swimming and stuff. And, of course, crafts and dramatics and things to do on rainy days."

"I'll bet you made a lanyard," said Miriam.

"I did," I laughed. "It was an awful mustard and dirty green color."

"Josh could show you. He was the master of lanyard making, weren't you, Josh?"

"And if I had one right now, I would throttle you with it."

"He went off to camp last summer thinking he was going to teach archery and swimming and they made him the craft counselor."

Josh reached over and pushed Miriam's curly hair down in her eyes with a swipe of his hand.

"Stop it," she whined, and I could see why she didn't mind if I dated Josh. They acted like teenage sister and brother.

"How about you, E.A.?" asked Miriam. "Did you go to camp in the summer?"

"Didn't everybody?" she answered.

"And I suppose you went to Waldemar."

At this, E.A. bristled. "I did not. With all those snooty girls? "I went to Camp Mystik. My friends and I thought it was lots more fun."

"Where is it?" I asked.

"Right here in the Texas hill country. I've got to take you over there and show it to you. It's even prettier than your New England or certainly Wisconsin."

I sat and listened in silence to the heated discussion among my three companions about the beauties of nature in the various parts of the United States. I was determined to someday see these places for myself now that I had left the East Coast.

In the meantime, the local landscape had flattened out and we approached Fort Worth. Like Dallas, it was remarkably clean and well kept, even in the marginal industrial parts of town we drove through to get to the residential area, but it was horribly flat to my eye, which is more used to the clutter and jagged buildings of New York.

Miriam and Josh lived only a few doors from each other. We dropped them and their luggage, met Miriam's parents and got back in the car for the drive west to San Angelo. I was disappointed not to meet Josh's parents, but Miriam had pointed out the neat ranch-style house where he lived. Now I had a permanent impression of where he grew up, including how he spent his summers.

"Thanks for the ride, E.A.," Josh said as he picked up his suitcase and headed toward his house. "And watch that lead foot of yours on the way to the ranch."

"Now, I didn't drive too fast getting down here," she protested.

We headed west toward San Angelo on Highway 84. The road, undulating slightly, was fairly free of traffic and E.A. let the speedometer climb until I didn't want to look anymore.

"You don't drive, do you, Sheila?"

"I never had any reason to. We always had the subway or taxis if we wanted to go somewhere in the city. I usually just walked around Brooklyn to school and church and shopping. Why?"

"Well, I have in mind teaching you to drive while we're down here. We've got lots of time on Friday and even Thursday morning before Thanksgiving dinner. On Saturday, I'm sure we'll go into town for lunch or tea at one of Mama's friends, but the ranch is a perfect place to learn. No traffic to speak of and you can stop and turn around almost anywhere."

She didn't ask me if I wanted to, just took it for granted that I would be thrilled; in fact, I was excited at the prospect. Not being able to drive and with no public transportation around the campus had left me feeling a little claustrophobic and I hated having to depend on asking friends for transportation. There were buses in Dallas, but the one mode of transportation directly to downtown, the streetcar, which the students had nicknamed the Green Dragon, had ceased to run in August before we got to school.

My attention was caught by what looked like a huge brown ball of branches. "What's that?"

"That my dear, is a real live, or rather dead, tumbleweed." E.A. broke into a chorus of the old cowboy song about drifting along with the tumbling tumbleweeds.

I joined it, thinking how strange it was; instead of singing along with my radio at home, I was right here on the edge of West Texas looking at the real thing. "And what are those bushes?"

"That's mesquite. Daddy always puts some in the fireplace because it has such a sweet smell."

The cityscape and riverbed gave way to broken land that led to the flats of West Texas. The highway threaded itself between low but rugged escarpments and outcroppings of rock. The winter aspect was stark, the grass turned to the same hay color I had seen on campus. As we traveled west, the land flattened and landscape by this time seemed sparse to the point of desolation. Yet, there was majesty in the broad sweep of level land, broken only by heroic cedars here and there. In some places, the flatness stretched to the horizon line in all directions, broken only by dots of red or black cattle.

Occasionally, there was a thick growth of jack pine with hummocks of prickly pear cactus huddling around their roots. I thought the thicket impenetrable until I saw cattle grazing nonchalantly between the trees, their muzzles clipping grass between the spiked plants.

E.A and I chatted some but mostly enjoyed the passing landscape.

The sky as evening drew near had turned into a breathtaking array of colors reflected on thin strips of cloud. I watched as the pale pinks turned to fuchsia and then orange, reflecting the color of the copper disc of the sun, hovering on the horizon. There was enough of something in the air—not city smog, but dust, I guessed—so that I could look directly at the setting sun. The surrounding sky was a clear turquoise, reminding me of Indian jewelry.

We came to a drive with two stone pillars flanking its entrance. The car slowed barely enough to make a right angle turn and clattered across a bridge of pipes that E.A. informed me was a cattle guard. As we topped a rise, I could see the house.

"I've never seen a farm house that fancy," I said.

E.A. laughed. "Down here, we would ordinarily call it a ranch house and it would be sprawled all over the landscape. But this isn't a ranch house or a farm house. Mama said that if Daddy was going to make her live way out here from town, she was at least going to have the kind of house she would have had in San Angelo. She bought this thing in some little old town in the hill country, had it sawed into two pieces and shipped here on trucks. Then they stuck it back together. That's Mama for you. They say it's the most traveled house in the world."

Mrs. Cabel had chosen a lovely example of Gothic architecture to cut up and move to this location. A wide veranda wrapped the front and sides of the clapboard house. The Victorian windows had broad panes, unbroken by mullions, and there was lacy woodwork decorating every opening and the eaves of the steep-pitched roof broken by a single turret. The house was painted a wonderful cream color and the trim was brown. The front door was an inviting dark green. Old-fashioned lilacs, dormant now, but familiar to me from the tiny backyard of our townhouse, flanked the steps to the front door.

A woman who reminded me of her sister, Aunt Mamie, was waving from the porch. She was dressed in silk pants and shirt, more fitting for a Florida vacation than the Texas prairie.

As she approached to introduce herself, I had the impression of a much cooler woman than her sister. She gave me an airy kiss as we shook hands.

"We're so glad to have you, Sheila." Cordelia Cabel shook my hand and immediately turned to her daughter. "E.A., what in heaven's name possessed you to wear that awful old plaid skirt?"

As we carried our bags into the house, Mrs. Cabel's interrogation of E.A. continued. I would have found it burdensome, but E.A. appeared to take it all in good humor.

A broad entry hall, hung with a chandelier of brass with round frosted globes over the lights, dominated the room. The stairway rose at our left, turned and then doubled back on itself. I could see a sunny kitchen through the door under the first turn. At my right, there looked to be a library with bookshelves and paneling. The homey smells of cooking meat and vegetables from the kitchen mingled with a sweetness coming from the fire in the library. This must be the aromatic mesquite, I thought.

Mrs. Cabel led us directly upstairs and into the bedroom of my girlhood dreams. There were twin beds of white painted wicker, covered with well-worn quilts made from tiny patches of flowered cloth in pastel colors. I recognized the wedding ring pattern, like the quilt my aunt used for warmth when she lay on the chaise longue in her room.

The wallpaper was printed with pink and yellow flowers with Kelly green stems and leaves on a white background, and in the corner, next to an antique chest which probably had held toys at one time, was a fully furnished dollhouse. I longed to examine each tiny piece of furniture, with its rugs and dishes and flowerpots.

"You take the bed by the window, Sheila," said E.A.

"Dinner is in fifteen minutes," said Mrs. Cabel. "Just time enough for you to wash up after your trip. We must be prompt for Zulamae."

"That's our maid," explained E.A. when her mother left the room. "She practically raised me. I'll introduce you when we go downstairs."

After a quick turn in the bathroom, we went to the long, narrow kitchen, where a round, dark woman, wearing a blue-and-white checked apron over a white starched cotton dress, stood at the stove. The dress looked to me like a nurse's uniform.

Zulamae opened her arms and E.A. rushed to receive a long hug. "Um-um. You do look good, Miz Eleanor Ann."

"Zulamae, this is my friend and roommate from school, Sheila O'Connor."

I was struck by the formal use of my name and E.A.'s with no mention of Zulamae's last name. I assumed I was supposed to call her by her given name.

"It's so nice to meet you," I said, holding out my hand. Her dark hand was as soft as velvet in my own. I had expected the calloused hand of a laborer. I also noticed the carefully applied red lipstick, a trace amount of which remained on E.A.'s cheek, which Zulamae brushed away as soon as she shook my hand.

"Tell me what's goin' on, girl," she said and went back to tending her pots and pans.

E.A. pulled up a kitchen stool and gestured for me to take a chair beside a small plank work table in the kitchen. She began a thorough account of most of what we had done at school the entire fall. "I intended to write, but you know me, I didn't get around to it," she apologized. I noticed she left out any reference to boys.

"And?"

"What?"

"I guess you haven't had a date since you got there," said Zulamae, nodding her head sagely and stirring something on the stove.

"Well ..." E.A. blushed.

"Uh-huh. Tell me."

This was all E.A. needed, as she began a detailed description of Chuck Bolton and his exploits on the football field. I thought some of the things she described sounded more like what I had seen Fred Benners do than Chuck, but I couldn't help but smile at the recitation.

The clock crept toward six o'clock and finally Zulamae interrupted. "You girls put some ice and water on the table. I've got to lift dinner. Your Mama doesn't like a meal to be late."

E.A. pushed open the swinging door from the kitchen to the dining room. A huge round table dominated the center of the room with another wonderful chandelier hanging over it. There was tall wainscoting on the walls that matched the huge pocket doors separating the dining room from the library I had seen when I walked in. The wainscoting was topped by a shelf that displayed a lovely collection of Flow Blue china pieces.

We filled the glasses set at each place on the snowy damask tablecloth. A silver basket of fall colored gourds was in the middle of the table.

The sliding doors opened and Mr. and Mrs. Cabel came in with a tall young man dressed in Levis and a plaid shirt. I was introduced to E.A's brother, Sam. Casually dressed as he was, there was a suggestion of the military in his bearing and his closely cropped hair. He didn't smile and neither did I. I felt as though I was being introduced to a five-star general.

As dinner began, Mr. and Mrs. Cabel and I started a polite conversation between bites of roast beef, mashed potatoes and green beans. The conversation reminded me vaguely of Rush Week. I described something of my home and what my uncle did. They obviously already knew about my parents, and carefully made no mention of them. Sam, I discovered, must be the strong, silent member of the family, much the same impression his father gave me when we first met in the dormitory. I was mistaken about both of them.

"I hear your university has let Negroes into the Theolog School," Sam said, addressing his sister in an accusatory tone, as though she had been responsible for this action.

"Oh, I didn't know."

Mr. Cabel put down his knife and fork. "You're kidding?"

"That's what I read, Pop."

I was unprepared for the lecture that followed in Mr. Cabel's quiet voice. But there was fire in his words. He strongly objected to Negroes going to school with whites under any circumstances and deplored the fact that if this started in universities, it wouldn't be long before the races were mixing in public schools. He ended by looking directly at me and saying, "Don't you agree?"

"Well, actually, we had several Negroes in our school at home," I managed to choke out. "They were really very nice." I was appalled at my weasely tone of voice.

"And you went to a Catholic school, didn't you?"

"Yes, I did."

"You know the Bible is against it?"

I shook my head.

"But I guess you people don't study the Bible, do you?"

"Actually, we do. We just use a different translation." I felt backed into a corner, but wanted to defend myself without being impolite. I wondered where this conversation was going and didn't know how to stop it.

"Well, in our Bible, it says in plain English that the Niggers are the children of Ham, and …"

Mrs. Cabel had had enough. "Harold, don't use that word!"

"Nigger?"

She gave a toss of her head toward the closed kitchen door and I realized Zulamae would have heard all of the conversation.

"Zulamae knows exactly how I feel about it, and besides, they use that word all the time."

"And you're not one of them."

That ended the conversation and dinner sat heavily on my stomach until E.A. brought up the subject of teaching me to drive. I was relieved and able to eat every bit of the delicious warm apple crisp and vanilla ice cream Zulamae served us when she had cleared the dinner plates. I could even look her in the face and smile my thanks. She seemed as jolly as ever.

At breakfast, E.A. told her brother about the plan to teach me to drive. Sam derided E.A. as a driving teacher, calling her "Miss Leadfoot," echoing Josh's admonishment to us. Nevertheless, he was persuaded to drive E.A.'s Oldsmobile into San Angelo to visit friends early Thanksgiving morning, leaving the second pickup truck for her to begin teaching me on a standard shift vehicle.

As we left the house, Mrs. Cabel admonished all of us to be back by noon. "Thanksgiving dinner is at one o'clock and we don't want to make Zulamae late. She still has to go home and cook for her own family before tonight."

E.A. drove out one of the ranch roads to a deserted spot, parked the truck, turned off the key and climbed down from the driver's seat. "OK, it's all yours."

Reluctantly, I stepped down from my side of the car and we exchanged places. My hands were sweating.

"So what's the first thing you do?"

"Turn on the key?"

"Yep."

The dusty red truck made a grinding sound and then did nothing. Then it coughed to a start and made a brief lurch forward before dying.

"Lesson one. That pedal on the floor at the left? It's called a clutch. If you're driving a regular shift car, push it down with your foot before you turn on the key. It's also a good idea to put your foot on the other pedal at the same time, the square one. That's the brake; it stops the car."

I pushed down hard with my feet on both pedals.

She then spent ten minutes showing me how to shift gears, my feet firmly on the clutch and brake. I learned the "H" position, how to shift into reverse and began to feel the difference when shifting into reverse and shifting among the other three gears.

"Now, when you turn the key, let up on the brake pedal and put your foot gently on the gas pedal; that's the long one. And for now, just be sure you have the truck in neutral."

This time, the engine sputtered into a not so gentle purring sound.

The first three times I tried to shift gears to move the truck forward, the exercise ended in the same lurch forward and a dead engine. E.A., her hands firmly pressed against the dashboard to keep her from bouncing against the windshield, gently instructed me until, at last, the cab of the truck eased forward with the two of us as passengers.

Now more used to the movement of the car, I felt a powerful surge of pride. However, my eyes were fixed on the six feet of road ahead of me as though if I blinked I would end in the bar ditch. Gradually, I became less afraid. I glanced in the rearview mirror and noticed I had already begun to raise a cloud of caliche dust from the road's surface.

Moments later, I also saw a larger cloud of dust approaching us, evidently one of the ranch hands driving toward us. Panic rose in my throat.

"Just take it easy and stay on your side of the road."

"Is there room for two of us?" I asked, my throat as dry as the road surface.

"Oh sure, that's just Dave coming in from the east pasture.

Dave passed us in a blur, but he must have waved, because E.A. waved back, flashing her bright smile.

Instant relief flooded through me when I realized he really had passed us safely and I could still see the road through the dust he left behind.

"Now stop," said E.A.

I halted the truck in the middle of the road and looked at her with eyebrows raised in a question.

"Turn the truck around."

"Huh?'

"Well, you have to learn to back up and turn around."

I looked out the window and the bar ditches on both sides of the road looked like the Grand Canyon. I was convinced I would end by depositing the truck in one ditch or the other.

"Come on," coaxed E.A. "Put you foot on the clutch and do you remember where I told you reverse was?"

I did, but the gears made a grinding sound that startled me. I was sure I had damaged the truck.

"Now turn your wheel and back up."

I took my foot off the clutch too quickly and the truck lurched backward, precariously close to the ditch.

"Whoa! Brake! Brake!" Even E.A. sounded alarmed.

All I succeeded in doing was killing the engine, but my tutor had no sympathy for me. She made me start the engine, keep my foot on the brake to prevent us from toppling into the bar ditch and then inch forward until I was almost at the other ditch. I had to back up again to accomplish the turn. I realized I was sweating and there was grit in my mouth. I would be a lovely sight for Thanksgiving dinner.

But the driving lesson continued until I could stop and start the truck and even back it up and turn it around. After an hour, E.A. took pity on me and drove back to the ranch house. "Tomorrow, you get to drive my automatic shift. It's going to feel like a breeze after this old thing."

I certainly hoped so.

When we reached the house, Sam was standing on the driveway talking to a young man. Dressed in blue jeans, a work shirt and boots, I thought he must be a ranch hand, but I was struck by his graceful body. He was of medium height, with broad shoulders and a narrow waist and hips. He had been leaning against a dusty Ford pickup with his back to me. I couldn't help but notice his high firm bottom. He straightened when he heard our doors slam and seemed to stand at military attention. He swept the worn Stetson off with a courtly flourish.

E.A. introduced me offhandedly to him. "Hey, Jim Ed, this is my friend, Sheila O'Connor from school. Sheila, this is Jim Ed Roberts. He lives down the road."

She continued on into the house while I acknowledged the introduction, holding out my hand for his firm handshake. The lovely physique was topped by a freckled face, with surprisingly good cheekbones and a shock of red hair that could only be described as carrot red.

I followed E.A. into the house.

"He's cute," I said. "Does he work for your Dad?"

E.A. gave her raucous laugh, "Gosh no. His dad owns more of the county than even mine. He's a classmate of Sam's at A&M."

"Well why don't you date him?"

"Lord, it would be like dating Sam. Although Jim Ed's always hanging around and sometimes he takes me to the movies. But I'll get you a date with him if you think he's so sharp."

I was almost tempted and then thought of Josh. I shook my head. "I think I'll stick with what I've got."

The house was filled with all the familiar smells of Thanksgiving dinner: roasting fowl, sage, and onion. E.A. and I hurried upstairs to freshen up and change out of slacks into skirts and sweater sets. Each of us had on a single strand of pearls and the ubiquitous earrings. E.A.'s sweaters were pink and I wore the blue ones I had purchased in the fall. Thick white sox, turned down in a double fold, and penny loafers finished our outfits. I could feel the hem of my wool skirt catch on the top of the socks as I went downstairs.

At this meal, the conversation was kept safely to noncontroversial subjects, until Mrs. Cabel inquired about the girls we had met at school. E.A. enthusiastically described Miriam and Paula. The Cabels seemed uninterested in Miriam, but were curious about Paula and her father's Foreign Service background.

"She sounds interesting. I'm sorry she couldn't come down for Thanksgiving with you," said Mrs. Cabel.

"Oh, she's off with her friend Susan, from Houston."

"What are they? A couple of Lesbos?"

E.A. put down her fork, still full of turkey, and frowned. "God, Sam. You can be such an oaf."

"That's silly." I burst out. "They are both perfectly nice."

Sam, sitting on the other side of the table, snorted.

I blushed. I suppose being perfectly nice didn't have anything to do with one's sexual preferences. But I had been taught all about perversion both from the nuns and from my friends, and I knew those people could not be "perfectly nice."

"At least, if they're queer, you don't have to worry about their virginity over the weekend," Sam added to the conversation, and once again Mrs. Cabel changed the subject.

The afternoon was spent watching football on the Cabels' new television set in the library. We watched the traditional Turkey Day game between the University of Texas and Texas A&M. Texas won, so both Mr. Cabel and Sam were disappointed in the outcome.

The rest of the weekend passed in a flurry of social activities, with my driving lessons sandwiched in between. E.A.'s Oldsmobile was considerably easier to drive, and I found myself driving fast enough to raise my own rooster tail of caliche dust, but I demurred when she suggested I drive into town.

San Angelo was a surprise to me. Nestled in the confluence of three rivers, the Concho, the Middle Concho and the Colorado, pronounced in Texas Colo-RAY-do, to distinguish it from the great Colorado River that flowed through the Grand Canyon. This town, nestled in a still-green valley, was a true oasis in the barren landscape. Huge cottonwoods and elms lined the streets, as well manicured as those in North Dallas. In the neat downtown area were the Cactus Hotel and the Hemphill-Wells department store.

Entertaining was all done at home and the women, along with their maids, had become marvelous cooks. I was introduced to a host of unusual and savory dishes. Everywhere we went, there was food and gossip. The community of ranchers, the natives of San Angelo, was proud of its heritage. I learned about the settling of the country and building of the ranches before and after the Civil War, about the "Buffalo Soldiers," black Union troops who had been stationed at old Fort Concho and stayed to become foremen and ranch hands. Oil and gas in the Permian Basin west of the town had provided a degree of wealth to the community that seemed to insulate it from economic insecurity.

Within this cocoon, though, I could see a genuine love for and interest in each other. The fact that absolutely everything about you was known and a matter of open discussion daunted me. Not knowing or remembering the names, I learned who was pregnant again, who were going through a rocky time in their marriage, which couples were likely to swap mates and who had a "problem," although alcohol and drugs were never mentioned. Yet, here was a community that genuinely supported its own. On top of this was the thick patina of southern hospitality, and instead of being put off, I found I was drawn to it. I could see where E.A. had acquired her open, trusting and friendly personality.

Although it added another thirty miles to our trip on Sunday, E.A. and I took time to go into the Cactus Hotel on Sunday for fried catfish, and I learned the true taste and meaning of that southern delicacy.

We bid good-bye to the Cabels and took off, driving northeast to Fort Worth. We were later than we had told Josh and Miriam we would be, so E.A. pushed beyond the speed limit. Each time we would come up behind a slow traveling car, she would mutter about Sunday drivers.

Twenty miles west of Fort Worth, she began to whip around a Nash Rambler when I saw another car approaching on the other side of the road. E.A. gunned the motor and made it though the opening with inches to spare. I braced my hands against the dashboard they way she had done when I was driving. What she didn't notice was the Texas state trooper in a wide space next to a long country driveway. I noticed him and then so did she as he made a U-turn and his lights began to flash.

"Oh, shit."

I was speechless.

E.A. pulled over, opened her window and gave the officer her dazzling smile. It didn't soften his grim expression behind the dark glasses and broad-brimmed hat. He leaned down to rest his arm on the window.

"In a hurry, M'am?"

"Yes, sir. I'm sorry; I'm a little late pickin' up friends in Fort Worth."

"Did you notice both cars moved onto the shoulder to let you pass?"

"No, sir."

"Had another young lady do the same thing last week. Wasn't so lucky.

Her head ended up being about this wide." He held the palms of his hands about six inches apart.

E.A. was shaking by now, both from a reaction to the close call and to the description.

The trooper took out his pad and wrote a ticket. It was for $44. He handed it to E.A. "You drive, Miss?" he asked, looking at me. E.A. nodded vigorously. I was too stunned to answer.

"You better drive the rest of the way."

He turned to go back to his car and E.A. quickly got out of her side of the car. "Thank God he didn't ask to see your license," she said. "You've gotta drive, Sheila."

Reluctantly, I obeyed. My mouth was as dry as the Texas landscape. My hands were clammy and my stomach quivered. I shifted into drive, grasped the wheel and drove the last twenty miles at forty-five miles an hour.

E.A. asked Josh to drive.

My fear and horror at what almost happened abated as Josh, his steady hands on the wheel, drove a dignified sixty miles an hour toward Dallas. This time I was sitting in front with him. He opened the conversation by telling me his parents were sending him to New York for Christmas to look at Columbia. He would be staying with friends in town, but wanted me to join them for at least one evening of fun.

For me, Christmas seemed to have come early.

CHAPTER TWELVE

Dallas, Texas
Wednesday, May 16, 1985

The cab driver left me in care of the doorman at the Hyatt. We had no more than stepped into the building and taken the escalator to the lobby when I heard E.A.'s voice.

"My God, wouldn't you know, she hasn't changed a day."

If E.A.'s voice had not changed, the woman had. The voluptuous figure I remembered from school days had puffed up, expanding like a balloon. The waist was still evident but the entire body was twice the width of the nineteen-year-old girl. The hair was still blonde, but had lost its natural look. I suspected that the roots would be grayer than the ends.

Skillful makeup retained only a suggestion of the once petal-smooth skin, but the honey brown eyes and the smile had changed as little as the voice.

E.A. held out her arms and I found herself moving toward the female embrace with an eagerness that surprised me. The full bosom was firm and the fleshy arms strong. The expensive silk dress was warm and slick under my palms.

My nose wrinkled at the wave of perfume, which rose to assault me. She never had learned just to use a dab. My eyes were stinging, but with tears. I knew I was grinning like an idiot.

"E.A., God, you look terrific!" I said. I stepped back to look the blonde woman full in the face.

"I'm as fat as Shelly Winters, but she seems to still be blowin' and goin' — and so am I."

"And I want one of those hugs, too," a voice said.

Miriam had been standing quietly to the side but she moved with dignity and purpose, reaching up to give me a quick hug and a warm cheek to cheek kiss.

Miriam's maturity had obliterated her waistline and squared the oval face with a heavy chin. I doubted that Miriam weighed more than ten pounds more than she had thirty years ago, but she looked matronly. Her hair still curled into thick crests. The blue-black had given way to steel gray. Miriam's eyes were the same deep confident brown, slightly crinkled at the upturned corners

E.A. immediately took charge. "Miriam, go with Sheila and get her stuff stowed in her room. I'll go to the bar and grab us a table. It's getting on to four-thirty and the workin' crowd shows up to fill up the place. I'm ordering margaritas for everyone. They make the best."

With that, she turned on a spike heel and left the two us. We shrugged at each other and knew we would do exactly as she ordered.

"Yes, sir, General," Miriam whispered.

During the trip upstairs, the tipping of the bellman, a stop at the bathroom and the trip down, we filled in the gap of some ten years or so since we had stopped communicating except for the perfunctory holiday card.

I talked about my job, Elise, and living in Manhattan with Hugh. Miriam talked about her quiet life in Tyler, Texas, with her husband, Manny Gold. She reported on the three sons, Joshua, a fledgling correspondent for a Chicago paper, living in Moscow; Jacob, who was teaching and getting his doctorate at Stanford; and Andy, who just graduated from Rice with a degree that he hoped would lead him into industrial design. He was in New York City "finding himself," according to his mother. The last statement was accompanied by a look of exasperation familiar to me whenever I happened to be staring into the mirror and talking to Elise at the same time.

Unconsciously, we rushed through our own stories, knowing that once we were back with E.A., she would dominate the conversation.

"Over here, girls," she hailed, and we responded like automatons.

E.A. sat on a banquette, the silk of her summer print dress spread around her like a picnic blanket. Three balloon glasses edged in salt and filled with a milky but translucent liquid stood frosted in elegance on three cocktail napkins. E.A.'s already had a lunette of bright red lipstick on its edge.

Miriam took the chair next to Eleanor Ann, a somber counterpart in her black Chanel suit and white blouse. The only relief was a stunning black, red and silver pin on her shoulder. The design was contemporary and unusual, obviously a purchase from some exclusive store.

I was suddenly conscious of my own New York look, dressed in my favorite traveling outfit, an Armani pantsuit in navy and gray twill with its off-center closing. What a strange threesome we were today and had been from the very first day we met.

"Well, hell," said E.A., "I hope your margaritas are still cold. I told the fucking waiter to bring mine and wait to bring yours 'til you were down, but the idiot brought them all at once."

The word "fuck" rolled off E.A.'s tongue as easily as the tequila rolled onto it. I knew E.A. spoke one way in polite company and another way with intimate friends. The use of the word suddenly transported me back to the first time she ever used that word. I grinned.

"What?" said E.A.

"Nothing." I shook my head

I knew that Miriam Gold and Eleanor Ann had kept up a friendship over the years, seeing each other at least once a year and often more. Since Dallas was about the same distance from Tyler and San Angelo, the couples often would meet and spend the weekend in the city when the children were small enough to be left with grandparents.

I had seen E.A. on two occasions through the years, always when Jim Ed and E.A. came to New York for shopping and the theater. I had watched E.A. blossom into motherhood with the adoption of, first, her son and then the daughter of whom she was so proud. The blossoming swelled into plumpness and then steadily increased into fat as Eleanor Ann worried about the son, Harold. The boy did not seem to be able to stay out of trouble. First, it was school; then he began stealing.

I suspected drugs or alcohol might be involved, but the Robertses stoutly dismissed the idea. E.A. turned to food the way an alcoholic turned to booze. I wondered if she ate at the problem eating her. And she spent money. I was sure the rather unflattering print dress cost a fortune.

"Earth to Sheila!" E.A.'s teasing voice called me back to the present. "What in the world were you thinking about?"

I looked up into the smiling faces of my friends.

"What in the world were you woolgathering about?" asked E.A.

"Oh, just a lot of memories. Remember rush? What a week that was and was I glad when it was over. It all seemed so desperately important at the time." There was a silence then as each woman toyed with her glass, perhaps reliving some of the emotions of that turbulent week or ruminating about the change in times and mores.

"Have either one of you heard from Paula? When is she coming?" I asked.

E.A. sat up straight on the banquette and cleared her throat as though to make an important announcement. "She's supposed to be here this afternoon. Miriam can tell you the rest."

"E.A. asked me to try to get in touch with her," said Miriam. "She was the first one of you two we tried to reach because we didn't know how long it would take to get Paula in Calcutta. As it turned out, she was almost the easiest to reach. Everybody knows about the clinic she works in. Well, anyway, I got right though. At first she just said there was no way she could come. I told E.A. and gave her the number. She called back and talked Paula into the trip."

"I guess I wheedled," E.A. said. "Anyway, pretty soon she said she would think about it. Then about a week later, she called me and said she had made plane reservations, but still didn't know if she'd make it. If she comes, she's supposed to be in this afternoon, as I said. I told her to call our rooms, and if we weren't there we would be in the bar."

"And so we are," I mused. E.A. was always a marvel to me. The woman seemed so ditzy, but let her get an idea and she banged away at it until she made it happen. Her only defeat I could remember was the unsuccessful attempt to get me into a sorority. Sometimes I thought it was a particularly Texas trait not to let anything stand in your way, "come Hell or high water," as the saying went.

As though on cue, I saw a compactly built woman with gray hair cut in a rather masculine shingle making her way across the bar to us. The clear eyes were unmistakable. It really was Paula.

How appropriate, I thought. Paula was always there when she was expected and always there when needed, quiet but with a certain incalculable force.

E.A. saw her almost as soon as I. "Paula," she hailed, "we were just talking about you. I'm so glad to see you. So glad you got to come." E.A. was on her feet and soon grasped the other woman in that enveloping embrace. Over E.A.'s shoulder, I could see Paula's expressionless face turn from bland to a shy smile, accompanied by what was certainly a blush and could have been a trace of tears. She returned E.A.'s hug with one of her own.

Miriam and I rose and also hugged Paula. I could smell the lingering odor of E.A.'s makeup and scent on Paula's cheek.

While the greetings took place, E.A. hailed the waitress, "Miss! Miss! We need some assistance here. We have a weary traveler who definitely needs something to drink. What'll you have, Suzy Q?"

Paula settled herself in a chair. "Uh," she said and shook her head back and forth as if clearing her mind. "Just some Perrier and lime, please," she said.

"Now, honey, you gotta have something more than that after all your traveling."

"No, she doesn't, E.A.," Miriam said, "not if she doesn't want it." She was laughing, but her tone was firm.

"Well, I certainly want another round and you look a little dry over there, too, Sheila."

"I'm going to switch to Perrier and lemon," I said, addressing the waitress.

"I'm fine for now," said Miriam holding onto the stem of her margarita glass, capping its top with her other hand.

"Well, I'm switching, too," said E.A. "but make mine a vodka martini on the rocks with a lemon twist."

"E.A.," Miriam said, "now that we are all here, brag about your daughter and my goddaughter."

"Goddaughter?" I laughed.

"Absolutely. And what's wrong with a Jewish godmother? You get a godmother and a yenta all rolled in one."

"But," Paula asked, "didn't you also have to promise to raise the little bugger as a Christian?"

"Well of course, but that was the easy part. Can you imagine E.A. and Jim Ed doing anything else? It's the only time I can remember being in a Christian church and the experience was quite delightful. She was a lady and didn't cry at all. Just looked up at the minister with adoring eyes."

"Speaking of angels!" E.A.'s face took on that special maternal glow some women have when they talk about their children. I turned to see a young woman crossing from the lobby into the bar where we were sitting. She was a lovely girl. Not tall, but slender and tiny boned, her hair a mass of brown ringlets, which were natural instead of the perms so many girls affected these days. Her eyes were dark and snapping.

"Manny says she looks more like my daughter than E.A.'s," Miriam said, and I wondered if she secretly thought of Edwina as the daughter she so wanted after three boys.

Edwina strode up to the table, and before her mother could introduce her said, "Now don't tell me. I want to guess. Aunt Miriam I know, and Mom." She drew the word out for emphasis. "So, this must be Paula and you're Sheila." She stood between the chairs of the two of us unfamiliar to her, but correctly identified us, laying a hand on each of our shoulders in the process.

"Oh, you're so smart," her mother teased. "Pull up a chair and have a glass of wine."

"No margaritas like you're having?"

"If you want. I guess a college graduate can have anything she wants."

"I wish," the girl said, and I wondered what unspoken desires the casual remark covered.

We were all watching the girl, smiling, and I was aware that Edwina also had been assessing her mother's friends.

"Now, what was your major, Edwina?" I asked.

"I was history and government, but what I really would like to do is be in the Foreign Service or a foreign correspondent."

"So, what do you want to do after graduation? Go to Georgetown or someplace like that?" I asked.

"What I would really like is to go to Columbia first. That is if I can get into the J-school. I've applied, but haven't heard. What I can't make up my mind about is whether I would like to be a correspondent. I think I know what it would be like working for the government, but I don't know what it would be like to work for a newspaper." A perplexed vertical line appeared between her perfect brows.

Oh, to have such tender worries, I thought, but what I said was, "You should talk to Paula about the Foreign Service. She grew up in it."

I remembered the morning I asked Paula the same question and she gave Edwina much the same answers she had given Miriam and me, especially about the isolations.

"I tell you this because I see it in a lot of Foreign Service people and even in the journalists I meet overseas. Of course, with them, there is the added spice of sometimes being in danger or meeting with dangerous people, but it is the temporary nature of the life that seems to appeal to a lot of them. Just be sure of your motivations. It took me years to figure mine out."

The girl regarded Paula with wide, sober eyes. Her mother broke in, "Leave it to Paula to get the serious stuff into the conversation. I'm starving. Edwina, can you eat with us?"

Edwina immediately relaxed, blushed only slightly, screwed up her face as though to dismiss what she was going to say. "Can't. Thanks. Got a date."

"A serious date?" I asked.

Edwina smiled at me. "Cute, but no commitment yet on my part. Or his. He's thinking about going to Georgetown." She raised her eyebrows meaningfully to me.

E.A. watched her daughter cross the bar toward the lobby. Then she turned to us again.

"Can you believe? She met this guy on a blind date." She grinned at me mischievously, "He's a darn sight better catch than the one you had, Sheila. What a dog."

"Speaking of freshman dates and someone who could not in any way be called a dog, did all of you read Josh Cooper's book?" Paula's question ran through me like electricity.

E.A. leaned toward Miriam. "You, my dear, did have the inside track with the prize from that grab bag of freshman dating. Oh, my stars, was he pretty!

"Here we go again," said Miriam, rolling her eyes. "E.A. is never going to let me live down having blown off, so to speak, a Pulitzer Prize winner and turned him over to my buddy Sheila."

Paula looked at me with curiosity. "Sheila, when he was in New York, did you and Josh ever get back together?"

"Yes, as a matter of fact, we did. Of course, by that time I was out of school and working, but we did see something of each other."

The answer sounded rehearsed.

"Probably at the library," teased E.A. "Sheila was always sneaking off to the top floor of Fondren Library to talk books with him. She didn't think I knew where she was going."

I didn't want to prolong the conversation so I fumbled in my purse for my credit card to pay the check. The others protested, finally tossing bills my way to pay for their part. Then we started for the elevator to freshen up before dinner.

As we had in the dormitory, E.A. and I occupied one room in the suite E.A. had reserved in the hotel, and Miriam and Paula took the other room. Most of the hour before going to dinner was taken up with unpacking and hanging clothes, arranging cosmetics and toiletries in the bathrooms, washing faces and reapplying makeup, and finally putting on fresh clothes, all interlaced with snippets of conversation.

E.A., in another silk dress but this time an attractive dark print with large puffed sleeves, excused herself, closed the door and engaged in a murmured telephone conversation, inaudible to the rest of us in the sitting area of the suite.

I looked at my friends. Paula had changed to a plain black pantsuit; Miriam had on a black dress, adorned with another of her spectacular collection of pins; and I sat across from her in black silk pants and a buff colored silk jacket over a printed shell. I must have frowned.

"What?" asked Miriam.

I shook my head. "We've yakked all afternoon about old times and our kids." I gave Paula a nod, "You missed most of that, lucky you, and E.A. has yet to say a word about her son. What's his name?"

"Harold," said Miriam.

"Oh, sure, named for E.A.'s dad."

"Anyway, when I mentioned him, she just said he was away and that was all. Is he in school somewhere?"

"He's in prison in Palestine, Texas," said Miriam succinctly.

CHAPTER THIRTEEN

New York City
Wednesday, December 19, 1951

When the plane landed, the sky was a smooth white as though someone had covered everything from horizon to horizon with butcher paper. I hoped for at least a few flakes to make halos around the bright Christmas lights of New York. The air, as the stewardess opened the door, bit my nostrils with a sharp promise of snow to come.

As I started down the metal stairway from the door of the American Airlines plane at La Guardia, I could see my Aunt Grace just beyond the chain-link fence of the gate. She was scanning the people descending from the plane and I had to smile. She didn't recognize me.

The week before, I finally had paid the last installment at Neiman's on the full- length white cashmere coat E.A. had convinced me to put on layaway in October. My hair, now short, was partially covered by the face veil of a small butterscotch velvet hat.

I wore long suede gloves of the same color and the only piece of clothing she would have recognized was my brown opera pumps.

I waved and watched her eyes widen and her jaw drop as she recognized me.

She gave me a huge, warm hug and said, "Well, I see stylish Dallas has already had an effect on you. Do I see Mamie Hamilton's fine hand in your choice of clothes?"

"Not hers, but her niece's."

The ride from the airport to Brooklyn, past the huge St. John's Cemetery, was as familiar to me as the palm of my hand.

"I have really missed you, my love. I miss having a woman to talk to now that your mother is gone."

Aunt Grace was the only member of the family who even mentioned my mother. I was grateful to have one person whom I could ask questions about what mother had been like as a girl my age.

Uncle Howard was still in Manhattan at the office, so we had time for a cup of tea. We sat at an antique tea table she had in the front room by the window looking out on the street. The view through the lace curtain gave me a conspiratorial feeling of privacy. We could spy on the world and not be seen. As we drank English tea from my grandmother's Limoges china decorated with pink apple blossoms, I found myself pouring out a flood of minutia about my semester in Texas, describing Eleanor Ann and the other girls, and relating what we had done both in school and at the ranch, including my prowess at driving an automobile. I shyly scattered references to Josh into this verbal mix.

"And this young man—Josh is it?—I gather he's going to be up here during the holidays."

"Yes, he graduates this year and he's coming up to look over Columbia for graduate school."

"Will he be here by Christmas? Would you like to invite him to eat with us and go to Mass afterward?"

I hesitated. "Actually, he's Jewish, like Miriam." I thought I saw the barest lift of Aunt Grace's eyebrows and wondered if it indicated disapproval or just curiosity. "Anyway, he's not coming until the day after Christmas." I took a sip of tea. I wanted a cigarette.

"That's interesting." The statement revealed nothing but seemed to hang in the air.

"I don't suppose I ought to mention that to Uncle Howard."

"I don't think I would."

My uncle often referred to the law firm where he was a partner as a "white-shoe" firm. That was his shorthand for a firm that was totally Anglo-Saxon. Other than this, he rarely made reference to anything even touching on one's race or religion

My mind was skipping over Christmas and dwelling on the week Josh would be in New York. I looked forward to New Year's Eve with the sort of anticipation I had for Christmas when I was a child. Josh already had intimated he wanted me to go downtown with him to Times Square. I had never been allowed to go before and had only seen the celebration on the first television set my aunt and uncle bought three years ago. I wanted to be there in person, to see the lights in color instead of black and white, and feel the gaiety of the crowd, and I didn't want anything to keep me from experiencing that with Josh Cooper.

During the two and a half weeks of school between Thanksgiving and Christmas vacation, Josh and I had been inseparable. Gone were my fears of his paying any attention to what his parents would think and gone was any thought about Miriam's possible interest in Josh. She was completely absorbed with seeing Manny during the holidays and Josh made his intentions toward me increasingly clear. The shared cigarettes on the stairway had given way to shared kisses and a deepening intimacy.

Like clockwork, at 5:45, my Uncle Howard walked up the steps of my aunt's townhouse. He hung his grey fedora and long overcoat on the mirrored hall tree. Then he gave me a stiff hug and a brief kiss on my cheek. I could smell tobacco smoke on the collar of his gray suit. I hoped he couldn't smell the smoke from the cigarettes I had smoked on the airplane still clinging to my hair.

"Hello, Princess," he said. There was that endearment again that rankled me so. "Glad to have you home." He headed straight for the sideboard that held whiskey and glasses. Aunt Grace had put out a silver bucket of ice and some canapés.

"Now, missy," Uncle Howard said, "I'm playing bartender as usual, and since you're all grown up and a coed, what would you like to drink?"

He had a bluff manner, which always reminded me of either Winston Churchill or the British bulldog. Uncle Howard was not at all British, but his prep school upbringing had left him a hopeless Anglophile. I asked for some scotch with a lot of soda. The answer seemed to please him.

"And you, my dear? Fancy a drink?" Aunt Grace asked for sweet sherry, which he poured, and then mixed a very dry martini for himself.

I wondered how long we would spend drinking before food was mentioned.

Aunt Grace may have wondered the same thing, because halfway through her own glass of wine and as my uncle rose to mix seconds, she said, "Don't think about having another drink. I called Luigi and said we'd be down by six-thirty. Tea's the limit of my cooking for one day." Luigi was the owner of our neighborhood Italian restaurant. They didn't really make reservations, but I knew her remark was to forestall another cocktail. We put on our coats and walked down to the corner of Court Street to be greeted by a smiling Luigi.

During the meal, where I had my favorite, Luigi's special lasagna, the adults quizzed me about school and what I had been studying. Aunt Grace brought up my social life.

"And I guess there's a young man. Friend or boyfriend?"

"Just a friend," I said but knew there was a blush and a sparkle to my eyes that would give away more than I wanted to admit.

"But I gather he's coming to New York over the holidays?"

My Uncle, who had looked up from his dinner when Aunt Grace mentioned Josh, gave me a rather hard and inquisitive look.

"Oh, not to see me," I hurriedly said to him. "He hopes to be a graduate student at Columbia next fall, and he's really coming up to see friends who are already students there and get some idea of the lay of the land."

He didn't pursue the subject.

After dinner, my Uncle carried my suitcase upstairs. The house had an entry hall from which rose a steep, uncarpeted staircase to the second floor. Its dark wood risers and treads and turned oak balusters gleaming in the lamplight. On the right of the hall was a living room, with the dining room beyond. The kitchen was behind that and looked out on our small, neat yard, Aunt Grace's pride, filled with as many various flowers as an English garden—hollyhocks and larkspur in the summer, spring tulips and iris from dark purple to palest peach. Behind the back garden ran a narrow alley, barely wide enough to accommodate the cats that nightly yowled their defiance into the darkness.

All of us were tired, so after dinner I went to my small bedroom at the head of the stairs. As I put on my nightgown, I heard Uncle Howard go back downstairs so that he could, I was sure, continue his drinking long into the evening.

As I looked around my bedroom, I couldn't help but contrast it to E.A.'s. Mine was not appreciably smaller than hers, but it lacked the indefinable air of comfort and security that I felt in her room. Mine contained only one twin bed, painted white with a panel of white caning in the headboard. A matching dresser was on one wall and a small white writing desk sat before a window that looked out on the front walk. Between my bedroom in the front and my aunt and uncle's in the back, a narrow, windowless bedroom had been divided into two generous bathrooms. Mine was tiled in strawberry pink and white. Theirs was done in a rather pasty green.

There was something forlorn about my neat bedroom with its four-shelf bookcase, crammed with all the reading I had done on lonely days in high school. I glanced at the door and noticed that the old-fashioned key to the door had disappeared a few years ago. That key had been a bone of contention between my uncle and me. There was a time in high school when I had insisted vainly on having a key to lock my door, but that time was past. I sat down on my bed and ran my hand over the ridges of my grandmother's green and lavender patch quilt, but it only reminded me more strongly of the ghosts and memories that seemed to suck the air from the room.

My wish for snow finally was granted after a week. It began falling the day Aunt Grace and I went into Manhattan to finish the last of the Christmas shopping. This, along with tea at the Plaza Hotel, had been a ritual for my mother and me for as long as I could remember. The waiters at the Plaza were used to the well dressed little girls who often came for tea. They were especially nice to me, I thought.

When Aunt Grace moved back from Texas, she joined us each year and she and I had, without discussion, carried on the habit. This year, dressed in my collegiate sweater and skirt instead of my school uniform, I noticed the waiters not only treated me as an adult, but I could see the younger ones looking at me with that calculating look I often saw boys giving girls as they walked across campus. It gave me a rather giddy sense of power. Regardless of what my aunt thought, I pulled out a pack of cigarettes.

"May I?" I asked, rather as an afterthought.

"Certainly."

Before the cigarette reached my lips, one of the waiters was at my elbow with a Zippo lighter. I smiled my thanks, and he grinned.

When we left the hotel, my aunt hailed a taxi to take us home. The new snow was beginning to fall again and it crunched underfoot.

By Christmas Day, it had melted into slush. The ubiquitous city dirt, unnoticed on dry pavement, colored the piles of icy debris at the curbs and dotted even the snow on the tiny plot of grass before the house with bits of soot. I had so hoped it would be lovely and white when Josh got to New York.

As it was, the rest of the week passed with no word from him. I had thought I would hear the day after Christmas. Finally, by Saturday, the phone rang in the late afternoon. I raced downstairs to the hallway to answer it. I was home alone, having refused to go to the movies with my aunt and uncle, just in case Josh did call.

"Hello?"

"Sheila? Josh."

As though I didn't know.

"Hi, how was your trip up?" My voice was breathless from my dash downstairs and because my elation had sent my heart rate soaring. I thought I sounded like an idiot.

"Oh, fine. I got here Sunday."

A stab of irritation brought the heart rate back down. What had he been doing all this time?

"My buddies from Columbia have been great. I've been all over the campus, but of course, everything is closed this week. But I've got a commitment from one guy to share an apartment, and I've got a couple of leads on jobs. Before I leave next Wednesday, I hope to nail down something."

I became impatient with all this reporting; all I really wanted to know was when I would see him.

"Uh-huh," I said with what I hoped was enthusiasm. I could see through the windows in the front room that it had begun to snow again.

"Say, we are all going to have dinner near Washington Square at this

Italian restaurant. What's the name of it?" he said to someone else, his voice fading away as he turned his mouth from the phone. A feminine voice said something I could not understand.

"Anyway, why don't you come down and meet us?"

"When?"

"Well, now, if you can. Here," Josh said, "talk to Anita. She'll fill you in."

"Hi."

"Hi," I answered wondering what her relationship to Josh was. She explained where the restaurant was, gave me its name and what subway stop was nearest. "Wait a minute. Josh is yelling at me." She put her hand over the mouthpiece and I could hear nothing but garbled sound. "He wants to know if you can come on down?"

For a second, I hesitated. He could have asked me himself, but after all, wasn't this exactly what I had been praying for all week?

"Be there in thirty minutes," I said.

"Great. Josh told us all about you," she said before she rang off.

That was encouraging.

I wrote a note for my aunt and uncle, telling them where I was going and that "a friend" would see me home. Then I pulled on snow boots, my heavy coat and a matching knit hat, gloves and scarf. I locked the front door and headed to the subway station. The long oblong shadows cast by buildings and a winter sun turned a slate blue against the new snow cover. The air smelled as icy as a sno-cone. For the first time, I felt adult and free. I had never been happier in my life.

The restaurant was down a short flight of stairs from the sidewalk. The air was laced with after-dinner smoke and fresh garlic. By the time the major domo saw me, my eyes were adjusted to the darkness and I looked around the room for Josh's familiar face. The walls of the restaurant were covered in a fancy red and white wallpaper. The white background and the snowy tablecloths reflected the glimmer of candles stuck in old Chianti bottles. Remnants of former candles dripped in now-hardened strings down the sides of the bottles, giving them a Joseph's coat of color.

"You're meeting someone?" He had a slight Italian accent.

"Yes."

"Is it the table of people there?"

Slightly behind a pillar, I saw a table with five young people and one of them was Josh. He looked up at about the same time and came to greet me with a quick kiss.

As I pulled off coat, hat, scarf and gloves, I realized my hands were shaking. Partly, I thought, from the excitement of being with Josh and partly from being in the midst of all these older friends of his. From my earlier conversation with Anita, they knew something about me but I knew nothing about them. I felt in deep water.

Josh introduced me to the others, all graduate students at NYU except for Anita, who was at Columbia. She had long straight, dark hair and horn-rimmed glasses, exactly my idea of what a grad student should look like, but she had a friendly smile. Her date was Walter, slender and blond with a swimmer's build. I learned later he was from California, and I suspect he had spent a good deal of time on the beach.

Terri had flaming red hair and squinted her green eyes at me when we were introduced. "I'm from Brooklyn, too, and you look familiar. Did you go to St. C's?"

I said I had and we played a game of small world for a minute or two. This made me feel marginally more comfortable.

Her date was a surprise to me. Tony was from Marblehead, Massachusetts, with a decided "down East" accent, and, although he was very fair, he was a Negro.

Josh poured me a glass of red wine. Although I was no connoisseur, I liked the smooth taste and guessed that it wasn't the cheapest thing on the menu.

Josh confirmed it. "Drink up. We're indulging in the good stuff tonight."

"Celebrating what?"

"Celebrating the fact that I got a letter just before I left home telling me I was accepted. How about that?"

I gave him an impulsive hug, while everyone clapped and cheered, either from the acceptance or my show of affection; I couldn't tell which.

The waiter strode up to the table with purpose. I supposed he had waited for us to order until all the seats at the table were filled. Josh and I both ordered pasta, his Alfredo and mine with white clam sauce. Suddenly starved, I reached for the sliced Italian bread in the basket on the table and spread it generously with butter. The salad came quickly, for which I was grateful, its dressing just the right mixture of olive oil and vinegar. We all lit cigarettes between courses.

The conversation veered from everyday topics to a literary discussion and I realized that this was my fantasy of what college was about, not the parade of sororities, clothes, haircuts and sports I was used to in Texas.

"Hey," said Tony. "I was in the library a couple of days ago and ran across this fantastic collection of short stories by some Russian. Named Natikoff or Nabikov or something. Anyone heard of him?"

Anita was quick to answer. "Nabokov. He's at Cornell now. I heard him lecture when I was there. Fabulous."

"Why is it," asked Tony, "that all these Eastern Europeans, like Conrad, can use the language better than native English speakers?'

"Beats me," said Walter. "I'd give anything to write as well as somebody from Michigan."

"You, of course, are referring to your favorite, Hemingway," said Josh.

"God, I think he's so pedestrian, except maybe for some of the really early works like his short story 'Turn About,'" said Tony.

"I really liked that story. I never had heard much about Hemingway's short stories," I said, taking a stab at being part of the conversation and grateful we had been required to read the story in Freshman English.

"Now there, Josh, you have a young lady with good taste," Tony said, waving his fork at Josh.

I was afraid I was blushing and glad for the candlelight.

"I still think Fitzgerald has it all over Hemingway," said Terri.

"Well, maybe *Gatsby,* but that's another story," said Anita.

The group all laughed at her inadvertent joke. She pursed her lips and took a drink of wine, looking as though she didn't appreciate being made fun of. "But none of them can hold a candle to Faulkner."

"Lawrence can," interjected Josh.

"Oh, maybe *Sons and Lovers,* or even *The Rainbow,* but not much else."

"I disagree," said Josh. "You know what work of his I like best? *Lady Chatterley's Lover."*

This observation received catcalls and protests from the table.

"I know what you liked about the book. You liked what Melors and M'lady were doing in the barn," teased Walter.

"Not so. Now listen to me. I think it's a superbly plotted novel. You know from the very first page just what all these people are like and you're pulling for her all the way. The plot just unfolds like a Greek tragedy."

"Comedy, really," said Terri.

The discussion went on until I had to pull at Josh's sleeve. When I got his attention, I whispered we had better be going. In the note I left, I said we would be home by ten-thirty, and it was already ten.

Terri overheard me, turned to Tony, gave him a quick kiss and said, "I need to go, too. I'll ride the subway with these guys. You don't have to see me home tonight."

"Damn," said Tony. "I was hoping for a little subway time with you."

Everyone laughed and began to struggle into coats and mufflers. The men left some cash on the table for the waiter and we all made our way out into the snow. At the door, Josh and Terri and I headed for the subway station as the other three made their way to their respective apartments.

The snow was falling gently again, muffling all sound except the crunch of our footsteps. Josh's dark hair and Terri's curls were dotted with the white stuff like eighteenth century aristocrats just beginning to powder their hair.

When we got on the train, Terri sat in the seat in front of us, legs stretched out so she could carry on a conversation during the trip to Brooklyn. Josh put his arm around me and pulled me close. I suppose I was hoping for a furtive kiss or two on the way home. As it happened, I sat and listened to them carry on a long conversation about Renaissance poetry, which I knew nothing about.

I spent the time upbraiding myself for being silent all evening. I had scarcely said ten words at the restaurant, finishing my dinner long before anyone else, since that was all I knew to do with my mouth. The wonderful feeling of adulthood and freedom I felt on the way into town sank into a pool of self-disgust and callowness. I certainly couldn't keep up with these graduate students.

At our mutual stop, Terri waved good-bye and turned toward her home. Josh and I began to walk the two blocks to my house.

"I hope you had a good time. It's hard to get a word in edgewise with that bunch."

"I know."

"They are pretty full of themselves. I love some of the conversation and then I get tired of all the pretentious talk. That seems to be the way in graduate school, so I better get used to it."

"I did feel like the freshman I am, but it was interesting."

Josh stopped walking and pulled me to him. I could see snowflakes clinging to his eyelashes. The kiss was long, deep and satisfying.

"There, that's more what I had in mind for the ride on the subway."

I giggled. "So did I."

"I'll make it up to you New Year's Eve. If it's okay by you, I'll come out and get you about five. We can go downtown and have something to eat near Times Square and then watch the countdown. If it's as cold as it is this evening, we can go to Walter's apartment for a while, if you don't mind being with that mouthy crew again."

"No, that's fine."

"He has a walk-up apartment in a building in that really raunchy section of town off 42nd Street."

"Is it safe?" I was used to being in the theater district, but only during show times and with either my uncle or Aunt Grace.

"Oh, I think so. Anyway, the streets will be crowded on New Year's Eve."

By this time, we had reached my aunt's front steps. "This is it," I said, and turned again toward him, offering my face. His first kiss was soft. For a second, I thought I saw movement at the window of the front room, but then he kissed me again and I closed my eyes.

Josh suddenly released me and I realized the front door was opening and Uncle Howard stood there, a silent, black outline against the light of the front hall.

"Good evening, sir." Josh kept his left arm around my waist, guided me up the steps and held out his right hand to my uncle.

"Josh," I said hastily, "This is Howard Finnerty, my Aunt Grace's husband."

"I'm Josh Cooper, sir."

"Good evening." My uncle's voice was cooler than the outside air and precise, as though he was trying to enunciate clearly, but after a moment's hesitation, he did shake Josh's hand.

"I hope we haven't kept you up too late."

"Sheila's note said she'd be in by ten-thirty."

I heard the tone of rebuke and cringed although I knew it was barely ten forty-five.

"I've asked her to go to Times Square with me and my friends on New Year's Eve, if that's all right with you and Mrs. Finnerty."

I had given no thought to whether they would let me go or not. Now I felt a moment of panic.

"I suppose so. She's an adult now. Old enough to do anything she wants."

He opened the door wider to me, but did not ask Josh in. After all, it was late. I gave up any thought of asking Josh out to visit with my aunt and uncle.

"I'll see you day after tomorrow," Josh said to me, and backed down the three steps.

"Good night Josh, and thanks," I said, my voice sounding forlorn and muffled in the snowy evening. He waved and smiled. I followed my uncle into the house.

"Sheila."

"Yes?"

"How well do you know that boy?"

"Pretty well. We've gone out quite a lot since November."

"Have you met his family? Do you know anything about him?"

I leaned back against the wall of the stairwell. "I know quite a lot. One of my friends in the dorm introduced me. They grew up together in Fort Worth, Texas. I've met her parents and seen where they lived." *Were all lawyers full of questions? And what business was it of his anyway? It would have been different if he were my father.*

"It's a nice neighborhood?"

"Of course. He's a fine student, too. He's going to graduate school next year here at Columbia. We were out with friends of his who are in grad school at

NYU already." I thought perhaps academia would put his fears to rest.

"What's he studying?"

"He wants to be a writer."

My uncle sniffed dismissively. "Isn't a senior a little old for you? Most seniors don't pay any attention to freshmen."

"I never thought about it," I said flippantly.

He bridled a little at the snippy answer and I headed back upstairs to my bedroom. If he intended to say anything, he didn't. I could hear his steps going back to the kitchen as I closed my door. I supposed he was going back for more scotch before going to bed.

I closed the door and automatically reached for the key to lock the door and remembered there wasn't one. I didn't think it would matter. I knew that soon I would hear his footsteps, leaden with liquor, climb the stairs and proceed down the hall to his own bedroom. Surely he wouldn't bother me, anyway.

My thoughts turned to Josh and how different I felt in his arms. I wanted desperately to have him make love to me, but was even more desperately afraid of getting pregnant. I undressed and got into bed.

CHAPTER FOURTEEN

On Sunday, I heard none of the homily at church and only half paid attention to the bridge game my uncle and I played with Grace and Howard. My uncle was an excellent bridge player and this was the one activity we enjoyed doing together. Aunt Grace had asked Mr. Holland from next door to make a fourth. Mr. Holland was rather sweet but ancient and said little. I thought he made an excellent dummy. Today, I had drawn Uncle Howard as a partner. He was irritable, probably at my inattention.

"Sheila, didn't you see me discard a diamond?"

"Sorry."

"Where's your mind, Princess?"

Aunt Grace smiled. "Have you heard from your young man? I want to meet him."

Drat. She had guessed why I was preoccupied and she would bring it up. I tried to sound nonchalant. "Haven't heard a word."

"I met him. Handsome little Jewish boy," said Uncle Howard.

My trick," I said, as I trumped Aunt Grace's ace. Maybe that would make up for failing to lead diamonds earlier.

I hoped Josh would call, just to talk that evening. He didn't. I listened to the radio in my room alone, read the Christmas issue of *Mademoiselle*, and finally fell asleep.

Finally, by three in the afternoon on New Year's Eve, Josh called to finalize the arrangements. He said he would show up on my doorstep at about five o'clock. Having been in a state of nervous anticipation for two days, I was relieved to see his tall figure coming down the block from the subway station. My uncle was hovering in the background and I pulled on my coat and began to put on scarf and mittens, anything to affect a quick getaway. My uncle had said little to me in the last few days and I had not offered much on my own.

However, he opened the door to Josh and offered his hand in greeting.

"Good evening, Mr. Finnerty."

"Good evening, Josh. Aren't you a little early to go to Times Square?"

"I promised Sheila dinner and then we're meeting some friends at their

midtown apartment before we all go to Times Square for the great countdown."
He smiled his charming smile and I thought my uncle relaxed a little.

About that time, Aunt Grace came rushing down the stairs. "Josh, this is
my Aunt Grace."

"How very nice to meet you." Aunt Grace held out a hand but looked like
she would prefer to hug him. Josh responded with his charismatic smile.

"And when will you be home?" asked my uncle.

"I suppose we might go back to the apartment for a while to let the crowd
clear out. Then I'll have her home by one o'clock if that seems like an acceptable
plan to you?"

"That's all right, I suppose."

"Oh, that's fine," interjected my aunt. "Have a wonderful time, children."

"Good. Then Sheila, let's be off."

I gave my aunt a hug and my uncle a perfunctory kiss good-bye as Josh
and I started for the subway. The air had cleared and the day had been sunny, but
it was considerably colder.

"I know I promised you a dinner with just the two of us, but Walter and
Anita are having everyone over for dinner and I said we'd come. I hope you
don't mind?" Josh looked at me with a worried frown.

I did mind, but said, "No, that's fine with me."

"You sure?"

I looked at him and smiled, just glad to be away from the house and with
him. "I'm sure."

We took the subway to midtown and made our way to Walter's apartment.
Anita, Walter, Terri and Tony were already there.

They all greeted me like an old friend and Anita gave me a quick hug.
"Hang your stuff on that hook there," she said, indicating a row of hooks beside
the door that held the coats and hats of the guests.

The one-room third floor walk-up was furnished with a mattress on
the floor, huge pillows and a motley assortment of crockery and tableware in
the Pullman kitchen against one wall. There was a bathroom with a stool and
lavatory, but the shower consisted of a round rod with its curtain suspended over
a floor drain by the kitchen sink. The walls were a strange yellow, and I smiled as
I imagined that the color was chosen from whatever the paint store had on sale.

It wasn't long before I realized it wasn't only Walter's apartment, but
Anita lived there, too. There was one neat section of orange crates with her
books and personal items. Her clothes hung from hangers suspended on pegs in
the wall above the crates. She obviously slept in the bed with Walter.

Walter spread a thick pad of newspapers over the carpet worn so thin its color was hard to identify.

"Come on, everybody," Anita said, "Soup's on." She plunked down a huge platter of boiled shrimp and bowls of red sauce on the papers. Terri was right behind her with a bowl of green salad and a basket of crusty bread. Whatever reluctance I had about missing dinner just with Josh vanished as the briny smell of the shellfish mingling with the spices Anita had used to boil them in hung like pleasant incense in the air.

The six of us sat cross-legged on the floor and peeled the cooked shrimp onto newspapers. The shells piled up as the red sauce disappeared. We ate salad and bread off of paper plates with real forks, no two alike.

I sat between Tony and Josh, and while Josh talked to Anita, I asked Tony where he lived. Terri, of course, lived in Brooklyn with her parents. Tony described his cramped student sponsored housing, and Virginia Hall seemed palatial in comparison.

"I'm so glad to be able to come over to Water and Anita's and stretch out." To emphasize, he stretched out his long legs which went halfway across the tiny carpet.

"How did all of you meet? In class?"

"I met Terri my first year here in Restoration Drama. She was a friend of Anita's from somewhere. Anita and Walter both went to Cornell and met there."

I glanced at Walter and Anita. They still seemed like such a mismatched pair, he so West Coast and athletic and she the quintessential Eastern intellectual.

When we finished the last of the boiled shrimp, Anita made coffee and we all lit cigarettes as she passed cups and a plate of brownies.

Anita began to gather up the forks and the bowls that held the remnants of red sauce left on the floor.

"May I help?" I asked. Terri was in some sort of deep discussion with the guys about which courses Josh should take in the fall.

"Sure, will you roll up those newspapers? I'll have Walter toss them down the trash chute. If we don't get them out of here, they'll start to smell.

"Come on, guys," said Tony, "We don't have enough beer to last until midnight. We don't want to run out of supplies. Besides, Josh can buy this round. He's still on the parental dole."

The three of them struggled into their coats, taking the trash including a bag of empty beer bottles with them.

"You do have your wallet, don't you, Cooper?"

I could hear their laughter echoing down the dingy hall.

"Yeah, what we all need is a little more beer," said Anita.

Terri laughed. "I don't think that's what Tony meant by supplies."

Anita was wiping the last of the forks. She dropped them in the drawer and said, "Oh, damn. I forgot to tell Walter to get me cigarettes."

"Do you two need any?" she asked as she was halfway out the door with her coat and purse.

We both shook our heads. When Anita was safely down the hall, I asked what sort of supplies Tony was talking about. I had visions of marijuana showing up at the apartment.

Terri laughed again. "Condoms. He told me on the way over here that he was out."

"Oh," I said, and knew I was blushing.

"He's always careful that way." She looked at me with curiosity. "Aren't you and Josh doing it?"

"No."

"God, I would if I were you. He's so gorgeous."

"Anita lives here, I gather." I wasn't sure this was exactly a change of subject.

"Yep"

"They seem to me to be such an odd couple."

"Jeez, aren't they though? But he's stuck by her through thick and thin."

"I see." But I didn't.

"They don't have to worry about condoms, but it's a sad story." She lit a cigarette and handed me a book of matches so I could light my own. "She had this boyfriend at Cornell who Walter thought was a drip, but it turned out he was just a complete jerk. The first semester she was in grad school down here, he came for Thanksgiving and knocked her up. Then the drip didn't want to have anything to do with her. She found this guy who would do an abortion. It was like something out of a 1930s detective movie. She got this number from somebody and called it. All they said to her was, 'I'll call you back.'" Later, somebody called and she was told to come alone, but I went with her anyway. We went to this dingy brownstone down around 33rd Street and Second Avenue. It was awful. The place was filthy and she said even this so-called doctor's fingernails were dirty."

She took a drag on her cigarette, exhaling through her nose. When the long plumes of smoke had subsided, she shook her head as if to shake off the memory. "There was this waiting room with all kinds of people in it. I guess he had a regular medical practice, too. Anyway, they told me I couldn't stay, so I left and found a coffee shop until she came out. She paid that butcher a thousand dollars. Cold cash."

"A thousand dollars?" I gasped. "Where did she get that kind of money? From her parents?"

"Are you kidding? She would have died rather than tell them. She's really a thrifty little soul and had some saved. She sold her grandmother's ring and the rest of us made up the difference. She keeps paying us back about ten dollars a month. I've told her to forget it but she won't. She says it's all her fault and she should pay for it."

I took a swig of beer from the amber colored Budweiser bottle. I couldn't imagine what it would be like to go through that. The enormity of what Anita had been through struck me like a fist. Abortion was the sort of sin I didn't even want to think about. "Why didn't she have the baby and put it up for adoption?"

Anita just shrugged and rolled the end of her cigarette around in the pile of butts in the ash tray. "The worst part of it was the asshole of a doctor made her let him screw her before he'd do the deal."

Whatever horror I felt at the prospect of abortion was overwhelmed by shock and disgust.

"The upshot of all this was she didn't have the baby but she did get an infection. By the time we got her to a proper doctor, it was a miracle she lived. But, she can't have any kids now," Terri said, lighting another cigarette. "Anyway, Walter saw her through all of that. He was the one who really nursed her. He moved her in here and saw that she got safely to class and back. She made it through the semester with his help, and, she's been here ever since. End of story."

Terri tossed her red hair from side to side as though to put a period to the subject, and then said, "Do you know they say they're working on some sort of pill you can take and you can have sex and not get pregnant?"

I thought I had read something about it and started to say so when we heard the boys' voices in the hall. Anita came in at the same time. Now that I knew the history of the Walter and Anita saga, I felt like a member of the group.

The condoms weren't in evidence, but my visions of marijuana turned out to be prescient. It was Josh who produced the glassine bag and the white papers. I watched as he expertly rolled a joint. He lit it and offered it to me. I shook my head and he grinned. "I'll teach you how to like this as much as you do tobacco."

I was vaguely disappointed and at the same time excited. All this seemed so cosmopolitan—a world away from my staid Brooklyn neighborhood.

Josh brought up the subject of movies. "So who do you think will win the Academy Awards this year? *African Queen* is my pick for best picture."

"Talk about original screenplays," agreed Walter.

"I think best actress will be the hardest choice," said Terri.

This was something I knew about, I was able to interject my own opinions. "I thought Vivien Leigh did a great job in *Streetcar Named Desire* but here she is, a British actress, again playing a southern belle."

Anita said, "I thought Kim Hunter was stronger in *Streetcar*."

Josh agreed, "And I can't ever quite like a movie based on a play as well as the original, especially when I've seen it on the stage."

"I thought Jane Wyman's performance in *The Blue Veil* was stunning," said Anita, staring at the floor. Terri and I quickly exchanged a glance and looked away. The movie was about a woman's agony in giving up a child for adoption.

"Didn't anybody like *An American in Paris*," asked Walter? We all just stared at him a moment. "Guess not."

"Sure," said Josh, "I loved it and the dancing was spectacular, but not for an Academy Award."

Terri quickly said she thought Leo Genn ought to get the Oscar for best supporting actor for his performance in *Quo Vadis*. I agreed.

"Sheila, do you remember seeing that awful old film they showed us at St. Catherine's? A really terrible print of Shakespeare's *Julius Caesar* but Leo Genn was a standout."

I laughed. "The film was awful and he was great. In fact, he's all I remember about it."

"I thought the only films they showed you at that convent were those dreadful films the Army made during the war about venereal disease," said Tony.

Terri threw her empty cigarette package at him. "Oh, shut up."

"Well, I do remember those, too," I said.

"Come on," said Josh. "It's time we made our way down to Times Square."

We bundled up and walked out onto the street. I had never seen so many people in Manhattan at that time of night, even at the height of the theater season.

We jostled and elbowed our way to the edge of Times Square. The bitter cold was only bearable because we were pressed in among thousands of bodies. It was as though the more than seven and a half million inhabitants of New York City had all come downtown at once. Josh held my hand as we made our way through the crowd to a place where we could stand and see the crowd. He was tall enough to keep the other two couples in sight until we found a spot. Josh pulled me around in front of him and wrapped his arms around me, resting his chin on the pom-pom of my knitted hat.

The crowd was a happy one, although the amount of alcohol consumed both in celebration and for warmth must have been enough to fill the lake in Central Park.

I could hardly wait for the minutes to pass. I wasn't sure whether I was more excited to see the crowd, the Times Square ball poised to drop or the New

Year's kiss I was sure would accompany the first moments of 1952. This was the happiest night of my life.

The moment finally came. We all shouted out the countdown with the crowd and as the strains of Guy Lombardo playing *Auld Lang Syne* came over the loudspeaker, I got the hoped for kiss and all six of us joined in the last strains of the song. The fireworks overhead sparkled and I was sure my eyes were just as bright.

We hurried back to the warmth of the apartment, and the kissing which began in the square continued. Anita and Walter were lying on top of their mattress. The other four of us made do with pillows on the floor.

The necking became more and more serious and I didn't care. Josh explored all there was to know about my body above the waist and then slid his hand up my thigh. I wanted him to continue all the way to orgasm so badly I thought I would be sick. He pulled my hand down to his erection and I realized he had unzipped his trousers. But there was something about all this intimacy, including the noises made by the two other couples, that stopped me.

"I think I'd better get home. My uncle will probably be waiting up." I felt like a fourth grader.

"Sure." Josh made no objection, but began to rearrange his clothes. We slipped into our coats and made our way to the subway. There were still dozens of people riding home after the New Year's festivities, but we sat and kissed and groped oblivious to any stares.

By the time we reached my front steps, I was again in a fever of desire. Cold as it was, he pulled me down on the front steps, practically covering his body with mine, his left knee between my legs. I pulled away a little from his kiss. This time, even though there was no light, I was sure there was movement at the window.

"Please. I think Uncle Howard is still up."

"Sheila, I know it was awkward down there with the others. But the four of them are going some place in the country tomorrow. I'm going to be staying at Walter's apartment. Please come down and meet me. We can do whatever you want to, see a movie, get something to eat, or just stay at the apartment."

I wasn't sure what he was suggesting. Did he buy some condoms too when the guys went out for more beer? Was I ready to take that chance? I didn't know but I did know I wanted him terribly. "All right."

"Great!" He shouted the word as he got up and pulled me to my feet.

"Shhhhh!"

"I don't care."

I pulled out my keys and unlocked the door, leaning out and giving him a quick kiss before I closed it behind me. I turned and nearly ran into my uncle.

"Just how far have you gone with that boy?" His voice was rough with whiskey.

I hoped the truth of what I really had in mind for tomorrow didn't show on my face. "Uncle Howard, that's none of your business," I said with as much casualness as I could muster. "But since you are dying to know, we were just necking a little. Nothing serious."

He snapped on the light. I was sure how I looked: no makeup, bright eyed from the beer and the sex, hair awry. He looked furious.

"Oh, come on," I said with a note of disgust in my voice. I elbowed past him and went upstairs to my room. I heard him turn again to the kitchen. I took off my clothes and put on my flannel nightgown. The bed was cold, but my body was still warm from Josh's caresses.

I was half asleep when I heard the door open.

"You've been fucking him, haven't you?"

I rose on one elbow. "No. And go away. Get out of my room."

"Let's see just how far you've gone." He pulled the quilt, blanket and sheet off me in one swift movement. I shuddered against the cold.

"Stop it. Get off me."

I started to scream, but panic pinched my voice in my throat and the sound came out like a baby's cry or an injured cat. I pushed at his body and tried to roll away. He put his arm across my chest, leaning his weight on it and pulled up my nightgown with his other hand, feeling, I was sure, the residual wetness between my legs. He forced his knees between mine, the wool of his trousers chafing my legs and then I felt it. The pain was brief and the entry aided by the excitement Josh's love making had caused, but the rest of the experience was mind numbing. His thrusts were hard and impatient. I was still making incoherent sounds when he groaned and lay still for a moment before he rolled away from me.

The panic, the feeling that he might hurt me severely, even kill me, which had elicited those ineffectual screams, suddenly vanished and was replaced with a cold anger and deep revulsion.

"Get out of my room." My voice now was as cold as the outside temperature.

"Sheila, I'm sorry ..."

"I don't want to hear it. Leave me alone."

He got up heavily, turning his back to put his penis back into his trousers.

"Shiela ..."

"Go away."

When the door closed, I lay for a moment, not able to comprehend what had taken place. My mind seemed to be somewhere else. I wished desperately for time to run backwards, to be again on the front porch, eager for love and a proper mating.

I finally rose and went to the bathroom. To my horror I could feel semen running out of my body. I wanted to retch.

I ran the bathwater and washed again and again.

Thank God there was no sound from Aunt Grace's bedroom. I prayed he wouldn't confess to her what he had done to me.

Then, in clean pajamas, I went back to bed. I slept fitfully until about six-thirty when I got up, dressed and gathered up the sheets from the bed and stuffed them in the pillow case. I remade the bed with clean sheets from the linen closet. I gathered up some clothes to put with them, as though I was just going to do laundry, and started for the basement.

I paused at the kitchen door. My uncle was asleep or passed out, the bottle of scotch next to his elbow, his head on his crossed arms on the kitchen table.

I was startled to hear Aunt Grace's voice. She was looking over the banister. "Hi, early bird. You're up early after a late date."

"Hi, couldn't sleep. Thought I'd get some laundry done and get it out of the way."

"That's an energetic way to start the New Year." She looked doubtful, "Are you all right? Did you have a good time with Josh."

"Fabulous," I was able to say with conviction.

She smiled and came downstairs far enough to see my uncle. "Was Howard still up when you got home?"

"Yes."

"I hope he wasn't ugly to your young man. I'm afraid he was dreadfully drunk last night celebrating."

"It was okay."

She gazed at her husband with a deeply sad look. "That's good. When he gets that way, I never know what he is going to say or do. It's gotten really bad this year after you left. And then he never remembers any of it."

"Really?"

"Total blank."

I felt a moment of enormous relief. No one need ever know.

I put the laundry in the Bendix and when I saw the sheets, whatever relief I had felt was gone. There was no way I was going to go downtown to meet Josh. I couldn't pretend nothing happened. I didn't know how to get in touch with him at Walter's, so I did nothing.

I knew Josh would call my house looking for me, but I couldn't face him just yet, especially since he was expecting me to meet him at Walter's apartment.

I spent the next two and a half days watching whatever there was on my aunt's black and white Magnavox television. I could not remember from one hour to the next what I had seen. Like an automaton, I filled my aunt's Lalique ash tray with cigarette butts.

When the phone rang, I let someone else answer it.

On Wednesday, I went to the market and a movie with my aunt. If Josh called when I was out, my uncle didn't mentioned it.

On Saturday, she took me to LaGuardia for the flight back to Dallas. I was dressed as I had been when she picked me up, except that this time it was the inside instead of the outside of Sheila O'Connor that had altered.

CHAPTER FIFTEEN

When I arrived at the dorm after my flight, Mrs. Jackson told me that E.A. had left a message that she wouldn't be in until early Monday. I was too absorbed with myself for the information to register. When I was unpacking, I began to wonder why she would wait until Monday when classes were supposed to begin to drive all the way from San Angelo. She would have to get up before dawn.

I wasn't sorry to spend the weekend alone. Part of my consciousness had been sleepwalking since New Year's Eve. I wondered if Josh was back on campus yet, but did not want to call him. One moment I wasn't sure I even wanted to see him again; then the next I hoped the ringing telephone was for me. Then I wondered if he would ever call. After all, I had stood him up blatantly. On top of this, I didn't want to think about what might have been said between Josh and my uncle if he had called to find out where I was.

Paula and Susan had spent the holidays with Susan's parents. They drove in on Saturday afternoon in Susan's new Ford coupe. We all trooped down to admire the shiny black car with cream and black leather interior. Paula and Susan persuaded me to go to the movies and out to a restaurant on "Miracle Mile" for a hamburger. I felt marginally better after some distraction, food and a ride in the lovely car.

On Sunday morning, the three of us went to Holy Communion at Canterbury House. This Sunday, I couldn't make myself go to the rail for the wafer and wine. I felt soiled and damaged.

Father Heinz did not miss my omission. He made a point of coming up to me at coffee and putting his arm around my shoulder. He gave me a long look and I couldn't even smile.

"How was Christmas vacation?"

"Fine."

"Did you go home to New York?"

"Yes."

"Everyone well there?"

I nodded.

He looked skeptical, hugged my shoulders and said, "Will I see you next Sunday?"

"I think so."

"Come by sometime during the week, Sheila. I'm always here." He gave me another hug and moved away to speak to other students.

I took a long drink of the acrid coffee, which we used to say was probably left over from Father's Marine days aboard ship in the South Pacific. I was disturbed by his solicitous behavior. Did I look different? On the other hand, his offer for a visit gave me an oddly comfortable feeling. I couldn't imagine ever telling anyone, including some remote future husband, what happened. But, if I ever did tell someone, it would be someone like Father Heinz, who couldn't tell anyone else.

Back in the dorm, I settled in to read one of the books on my English syllabus I hadn't gotten around to reading. Dead week and finals were only three weeks away. Once, when I got up to go to the bathroom, I caught my reflection in the mirror and stopped. This was perhaps what Father Heinz saw. There was a dead look behind the blue eyes that stared back at me.

Josh still hadn't called by Sunday evening.

At nine-thirty, Paula and I were sitting in my room, taking a break and having a cigarette when in walked E.A. She was flushed and she was frowning. She tossed her suitcase and makeup case on the bed.

"My folks didn't call, did they?"

"No," I said. "I thought you weren't coming in until tomorrow."

"I wasn't going to. I'll tell you, but first I gotta go to the john."

When she returned, she plunged into a long narrative about what went on at Christmastime in San Angelo and didn't broach the subject of her return. During this recitation, Miriam arrived, looking radiant. When E.A. finally ran down, Miriam took up the conversation, telling us in infinite detail about her love, Manny.

All of this saved me from saying much about my vacation, and Paula, tired of all the romance, dragged Miriam off to their room.

"So, what?" I said.

E.A. flopped on the bed, her pink bunny slippers poking out from below the long pink flowered granny gown.

"Actually, I was going to spend the night with Chuck at a friend's apartment. I finally made the decision virginity had to go."

I was both amazed and felt a strange sadness that the two of us had made the same decision with romantic visions of how it would all go, and somehow neither of us got our wish.

"What happened?"

"Nothing, really. I can't explain it. It wasn't what I had imagined. He got … pushy."

We had been talking to each other, both from a supine position on the bed. I sat up where I could get a good look at her, alarm bells ringing in my head.

"Pushy how?"

"I don't know. Just movin' too fast."

"So you left?"

"Yeah. And was he pissed."

"I'll bet."

She was quiet for a minute, a forlorn look on her face. "God, I hope I didn't screw up everything. I hope he calls again."

I bit back any comment that I thought she was crazy to see him again. "Shall I turn out the light?"

She nodded and kicked the bunny slippers off, onto the floor between our beds.

Chuck called the next day and so did Josh.

I was going over Western Civ notes, sitting at my desk when a voice echoed down the hall.

"Sheeeeeilah. Phoooone. It's Jooooooosh."

My feet in their white socks seemed to drag themselves to the phone booth.

"Hello?"

"Sheila? Well, what the hell happened?" I tried to parse the tone of his voice. Was he angry, disappointed, perplexed or all three?

"I'm so sorry, Josh. I should have tried to call you, but I didn't have the number. Something came up." I realized that statement explained absolutely nothing.

"You had a fight with your uncle, didn't you?" When I didn't answer, he added, "And it was over me, wasn't it?"

"Did you call? Did you talk to him?'

"Yeah."

"Well, what did he say?"

"Basically he told me you weren't there and to leave you alone, permanently."

"It wasn't really over you, Josh. He's just drinking too much and cranky."

"He was certainly sloshed when I took you home."

I couldn't think of anything to say.

"So. What is it that you want? Do you want to see me again?"

"Oh, yes." The relief that flooded my voice made me sound like a gushing schoolgirl.

"Okay, then. So we forget about New York. Meet me at the Union for coffee about three. I should be through at the library by then."

He added, "Sheila, do me one favor, though. Just don't ever do that to me again. I thought I gave you Walter's number and I expected to hear from you when you didn't show. I hate having people spring things on me."

I started to retort and ask him why he hadn't called when he got to New York and why he hadn't called until so late on New Year's Eve, or even why he hadn't called when I didn't show up at Walters, but my relief at his having phoned me now pushed everything else out of my mind, so I promised always to let him know if plans changed.

He said he couldn't wait to see me and I was back on cloud nine.

The Student Union was in a World War II barracks building. The University had moved several of them on campus after the war to take care of the influx of men going to college on the GI Bill of Rights. The interior was made to look like some sort of Texas corral. There were wagon wheels set into the railings that divided the lounge from the coffee area. The dark oak tables, captain's chairs and banquettes, coupled with the dim light, cigarette smoke and smell of aging coffee, gave the place the atmosphere of either a roadhouse or an intimate bar, depending on your point of view. During the school year, there was always an ongoing card game and the nonstop buzz of conversation.

I waited just inside the door of the Union out of the wind. I could see his tall form huddled against the gusts as he turned the corner from the library. The minute he opened the door, he pulled me to him for a rather long and public kiss. My fears melted.

We found a table for four in the corner and sat beside each other. I loved the feeling of his warm arm and hip next to me. We held hands under that table and let our coffee get cold.

I started off with an apology for missing our date in New York. "I hope I didn't completely mess up the rest of your stay."

"I would rather have been with you, but to salve my hurt feelings, I got a ticket to *The King and I*. Now, aren't you jealous?"

"Oh, damn, I am. I really wanted to see Gertrude Lawrence."

"She was great, but it's Yul Brenner who would have really turned you on. I think maybe I'll shave my head. Would you like that?"

"Oh, stop!"

Josh lit two cigarettes for us a la Paul Henried and placed one of them between my lips. I didn't see E.A. until she spoke.

"Hey guys. Josh, you remember Chuck Bolton, don't you?"

"Sure." Josh rose a little from the banquette and extended his hand, "Chuck."

The men shook hands and E.A. and Chuck sat down opposite us. Chuck went to get their coffee and our "How was Christmas?" conversation turned to basketball.

Josh loved basketball and as we left, the four of us made a date to go to a game when the season started after finals. For the first time since New Year's, I felt that life was not only getting back to normal, but that things were going to work out just fine. If I could just forget.

A week later, I woke up nauseated. I lay in bed a while thinking back over what I had eaten the day before. The thought of a shower made me feel better so I went to the bathroom. Paula was already there. Our personal schedules had varied little from the first days of school.

"Hi."

"Hi." I made a face at myself in the mirror. "I don't feel very well. Something I ate, I guess."

"The twenty-four hour is going around," Paula said in her best professional nurse's voice.

I laughed, took the shower, dressed and went to breakfast. The food in the cafeteria looked unappealing, so I had tea and toast. I ate no lunch and little dinner.

The next day was a slightly worse version of the first. This time, nurse Paula advised, "Carry some soda crackers with you if you feel queasy. And try drinking 7Up instead of Cokes." She was looking at me with a frown, fingering the towel around her neck. "Do you think you ought to go to the infirmary?"

"That place? With an upset stomach? I'd come away with ptomaine." The last thing I wanted to do was see someone in the medical profession.

By the end of the week, I was vomiting in the morning. I was terrified that the dry heaves would echo off the white plaster walls and tile floor, booming down the hall, so I tried to time going to the bathroom early enough so no one was around. Once, Paula came in right after I had finished. I knew I looked pale.

"Are you all right?"

"I'm fine," I said, and fled to my room. After that, she stopped asking when she saw me, but I could see her eyes register the fact that I was losing weight. Eating was not an option.

I pushed out of my mind what might be happening to my body and concentrated on final exams. Josh was preoccupied with his own finals. Also, I was worried about my roommate. She was spending a lot more time with

Chuck Bolton than in the library during dead week. Dead week on campus was the week before finals began when nothing happened: no social activities, no *Campus* newspaper, no sorority or fraternity meetings or gatherings of any kind. Students were expected to have plenty of time to catch up on whatever they had not done during the year. To her credit, E.A. was diligent about keeping up with her daily assignments and papers. But she was doing almost nothing about review. In the middle of finals week, she panicked. Miriam and I calmed her down. I spent five hours helping her cram for English and Miriam did the same for Algebra.

When grades were posted the following week, she had made a C+ average, good enough to be initiated into her sorority. Miriam pulled down a four-point-oh and Paula and I teetered on the cusp of B+ and A-. I made another B in Western Civ. Obviously, history and law school, like my father, were not in my future.

The new semester started with the usual flurry of registration, finding new classrooms, buying books and poring over class syllabi. E.A. seemed to be out with Chuck at least every other night, sometimes returning radiant and sometimes pensive. I didn't ask.

If I was observing her actions, Paula was watching me, or at least I thought so. The nausea continued, but I was able not to throw up most mornings. I tried not to think about when I should be getting my period.

On the first Saturday in February, Josh and I had gone to an early movie, and since he was working on a paper, he brought me home well before the eleven o'clock closing hour at the dorm. I was sitting on the bed, reading a trashy novel called something like *The Green Door* when E.A. rushed into the room.

One look at her face and I immediately forgot my own angst. Her left eye had a cut above it and looked as though it would be a lovely shade of purple by morning. I thought I saw a bruise on her right arm just above the elbow.

"My God, E.A. What in the world …?"

"I'm okay. I'm okay," she insisted. Then she looked in the mirror. "Jesus."

"I don't have any alcohol, but I think Miriam does, and some Band-Aids," I said, jumping off the bed and heading for the door.

"Oh, don't. Please. I don't want them to see me."

"It's all right. I'll just borrow the alcohol and we'll get that cut taken care of."

Miriam didn't have any alcohol, but nurse Paula had some and the Band-Aids. It didn't take her long to wander across the hall to see what was going on and Miriam followed.

Paula helped me pinch the cut together after I had cleaned it with a Q-Tip and alcohol, accompanied by howls from E.A.

"My God, what happened, E.A.?" Miriam was watching as we ministered to my roommate.

"I fell down running in the dark through the parking lot from behind the dorm," E.A. said firmly.

"Okay everybody got that?" said Paula. "That way, none of us lets on that what we really think is somebody nameless beat the crap out of her."

The brown eyes filled with tears.

When the girls were gone and we had turned off the lights, I asked the question I had been dying to ask all along. "You're not going to see him again, are you?"

"No. That's what the fight was about. I finally figured out he was just interested in one thing and I didn't like doing it."

"You don't think he'll try to hurt you, do you?"

"Hell, no. He's too proud. He'll just go off and find some other dumb freshman he can snow."

The disappointment, anger and irony in her voice seemed to mark the end of girlhood dreams. Most of mine were gone, too. But E.A. hadn't given up on her dream. She was soon going out with Chuck again.

Josh and I went out when we could, to movies, to get something to eat or sometimes just to the library to study and stop for coffee afterwards. I avoided places where there was too much intimacy, but on Saturday evenings, after a movie, we would sit in his car in front of the dorm and neck until closing time. After the first few minutes, I could forget what had happened and give myself over to the desire and the pleasure. He didn't suggest anything more intimate, as we had planned in New York, and I certainly didn't bring it up.

The second Friday in February, we went to the basketball game.

I hadn't eaten all day. The nausea I thought was getting better had hung around. I thought I was probably just tired from having stayed up late the night before to finish my weekly English essay due on that Friday. I had nibbled at tea and toast through the day, but I still felt lousy.

I must have been pale, because the first thing he did was give me a worried look and say, "Are you all right?"

I assured him I was and we walked to the Field House, one of the older buildings on campus, which held the gymnasium and swimming pool. Crowded with students, it smelled like chlorine and dirty athletic socks. We made our way through the foyer to the bleachers and climbed up to watch the game. E.A. and Chuck joined us.

Josh and I had both played basketball in high school so the activity on the court was familiar to me, unlike football. For the first half, I was as intent as he was on the running players. We cheered each point scored by our team. At the half, we had Cokes and I only drank half of mine. I hoped the sugar would give my flagging energy a lift, but during the second half the noise and closeness in the gym began to push at me. My attention wandered and I felt dizzy. I looked forward to walking back to the dorm in the open air. I was grateful the nausea was only slight. I didn't relish the idea of throwing up in the middle of the Field House.

At last, the final buzzer sounded. I felt unsteady walking down from the bleachers and grabbed Josh's arm. Even the slickness of the fabric of his windbreaker felt hot under my hand. He looked at me quizzically and then took me firmly by the arm as we joined the crowd exiting the gym.

I could see the doors open to the air ahead. But I only made it halfway there before a curtain of blackness descended somewhere between my retina and field of vision. My knees melted and I could feel myself sliding to the floor, sustained only by the crush of bodies around me.

The fainting spell only lasted a moment, but when I was again fully conscious, I was sitting on a bench in the hall of the Field House surrounded by a semicircle of worried faces.

"Chuck, if you'll stay with Sheila, I'll get my car and come around front," Josh was saying with authority.

"Where are you going to take her? The infirmary?" E.A. asked him.

"I thought I would, but I don't think she ought to walk even that far."

"I think she ought to go to the emergency room," Paula broke into the conversation. "She hasn't been feeling well for about three weeks, and I think a doctor ought to see her?"

I was too listless to argue, so soon Chuck and Josh were helping me to his car.

"I'll come with you," offered E.A.

"No," I protested, spurred by a rush of fear, but I wasn't sure where the fright came from. "Please don't. Please go back and tell Mrs. Jackson where I am and that I'll be late."

"Or," said Josh, "if we're delayed at the hospital, tell her I'll call her."

I don't know how long it took Josh to get me to Parkland Hospital, get me to the waiting room at Emergency, park the car and talk to the admitting office. All was a blur until I found myself sitting on a gurney with an impossibly young resident examining me and taking a history. I was embarrassed to think he was only a few years older than I and to make matters worse, Josh was standing just outside the curtained cubicle. The bright lights and smell of disinfectant made me feel like a laboratory specimen.

The doctor was thorough. He interrogated me at length about my eating habits. I told him I had not been feeling well and had lost my appetite.

He told me all my vital signs were normal and that in his opinion I had fainted from lack of food, and he admonished me to eat more regularly. Then he frowned at me and asked the one question I didn't want to hear.

"When was your last menstrual period?"

I opened my mouth to lie and only answered lamely, "I don't remember."

"Well, your breasts are slightly swollen, and with the nausea ... you're not pregnant are you?" he asked boldly.

The breath caught in my throat and I made a croaking sound that became uncontrollable sobs. I stared at him in horror; he stared back in curiosity and both of our expressions were mirrored in Josh's face. He had heard the question and pulled back the curtain in time to see my distress.

CHAPTER SIXTEEN

Josh didn't call the next day or all week. I didn't really expect him to. I went around like a zombie, and I felt like a fugitive from a horror movie. Friday, he called to ask me to go see *The Bad and the Beautiful* with him, as though nothing had happened. I welcomed the distraction, especially since the movie would not allow any conversation. I had resolutely pushed to the back of my mind what was happening to my body, which left my mind suspended somewhere between focus on my studies and terror.

We went to the movie and stopped for coffee. He was unusually quiet, but then, so was I. Finally, as we sat in the front seat of his car in front of the dorm, he said.

"I've been thinking a lot, Sheila. And I want to know. Are you pregnant?"

"I don't know. I guess so. I'm afraid so."

"I know it's not mine. Do you have a boyfriend in New York?"

"No."

"That doesn't leave much room, since I don't believe in Immaculate Conception."

I didn't say anything.

He hesitated, took a deep breath and said, "That only leaves one possibility."

Josh was sitting behind the wheel, staring out of the windshield. His whole body was rigid, as though he was holding his breath. I didn't want to voice the obvious, and I thought he probably didn't either. Finally, he let out a long sigh, almost a groan, and without turning said, "God. Your uncle?"

I knew I was going to cry and dug into my purse for Kleenex. He turned suddenly to me and put his arms around me. Instead of tears, all I felt was a terrible, vast and surreal sadness, as though I were trapped in a Salvador Dali painting with no escape.

"What are you going to do?"

"I don't know."

"The doctor at the hospital, along with giving me a lecture on the use of condoms, suggested you might want to talk to someone. What about your Aunt Grace? Is that absolutely out of the question?"

"I couldn't possibly. I would have to blame you or she would guess in an instant."

"E.A.'s aunt? What's her name?"

"Mrs. Hamilton. I couldn't do that, either. In the first place, she'd tell my aunt."

The thought of disappointing and embarrassing all these people had been growing to enormous proportions in my mind ever since I began to suspect what was happening to me.

"What about the priest over at Canterbury House?"

I shook my head.

We sat in silence for a moment and then he said, "Sheila, if it was possible, you know I'd marry you. I just don't see how I can right now."

I was overcome with the generosity and horrified at the prospect. "Oh, God, no, Josh. I wouldn't let you do that even if you could."

Just then, the lights on the porch of the dorm flashed, and we both got slowly out of the car. He kept his arm around me all the way up the steps to the front door.

"Anyway, if I can help, I'm still here," he said, and gave me a soft kiss.

I found myself clinging to him, feeling as though I was drowning. Only the presence of Mrs. Jackson made me let go and flee through the door and up the stairs.

The next day, E.A. joined her Aunt Mamie for some shopping. She invited me to go along but I refused. I had to face facts and do some thinking.

The silence of the Saturday dorm wasn't very comforting. My thoughts kept turning in on themselves. I kept coming back to the knowledge that I could not have this baby. What was it anyway? My daughter? My son? My cousin? Every time I thought of the inevitability of a pregnancy, the slow inexorable process that would culminate in seven and a half more months in a child I was responsible for, I felt nothing but panic and revulsion.

I got up and went to my dresser drawer. With my toilet articles was a small gray package with black lettering. I picked it up and went back to the bed. The little box, about an inch by a half inch was not full. I rolled it between my thumb and forefinger. There were about three single edged razor blades in the package and it gave way under the pressure, the end popping open to reveal the glint of steel inside.

It was as though a huge weight had been lifted from me. The decision was made and now I had to decide where to carry out the deed. I certainly didn't want to do it in the dorm bathroom. There were too many people coming and going and I didn't want my friends to find me. I contemplated going somewhere on campus, behind shrubbery or close to the utility entrance of one of the buildings, but that, too, was public. If I waited until too late in the evening, my friends would worry and call Mrs. Jackson. I decided to wait until dark and walk over to the relatively deserted park across the street from the sorority houses.

Then, I sat and stared into space. I didn't want to write a note. Perhaps I would call Aunt Grace, just to chat in the afternoon, not really saying good-bye.

All these ruminations were interrupted by E.A., who flew into the room and rummaged in her own drawer. She didn't say a word but left as quickly as she had come in. A few minutes later, she was back and plopped down on her bed with a look of abject joy on her face.

"Well thank the Good Lord, I just got my period. I was panicked I was pregnant."

All my newfound serenity evaporated. I stared at her. "What would you have done if it had been true?"

"I'd already called Sam and gotten the name of somebody to take care of things. All he had to do was ask around A&M. You know the guys all know these things and we dumb little girls don't know enough to get in out of the rain."

I was staring at her.

She gave me a piercing look. "Why?" she asked, squinting at me.

"Because I think I'm pregnant."

"Josh?"

"No."

"Well then …"

I wasn't going to tell anyone, but the story poured out.

She frowned at me, a look of incomprehension on her face and the brown eyes full of worry and sympathy. But she said nothing and went to her desk. Under some papers there, she found what she was looking for, a small piece of torn notebook paper with a telephone number on it. There was also an address and the name of a town I didn't recognize. "It's long distance. This guy is somewhere in Oklahoma. Look, I've got to go back down. Aunt Mamie's waiting for me. Don't do anything until I get back this afternoon, and we'll make some plans."

I nodded, feeling much as I had when she began making plans for me to go through rush. The feeling of relief, accompanied by a liberal dose of fear, returned. The combination left me almost catatonic. I turned on the radio and sat in a state of suspension to wait until she returned. But I did get up long enough to put the box of razor blades back in the drawer. I was ashamed of what she might think if she saw me with them

About five that evening, E.A. and I crowded into the telephone booth and I put through the long distance call, depositing coins in the slot when instructed by the operator. A gruff male voice, showing what I suspected was the effect of too many cigarettes and perhaps too much whiskey, answered the phone.

I began the rehearsed speech E.A. and I had devised. "Yes. I have a medical problem and I understand you are a doctor, is that right?"

"I can't talk to you now. If you want to make an appointment, you'll have to come to town and call me from here."

"When can I come?"

"Anytime," he said. "And bring a thousand dollars with you." Then he hung up the phone.

"What did he say?" asked E.A. When I told her, she squared her jaw and said, "Let me sit down."

I exchanges places with her and she thumbed through the yellow pages until she found the Greyhound Bus Line. She dropped a dime in the slot and waited a moment.

"Yes. I'd like to go to Durant, Oklahoma. Can you give me a schedule?" She motioned impatiently at me and I handed her the notebook and pencil I was holding in case the doctor had some instructions for me. She began to make notes: "Uh-huh. And what time does it arrive? You have to change where? Okay, and is that the same schedule for weekends?" Her voice was as efficient as a secretary's.

When she hung up she said, "Okay, here's the deal."

The bus schedule to Durant, Oklahoma, with one change in Sherman, Texas, was simple enough. Several buses ran each day. It was the money that stopped me and put me back into despair.

Back in our room, E.A. began to plot. "How much money do you have in the bank?"

"I've saved about two hundred dollars. I can use all of it, because my uncle will be sending my allowance next week." I nearly gagged when I mentioned the man.

"Okay. I'll call Sam. He promised me five hundred when he gave me the name. I'll tell him I need it and let him think it's for me."

"That still leaves me three hundred short."

"If Josh knew, you could ask him."

"He knows."

She looked surprised.

"The truth all came out at the hospital."

"Can you ask him?" She was once again the practical E.A.

"I'll have to."

CHAPTER SEVENTEEN

Early Friday morning, E.A. drove me to the bus station. She had invited herself to Mamie Hamilton's for the weekend and I signed out of the dormitory as though I was going with her.

When she left me in front of the station, I felt like I had the first day of school. E.A. leaned over, gave me a hug and pressed an extra twenty dollar bill in my hand. I bought my ticket and boarded the waiting bus.

Luckily, I got a window seat. The trip from Dallas to Sherman was only an hour and a half with a stop in McKinney, but the bus was stuffy and even though the smokers sat in back, just in front of the spaces reserved for Negroes, the smoke hung in a pall inside the bus. For the last month, cigarettes had tasted like something left over from a pigsty. What was worse, a fat woman in a flowered cotton country dress sat next to me and I was horrified to realize she was dipping snuff. She carried a small can that had held Vienna sausages in it, so that she could spit into it on occasion. I was grateful the majority of my nausea was behind me.

I kept my eyes fixed on the flat, uninteresting North Texas landscape.

In Sherman, I had time to buy a cellophane wrapped sandwich from the lunch counter and a bottle of 7Up. The forty-five mile ride from Sherman to Durant crossed the wide bed of the Red River. If I had imagined lush scenery with Montgomery Clift and John Wayne on horseback, what I saw instead was a deep cut of red sandstone and clay, the trees winter bare. The water wove a drunken course from one side of the bed to the other; it was the color of the rust showing around the bolts of the old green painted bridge we were crossing. I had a sense of fatality when we got to the other side of the gorge.

From the bus station, I called the number. This time, a woman answered the phone and I said I was in town and wanted to make an appointment.

"Honey, we can't see you until Monday," she said.

"But you have to," I protested, panic and tears in my voice. "I have to be back in Dallas on Monday and I only have enough money to pay you."

"Well, now wait a minute, sweetie. Don't cry. Hang on and let me see what I can do." It sounded as though she laid the phone down and I could hear muffled voices arguing in the background, and then footsteps. "Okay. We can see

you tomorrow. Just find a motel room and be here at ten in the morning. You'll
need a room anyway because you'll want to spend the night here tomorrow
night. Give me your name, now."

In a moment of panic, I lied and borrowed Paula's first name and Mrs.
Jackson's surname. It was the first time I admitted to myself that what I was
doing was illegal.

"See you then," she said and hung up. I looked around and walked toward
what I thought must be the center of town. A block away, I found the typical
southwestern Main Street: several blocks of one-story, false-front buildings with
small stores selling drugs, hardware, clothing and food. There was a two-story
hotel, but I didn't want to stay there. I could imagine the curious eyes of the desk
clerk. I walked back to the bus station and asked the man at the ticket counter
where I could find a motel.

Somehow, I felt less awkward being scrutinized by a ticket clerk than
someone in the hotel. He directed me to the highway and said I would find
accommodations there. The motel I saw was at the edge of town. It was more
what was called tourist cabins, and the tiny, detached wooden rooms reminded
me of the description of prostitutes' cribs I had read about in a novel.

The bored clerk in this establishment never changed expression when
I checked in for two nights, paying him ten dollars for the privilege. I had the
feeling he had seen this all before and would not even be surprised the next day
when I asked him for directions to the doctor's office. I spent the rest of the day
reading the book I had brought to read on the bus.

The woman had not said whether or not I should eat before coming to the
office, so after getting directions, I walked up Main Street to a café. It was dingy
and smelled of old grease, but the counter looked clean. I ordered tea and dry
toast. The waitress put down a dark green pot of hot water and a bag of Lipton's
tea in front of me. The cup and plate with toast had a green rim around the edge
and I was suddenly homesick for my aunt and Brooklyn. The local café, owned
by an elderly man and woman named Hearn, was a place we often ate when my
uncle worked late. It had this same institutional china, so plain and, for me, so
loaded with memories.

I looked around the various stores for an hour or two and then turned
left down the street to which the clerk had directed me. Two blocks further on,
I found the street named on E.A.'s piece of notepaper. The neighborhood of
old houses was rundown. The bungalows all had porches across the front. The
address I sought was one of these houses, with a huge elm in the front yard, a
chain porch swing and peeling white paint. I walked up the cement steps and a
brass plaque next to the door confirmed it was the doctor's office. I only hoped
the man was a real doctor.

I opened the door into a wide hall, the walls painted an impossibly sunny yellow. I suppose the color was meant to cheer up the patients. On the left, in what was once the front bedroom of the house, was the waiting room. On a mismatched group of chairs and couches sat two people waiting to see the doctor, neither of them my age and only one of them female. The normal looking patients, the shingles hanging on the wall, and the unmistakable smell of disinfectant, benzene, and sterile bandages made me more confident in the man's medical qualifications. I felt a moment of relief and realized I had been dreading the prospect of what had happened to Anita, and that the man might force me to have intercourse before the operation. The rather pedestrian medical appearance of the place reassured me.

The woman who evidently had answered my call yesterday was sitting behind a desk, wearing a nurse's uniform, complete with cap trimmed with a narrow black stripe and an official looking pin on the lapel. The thick makeup, eye-shadow and liner, along with false eyelashes, seemed to make the uniform look like a costume. I wondered if she were the doctor's wife. She smiled at me when I came in and said, "Paula?"

I nodded and she told me to have a seat. For forty minutes while the doctor saw the other patients, I read the ancient magazines in the waiting room, not really absorbing anything I read. No one else came into the waiting room.

"Come with me, Paula," the nurse finally said and ushered me into the room behind the waiting room. It too was the size of a large bedroom, a steel examining table on one side and a desk on the other. In between were old-fashioned doctors' cabinets painted white and filled with equipment, instruments and medications.

"If you don't mind," she said, "you can pay me now."

I took the envelope, thick with the money E.A. and Josh had given me and handed it to her. She put it in the pocket of her uniform.

The door on the hall side of the room opened and the doctor came in, wearing wrinkled trousers and a ragged white coat over a sport shirt. He was a hulking man with a lined, sad face. He didn't smile. He asked me when my last period was and whether I had had anything to eat. When I said tea and toast, he gave the nurse an exasperated look.

"I forgot to tell her," was all she said.

"If that's all you ate, you'll probably be all right," he said and turned to wash his hands in a lavatory.

The nurse pulled up a movable screen and helped me take off my skirt and underwear. I took off my shoes and left on my socks. She put a drape over me and helped me position myself on the table with my feet in the stirrups. Then she moved the screen and put a small, rigid mask covered in cotton cloth over my face. The metallic smell of ether at first seemed to stick in my throat and my lungs rebelled. Then, there was nothing.

"Okay, sweetie. Wake up, Paula. Wake up honey."

For a moment, I wondered who Paula was. The doctor had disappeared. The nurse was pulling at my arm, urging me to scoot back on the table and sit up.

"You aren't sick at your stomach, are you? Some people throw up all over when they have ether. I'm sorry I forgot to tell you not to eat, but I guess if you're not sick, it's all okay. Did you dream?"

"No."

"Some people on ether dream something awful. Do you feel dizzy?"

"No. I don't think so."

"Now, you'll bleed just like your normal period. If you do more than that, see a doctor, hear me?"

But don't tell them who did this, I told myself.

The nurse helped me dress and gave me a pad and belt. "That's it, honey. It's all over."

And as I walked out into the thin winter sunshine, I marveled at the fact that it was, indeed, all over. I went back to the diner for an egg salad sandwich, potato chips and a Coke.

That evening in the motel, between chapters of my book, I felt nothing. I knew I would always remember this and occasionally think about the child that could have been, but it was the overwhelming sense of being back to normal that filled my sense with a quietness that was like a balm.

The next day, I took the bus back to Sherman and Dallas. I had called E.A. to tell her when I was coming in. I had a vague hope it would be Josh who would meet me, but it was E.A.

"Are you all right?"

"I'm wonderful." I truly smiled for the first time in almost two months.

The euphoric feeling continued until the following Thursday when I woke with a temperature of 103 degrees.

CHAPTER EIGHTEEN

E.A. was frantic. She insisted I take my temperature. When she saw the reading on the thermometer, she flapped around the room aimlessly. Holding the instrument in front of her like a baton, she sat first on the bed, hopped up and finally sat at the desk.

"Look, Sheila, you've got to see a doctor."

"I don't want to."

"Oh, for God's sake. If what's wrong with you has to do with what you did, you could die. Don't you see that?"

I could see it, and in my present state of fever and chills, I wasn't sure I cared. "Sheila, listen to me. I'm going to call Aunt Mamie."

"Oh, please don't."

"I should have done that in the very first place. She knows about these things. She even takes girls to some place safe to have done what you did."

"But you didn't call her yourself. You called Sam."

"She's my aunt. I didn't want her to know and she would have told my folks. I couldn't face that any more than you could tell yours. I'm going to call her."

I was too sick to argue as she left the room. I lay in a pool of self-pity, knowing that my secret, which was no real secret at all, since E.A. and Josh knew, was now going to be known by more and more people. What would they think of me? This whole debacle must be punishment for some character flaw of mine. I huddled under the covers and shivered.

I heard the girls across the hall talking to E.A., and soon Paula and Miriam were looking down on me while E.A. wandered around the room.

Paula sat down on the edge of the bed. "You guys leave us alone a minute," she said to the other two. They left the room and Paula felt my forehead and then laid a comforting hand on my arm.

"Come on, girl. Tell me the truth. You've been under the weather for about six weeks now. What with tossing your cookies in the bathroom every morning, I thought you were pregnant." Her voice was low and confidential.

I knew the statement was really a question. I didn't answer but finally nodded.

"Does what's wrong with you now have anything to do with that and the fact that you were gone last weekend? I know you weren't with E.A. at her aunt's."

"I don't know. Maybe so."

Paula gave me the sort of look my uncle used to, when he thought I wasn't telling him the truth. "And?"

"E.A. has called Mrs. Hamilton," I said, as though that explained everything.

Paula, back into Nurse Jane mode, gave me a friendly pat and said, "Let me get you some aspirin."

About that time, Mrs. Hamilton swept into the room. She and Paula got me up and dressed sufficiently to get to the car. Mrs. Hamilton had already made an emergency call to her own gynecologist.

E.A. wanted to go with us, but she had a test scheduled for that morning and her aunt shooed her off to class.

"I wish to God E.A. had called me before you went off to Oklahoma," she said as she steered the car toward the Central Expressway. Obviously, E.A. had told her the whole story.

"Have you ever heard of the Gladney Home?" she asked.

"I don't think so."

"Do you remember a movie called *Blossoms in the Dust*?"

"I remember my mother wouldn't let me see it."

"It's about a place in Fort Worth where unmarried girls go to have their babies. Then the babies are adopted. I went there during the war when I was about your age. I got pregnant and the young man I was seeing was in the Army. He was killed in a training accident before we could make any plans to get married. I couldn't tell my parents, so I told them I had a job in Fort Worth, but what I really did was go to the Home and have my baby. Everything seemed okay, but Mr. Hamilton and I never had any children. I think about that baby all the time, and I've done a lot of work with them. But I've also done work with girls who made a different choice. There are not very many safe places to go even if you have the money. I often take them there. I would have been so glad to help you, Sheila."

"I didn't want anybody to know. Especially not Aunt Grace."

"We can talk about that later, but I urge you to tell her. E.A. says the baby wasn't Josh's and if what I suspect is true, you can't go back to that house again. Nobody is safe around a drinking alcoholic. Poor, poor Grace. Do you think she suspected anything?"

"She says he doesn't remember what he does when he's drunk. The next day he was hung over but acted like nothing had happened. I think if she suspected anything she would have asked me. All she wanted to know was if he was ugly to Josh when he brought me home."

Before we could continue, we were at the doctor's office. He was small, gray haired and gentle. When he finished, he asked me to come into his office alone.

I sat in a chair across from his desk, feeling my fever rise after the relief of the aspirin.

"Well, young lady," he said, when he had seated himself at the desk, "I'm going to ask the nurse to give you a shot of penicillin. That way you'll have a sore bottom to go along with your other aches and pains. But the happy news is I think all you have is a case of the flu."

I didn't realize how relieved I was. I had pushed all the worries about being sterile like Anita or dying from asepsis to the back of my mind.

"Now," said the doctor, looking at me over horn-rimmed glasses, "let's talk about what happened to you."

Slowly, under his gentle probing, most of the story came out. He talked to me about protecting myself in the future and suggested that in his practice, he had found it helpful to women like me to talk to someone, perhaps my priest or minister. "There are some wounds I don't know enough about to heal," he said and rose from his desk.

The nurse gave me the shot, which make me feel as though someone had taken a baseball bat to my buttocks. She also gave me more aspirin, so that by the time I got to the dorm, the fever had subsided.

Four days of bed rest made me feel close to human again. None of the girls mentioned what I knew was on their mind. I supposed they considered the case closed, but they did show a lot of interest in what I thought I would do during the coming summer, insinuating that surely I would not be going back to New York, or at least I would not be staying with Aunt Grace and Uncle Howard.

I still couldn't tell Aunt Grace what had happened, but when I had recovered from the flu, I did ask Father Heinz if I could visit with him. He was the only one I felt comfortable telling the whole story, because I thought there was a large part of it in which I was complicit. I didn't spare him the details.

Father Heinz let me tell the entire story without interruption. When I had finished, he said, "Do you feel guilty about this, Sheila?"

"I think I do. A little." I stared at a small painting hanging above the priest's desk. It was an old oil of a Cardinal, dressed in red, sitting at a desk. Its medieval connotation brought back a rush of fear and angst.

"Can you tell me why?"

"I think I made him mad."

"Sheila, the one thing a little girl or even young woman deserves to expect from her father or uncle or any older man in the family, is safety. When that contract, and it is a silent contract, is broken, the fault lies at the door of the adult. The adult should know better and act accordingly. Whatever you did or said, it was your Uncle who was the perpetrator. It just wasn't your fault. Accepting the fact that it happened and moving on is hard, but necessary. Do you think you can do that? Otherwise, my dear, you make the choice to hold on to your burden."

"I suppose." I looked away from the picture and stared at the priest. His blue eyes were filled with concern. I scrutinized his expression for any judgment.

I knew if I wanted to talk about it again I could go to Father Heinz. I knew it would take a while.

What it did do for me immediately was let me have the courage to call Aunt Grace. We talked for forty-five minutes on the phone. I told her I wanted to transfer to Columbia the next year, but wanted to live close to campus. She interpreted that correctly as also close to Josh and didn't question me further. We made some tentative plans for summer. I was sure to mention the possibility of my working in Dallas during vacation to make some money. E.A. had mentioned our staying with Mrs. Hamilton for the summer and getting a job at Sanger's. My Aunt seemed disappointed, but told me to do what I wanted about summer employment.

I went back to my room alone that Sunday evening and stood at the window staring out at the March twilight. Spring was near and I truly looked forward to it.

I would stay away from New York as much as possible until the fall semester. Tomorrow, I would look into the job at Sanger's and what I had to do to transfer and find housing for the fall.

CHAPTER NINETEEN

Friday, May 17, 1985

I awakened and looked over at E.A. and smiled. Perhaps the lump in the bed next to me was larger than at school, but the posture was familiar. From under the counterpane, only a wisp of blonde hair showed atop the pillow, pulled like a stopper into the cocoon made by the body curled into a tight C, her steady breath audible.

I slipped quietly from bed and closed the bathroom door. I had washed my hair the night before I left New York. I pulled it up in a fan behind my head. No use taking the time to wash it this morning. It would be fine in the chignon I usually wore. I cocked my head critically at my reflection, then made a face. I still looked like a little girl without lipstick. Or was it I was just remembering how untutored and naïve I felt those first few days at the University? No time to speculate this morning. I had to meet Behneke at ten.

I dressed in a hunter's plaid Armani suit and a red silk blouse to complement the narrow red bar in the plaid, gave myself a quick nod in the closet mirror and gathered up purse and briefcase. Eleanor Ann stirred in the bed by the window and breathed deeply. Her eyes were still closed. I hoped I hadn't wakened her and tiptoed toward the door.

"See you at noon. Good luck," E.A. rasped without opening her eyes.

"Kisses," I answered, automatically using the good-bye Elise and I used when we were speaking to each other.

The taxi drive to the complex of buildings that house Behneke's offices gave me the same kind of view I had from the airport. Now Dallas seemed homogenized, impersonal and repetitious. Perhaps, I was simply used to New York, the aging dowager of American cities, and here I was seeing for the first time the newness of a country growing almost too rapidly to absorb the expansion. The change made me sad and reminded me of the change a city can make in a person. Dallas had changed me and New York certainly had done the same for Josh Cooper. I shook my head to ward away the thoughts.

The offices of Southwest Tool and Supply were in one of the glass boxes. Theodore Behneke's offices were more inviting, the walls paneled in a warm walnut, the floors covered in dark green carpet, much the color of the entry and elevator lobbies. On the walls were prints rather than paintings, serigraphs by Vasarely and Korpi, really a remnant of '50s and '60s art, but bright, elegant and cool against the wood. The print behind the receptionist's desk looked like an Albers and I thought if it was, it was probably a real one.

I introduced myself to the receptionist, was asked to take a seat and told, "Mr. Behneke's assistant will be with you shortly." I declined something to drink. I wanted no distractions, and took the solitary moment to gather my thoughts, but before I could complete my moment of meditation, a tall, leggy blonde in a powder blue suit rounded the corner of the reception area and held out her hand.

"Mrs. Cauthron? I'm Lilah Bennett, Mr. Behneke's assistant. I think we spoke on the phone when you made your appointment."

"Yes, we did." I said. I really needed to get over this case of nerves.

I followed the assistant down the hall and through a reception area to the spacious office beyond. The man just turning in his chair from the piles of papers was shorter than I had imagined. He was a small, fit man in shirtsleeves and tie. His suit jacket hung over the back of his chair. He did not bother to put it on, but rose to greet me and his smile was open and genuine. Oh, that Texas openness, I thought, so different from the formality and wariness of New York. My nerves immediately began to subside.

"Hi, you must be Sheila," he said, the native twang evident in his voice, not quite as distinct as E.A.'s, but close. "I'm Ted Behneke, nice to know ya'."

"Nice to meet you, Mr. Behneke."

"Just Ted's fine. Is this your first visit to Big D?" Behneke took me firmly by the elbow and steered me to a sitting area with comfortable chairs and a large coffee table. He indicated one of the chairs for me to sit in, and he sat in one opposite me. Without consulting me, he turned to his assistant and said, "Bring us a couple of Cokes, will you, Lilah?"

He then turned his entire attention to me. "Diet or regular?"

"Diet, please."

"So, now, I didn't give you a chance to answer. What are you doing in Dallas other than trying to get your hand in my pocket?" Ted Behneke laughed as he said this, and the unmistakable twinkle in his blue eyes signaled at least some receptivity to the coming conversation about money.

I explained this was not my first trip to Dallas. That I had come from Brooklyn to SMU for my first year of college and that my roommate and my freshman friends were having our own small reunion. In the course of explaining, I mentioned E.A.'s name.

"E.A. Cabel? You mean Eleanor Ann Roberts?"

"Yes. Do you know her?"

"Jim Ed and I are both Aggies. I grew up in good ol' Fort Worth, but went to A&M." We were classmates and still have lunch sometimes. Who're the other ladies?'

I told him, using both of Miriam's names.

Lilah returned with the iced drinks, and I took advantage of the interruption to change the subject. I had done my homework. I knew a lot about Ted Behneke. He was a golfer, loved football, loved the Aggies (I should have guessed from his age he would have been in school with Jim Ed), but most important, he was an adoptive father. He and his wife, Gillian, had two children of their own and had adopted three others from various parts of the world, a girl from Guatemala, a boy from Jamaica and another son from the Gladney Home, one of the Roberts's and the Behnekes' chief philanthropies. The children now were all high school age or older. Their two biological children already had graduated from college.

It was this interest in children who were disadvantaged that made my boss, Gerald Chinn, so anxious to see if he could tap into the considerable Behneke resources.

I inquired politely about his wife and children, allowing him to brag a little and conveying to him that I had knowledge of his background. This is phase one of any good fund raiser's tactics, establishing a personal connection. I let him talk until he had exhausted the subject. It didn't take long, since he knew very well that was not the primary business of the meeting.

I segued into a brief but thorough explanation of the programs of the World Children's Fund and made the pitch for his help in securing one of those goals. I named the million dollar figure I hoped to get and firmly shut my mouth, sat back, took a sip of my Diet Coke and let the man think.

The nerves returned in full force. I slowed my breathing and did a little Zen exercise to center myself and not be tempted to interrupt the process that Ted Behneke was going through of mentally reviewing his financial options.

His gaze shifted imperceptibly toward me, and he smiled his open, Texas smile. "That's pretty strong, Miz Sheila," he said. After a pause he added, "How about half that and a promise to keep an open mind about the other half?"

I felt the tension I had tried to master with the bit of Zen evaporate completely and be replaced with an exhilarating sense of accomplishment. This was really more than I had hoped for. I felt a smile spread across my face in compulsive relief.

I held out my hand, "Deal."

He laughed. "So where's that dotted line I'm sure you want me to sign?"

My hand trembled a little as I extracted from my briefcase the donor card, already filled in with all but the dollar amount, fumbled for a pen, filled in the agreed upon amount and handed both to him.

As he signed his name, he returned once again to the earlier, more personal conversation. "Have you seen Jim Ed or just E.A?"

"Just E.A., but he called last night and I think he is just fine."

"How's that boy of theirs?" He glanced at me with the sort of sharp look I imagined he fixed on any employee from whom he expected a thorough and accurate report. I found myself responding in kind.

"From what I can gather, there is nothing but trouble there."

Ted Behneke gave me a long look, opened his mouth, thought better of speaking and turned his attention once more to the pledge card. He handed it carefully back to me.

"So, Miz Sheila, you're here visiting old friends. I remember Miriam from high school. Lord, she was a beauty."

"She's still very attractive."

"But I don't remember Gold. Is that his name?"

"Yes, Manny Gold. He was from Fort Worth too, but three years older. He and Miriam were childhood sweethearts."

"When I knew her, she was dating Josh Cooper occasionally. I couldn't forget that. They made a handsome couple. Did you ever know Josh?"

My stomach knotted again, and this time I did not have time to tap into the Zen. "I met him when he was dating Miriam." I was astonished to hear myself add, "Then we went out some when we were both at Columbia."

He nodded. "It was some sort of traffic accident, wasn't it?"

"He was run over by a New York City Transit bus," I added without expression, tamping down the feelings of anger and despair that still occasionally cropped up.

"Such a loss. Texas doesn't have that many Pulitzer Prize winners."

We took our leave of each other and I left the building with a feeling of disembodiment prompted by the success of the interview and the conversation about Josh. I found a taxi by the entrance. "Neiman-Marcus – downtown," I said.

I was unconscious of my surrounding during the trip to downtown Dallas from the suburban office complex. "Texas doesn't have that many Pulitzer Prize winners?" Was that all it meant? Was Josh some sort of ornament to hang on the Lone Star? Tears of anger surprised me. For so many years, my anger about his death had been leveled at him, not at something as abstract as fame and a literary prize. I suddenly had a clear vision of him that last day, the last day of his life.

CHAPTER TWENTY

Wednesday, April 9, 1952

The Wednesday before Easter found me again on the road to Fort Worth, this time just with Miriam and Josh. I was to spend the holiday with Miriam, and was nervous and excited in anticipation of meeting Josh's parents. This was one of the years that the Easter holidays coincided with the Jewish Passover and I was curious to experience it with a Jewish family. I looked forward to that, but not without anxiety. I realized I was terrified to meet the Coopers and about what they would think of his dating a Christian. I couldn't help but remember the comments made last fall by the girls at the football watch party about how Josh's parents would feel about him dating anyone but Miriam—especially a "goy."

"Stop that," Josh said.

"What?"

"You're biting your cuticles again." He gave my arm a gentle swipe that reminded me of Aunt Grace.

I twisted my hands in my lap. I hadn't bitten my fingernails since I was a teenager until the last month. Now I was desperate to grow them out before the SAM spring dance. I had gone from biting the nails to biting the cuticle and didn't think anyone had noticed. I should have known that Josh's writer's eye for detail would not have missed the habit. I felt the reprimand as though I was four years old.

"At least she's not biting her nails. Gotta look good for the big dance," Miriam said from the back seat. Now I was humiliated. Even she had noticed.

"Did you get that dress?"

I turned halfway around to talk over the back of the bench seat. "I did."

"You guys are going to be the hit of the dance. You should see that dress, Josh."

"Don't tell him about it! I want it to be a surprise."

"At least tell him what color it is so he can get you the right corsage."

"It's pale blue, and that's all I'm going to say." I had talked Aunt Grace out of a wad of cash to buy the dress. Some of it I used to begin to pay back Josh and E.A. But the dress was lovely. I could picture him looking incredibly handsome in his tux, waiting for me in the foyer.

At Miriam's, Josh helped us in with our luggage and said a quick good-bye, giving me his special smile. The Sapersteins greeted me warmly. Miriam's mother, Helene, was short, round and jolly, with Miriam's lovely eyes. Her father, Philip, was humorous and friendly, with a graying fringe of dark hair and thick glasses. We had met briefly at Thanksgiving when we dropped Miriam off at her house. Their warmth helped take the edge off my anxiety about meeting the Coopers.

Helene hurried us off to the bedroom to settle our baggage. She announced that she had asked all the Coopers for lunch that day and that we would be celebrating Seder the following evening at their house. This was all new to me, but if lunch and the Seder meal were as delicious as the smells filling this house, the weekend would not be wasted, even if the Coopers weren't thrilled with their son's current steady date.

While we were unpacking, Miriam asked, "Sheila, has Josh said anything to you about his plans for next year?"

"Only that he had been accepted at Columbia." I thought it was time I talked to my friends about my plans. "I guess I'm going, too. I've arranged for my grades to be sent up there and I think I've found some housing close to the campus. I'll miss all of you terribly. I hate the idea of leaving you. I hope I'm lucky enough to find friends like you there."

She gave me a strange look I couldn't interpret and I wondered if I had hurt her feelings by deciding to leave.

Before she could say anything, Helene came to the door and told Miriam that Manny would be in on the plane at four o'clock.

Compared to Miriam's family, the Coopers were rather subdued. His father, Alfred, was as tall as Josh, gaunt, with a rugged face and kind, sad brown eyes. His mother, Adele, was a slender woman. Josh had inherited her striking blue eyes and curly hair, but her eyes looked almost haunted to me. Both Mr. and Mrs. Cooper were cordial to me, if a little formal. I relaxed a little.

The conversation over the lunch of chicken soup, salad and fruit began with polite inquiries into what all the young people were doing and some of the usual questions about my background and family, but soon moved on to public affairs. There was much discussion of Senator Joseph McCarthy and his aggressive behavior. I was struck by the difference between the conversation at this meal and what had been of interest in the Cabel household.

Manny arrived at the Sapersteins just as Josh and I were leaving for the movies and a drive around the city, so that he could show me the sights of his hometown. I was surprised at Manny Gold's appearance. All I had seen of him was the picture Miriam kept on her dresser. He was smaller than I imagined, compact of body, but with a striking presence and serenity. If he wasn't handsome, at least he had just the sort of personality I would wish for her.

Josh and I got back to the Sapersteins about ten o'clock and Miriam came in just as I was climbing into bed with a novel. I was astounded to see she had been crying.

"Miriam, what's wrong?"

She sat down on the twin bed across from me and blew her nose on a Kleenex. "Manny has been called up. He reports to Fort Benning on May tenth."

"Won't they even let him stay long enough to graduate?"

"He's already talked to his professors. He's such a good student they told him to forget finals. A couple of them had him do some extra work. But he's going to miss graduation and everything."

"Is that what you're crying about?"

"No," she said. "I don't know what to do. He wants to get married now."

"You mean before he goes?"

"Uh-huh."

"But I thought you wanted to get married." I handed her several tissues which she just knotted up in her hands. I wanted to tell her to wipe her nose. "So?"

"We had it all planned. He was going on to grad school for three years while I finished; then we were going to have a big wedding and everything. Now, instead, I'm afraid he'll go off to Korea and get killed."

"Miriam. Think a minute. He may go to Korea, but he'll probably be fine. It just means all those long-range plans won't fit the facts. Do you want to get married now?"

She looked up with a look of deep consideration. Then she wiped her eyes, and her nose, I was glad to see. The lovely chocolate colored eyes began to sparkle. "Can we do it? Can we pull off a wedding in a month?"

Thoughts of war thousands of miles away gave way to wedding plans and we talked animatedly until exhaustion finally overcame us at two in the morning.

The next day, after a telephone conversation with Manny, Miriam told her parents what was going to happen. She didn't ask. She made a quiet statement. Mrs. Saperstein was dismayed at the prospect of such short notice to plan a wedding. Mr. Saperstein took a sober view of the prospect of a son-in-law going off to war.

In the early afternoon, the Golds and the Sapersteins gathered at the Coopers, along with Miriam's brother, David, his wife Anne and five-year-old son, Jacob. The men retreated almost in panic to the library. I heard Mr. Saperstein tell Manny, "Son, when women start planning a wedding, the best thing to do is get out of the way and keep your mouth shut. Sanity only returns after the ceremony." I heard Josh give a hearty guffaw.

In the kitchen, the women's conversation caromed between wedding plans and instructions to me on helping arrange the Seder food. In reality, the women had prepared most of it beforehand, just the way Aunt Grace would prepare much of Christmas dinner, but I was fascinated to help Miriam prepare the Seder plate with its bitter herbs, fruit and nuts, egg, greens, and roasted shin bone of lamb—Paschal lamb, I thought. Mrs. Cooper took special care to explain to me the significance of each item. I hoped her attention signaled at least some approval of the girl her son was dating.

Anne took Miriam and me by the elbows, pushing us toward the dining room door.

"Girls, come help me set the table. And let's talk about anything but the wedding." she said, pulling silverware from a drawer. The ritual of placing white linen, polished silver and sparkling crystal while women gossiped reminded me again of Christmases.

"So what do you think about Josh's fellowship?"

Miriam made a movement as if to silence her.

"What fellowship?"

"Oh, dear, I thought you knew. He applied to the writing program at Iowa when he applied to Columbia. He thought he wouldn't get in, but last month he heard that he had."

"And he's going?"

"Ask Miriam. Maybe he hasn't made up his mind."

"Miriam?"

"I'm not sure, Sheila. He hasn't said anything definite to me."

The meal, served at sundown, was delicious, the wine sweet and dark. I thought of the priest blessing the wine at mass. Mr. Saperstein recited the Kiddush over the goblets the four times they were filled during the Seder, and proceeded to pray over the matzah and other items of food, reading from the Passover Haggadah. A Jewish Missal, I thought. With Mr. Saperstein reading, the rituals of blessings, prayers and hand washing were easy to follow. Little Jacob was the most excited person in the room, since the youngest child has his own part to play in the ceremony. I felt very much at home.

The rest of the weekend was dominated, at least for the women, with more wedding plans, broken only by Temple and the second night of Seder on Friday.

Saturday afternoon, Josh and I escaped to the Art Museum. We stopped on the way back for a cup of coffee.

I finally brought myself to ask him if he thought his parents approved of me.

"Does it matter?"

"Well, I'd like them to."

"My Dad said you were cute and Mom said you were nice. Make you feel better?"

I stuck my tongue out at him.

"Ooh, save that for a better use," he said, and I groaned.

Even though it was still daylight, we had a long session in the back seat of his car. Slowly, my sexual longing for him was beginning to return. He was incredibly patient, letting my own needs overtake whatever memories of the winter seemed to intrude. If he was ready for full intercourse, he didn't say so, and I couldn't yet bring myself to want that. I wondered if I was just afraid of getting pregnant again or if I would ever be able to put away the memory of New Year's Eve. Or perhaps, since he hadn't said anything to me about the possibility of going to Iowa, I was beginning to be wary.

The wedding took place in the Blackstone Hotel ballroom the first Sunday in May. Mrs. Saperstein was still mumbling under her breath about the invitations not being engraved and the lack of availability of the ballroom at the larger, more popular Hotel Texas.

Anne was Miriam's matron of honor, and E.A., Paula and I were attendants, each dressed in pale green taffeta waltz length dresses, carrying bouquets of daisies. Manny's two brothers ushered, along with David and Josh.

Since Josh and I were the tallest, we were the last in but I still had a close-up view of the ceremony conducted under the wedding chupah. I paid close attention, wondering if I might one day be the bride in such a ceremony. At the end, Manny wrapped a glass goblet carefully in a napkin and then broke it with his foot.

As we recessed between the rows of white folding chairs set up in the ballroom, I luxuriated in the feel of Josh's tuxedo when I took his arm. The smell of aftershave and his body was an intoxicant.

There was champagne and dancing at the wedding dinner. I loved dancing the hora with the guests, Miriam, high above us, laughing from the chair held by the groomsmen. The heightened feeling of excitement and the thought that I now had no virginity to protect made me determined at long last to give Josh all I had wanted to give him since Christmas.

Josh wouldn't tell me where the bride and groom were spending the night, but he was delegated to take them there. He grabbed me as he slipped out of the room to get the car that was in the parking garage, properly decorated with a white shoe polish "Just Married" sign, balloons and tin cans. We drove to the front of the hotel, picked up the waiting couple in a shower of rice and drove them all the way to Dallas to spend the night near Love Field.

As we drove back to Fort Worth in the decorated automobile, people would honk and wave and we acted as though we were the bride and groom.

Josh pulled into a small park somewhere near his folk's house and reached across me to the glove compartment and took out a condom.

"I love you," he said, and kissed me deeply. I had waited since the first day I met him to hear him say that.

"Josh."

"Huh?"

"Just when were you going to tell me you were going to Iowa?"

"Who told you?"

"I heard it at Miriam's at Easter. That's almost a month ago."

"I'm sorry. I thought you had enough to worry about this spring and I didn't want to hurt your feelings. It's just such a once-in-a-lifetime opportunity." His eyes were ablaze with the kind of animation I had never seen there before, and I realized what the love of Josh Cooper's life really was.

"I do understand. This is what you live for, Josh."

"How about going to Iowa with me?"

Was he serious? Don't think so.

"So, are you coming back here next year?"

"No, I'll go on to Columbia."

"But you're not staying with your uncle, are you? He looked concerned.

"No. I've made other arrangements."

He reached for me again. "I think you'd better take me home, Josh."

A look of frustrated anger flitted across his face and then he was amiable Josh again. He tossed the condom back in the glove compartment.

We went back to Miriam's. The next morning, I packed my wedding finery and Josh picked me up in his car. As he let me out in front of the dorm, I said, "However, I want to wear my blue dress, so we're still going to the Sammy dance, right?"

"Sure," he said, as though nothing had changed.

CHAPTER TWENTY-ONE

The evening before Josh graduated was our last before he went to Iowa. By six-thirty in the evening, the heat had abated at least enough to allow Josh and me to be outside away from people. We sat on the edge of the fountain in the middle of the quadrangle, the sound of the water a proclamation that it stood ready to quench thirst, cool the air and water the earth.

Josh had his arm draped loosely over my shoulders and my hand was on his back, tracing the ridges of muscle on each side of his spine. His blue button-down broadcloth shirt smelled of Old Spice.

On the steps of Virginia Hall, he gave me the last kiss I would have from him for nearly ten years.

The room was empty when I got to the fourth floor. Most of E.A.'s things were packed in the beautiful yellow leather suitcases, except for a welter of clothes on the bed, which I suppose represented the amount of garments she had acquired over the winter.

I walked down the hall to the smoker where my three friends sat, much as we had the day we met. E.A. was sprawled on one of the chairs smoking a cigarette. Paula sat yoga-style on the divan and Miriam sat opposite E.A. in one of the chairs, her feet alternately on the coffee table or draped over the arm of the chair. Miriam had come back to the dorm for finals week. All three had Cokes, and I dropped my cigarettes on the table along with the silver Zippo lighter Josh had given me for my birthday in April.

I went to get a Coke from the machine at the end of the hall and joined the other three. The wheel of the lighter scraped across the flint as I lit my cigarette, then inhaled deeply.

How we had changed in nine months. A carat-and-a-half diamond sparkled on Miriam's left hand. She had permission from the Dean to return to the dorm after her short honeymoon. I smiled when I remembered how she looked in her wedding gown. I hoped she would always be as happy with her choice as she was that afternoon.

"So, did you get your good-byes said?" Miriam's dark chocolate eyes brimmed with sympathy. I wondered if she was feeling especially bad for our leave-taking now that her years of being separated from Manny were about to begin again if he went overseas.

"I really hope you get together again sometime, Sheila. Josh is such an unpredictable guy, but you seemed to be good for him. He seemed to concentrate more and he did even better in school this year. All he used to care about was jotting down stuff, writing for the paper and hanging out at the frat house."

E.A. didn't enter this conversation, but her quick eyes watched my every gesture and expression.

She squinted thoughtfully through the smoke in the room. "We've had some adventures this year. At Christmas, I thought we were all paired off for life." She looked at Paula. "But we've got to find somebody for our friend on the couch." She waved her cigarette in Paula's direction. "Here, we've had all the fun and she's just made good grades."

"Don't worry about me."

"But we gotta find you a friend," said E.A., and she and Miriam began to run down a list of prospects.

"I have a friend," Paula said quietly.

"Who?" E.A. sat straight up in her chair. "You've been holding out on us. You gotta tell us all."

Paula, after a moment of silence, put back her head and laughed her deep laugh that seemed to come from the bottom of her lungs. "God, I love you girls. You are still so damn naïve about sex."

Miriam and I straightened up in our chairs, too. I was sure my mouth was hanging open as far as E.A.'s.

"Well, you are. Even after all the things that happened to E.A. and Sheila and Miriam married."

"What are you saying?" demanded E.A.

"I'm saying it's been all year and you never have figured out that Susan and I ... that we have a special friendship."

"What the hell are you saying? That you're a *fairy?*"

Paula just laughed and wiggled her fingers to imitate flutter of wings.

"I never suspected," said Miriam, a mystified look on her face.

"I know. And I love you for it."

This conversation was interrupted by someone calling from the phone booth for Miriam. We had ignored the ringing phone, knowing the poor girls who lived closest to the center of the hall would always pick it up.

Miriam went off to the phone, hoping it was Manny calling from Georgia, and Paula said she and Susan were going bowling.

"You girls have a good time. You certainly bowled us over," E.A. called after her.

She got up and plopped down on the couch opposite me where Paula had sat. She propped her feet in their white sox on the coffee table, putting the soles against my stocking feet. The warmth of her transferred itself in a comforting sensation.

"So tell me, old dear. Are you okay with Josh not going to New York this fall?"

"I think so. I know there's a chance Josh may find someone else. But there's also a chance he might end up in New York. Most writers do at some point."

"I was thinking more about being that close to good ol' Uncle Howard. I'm scared for you to go back to that house."

"I'll just spend some weekends there, maybe, and see if I can see Aunt Grace more in town."

"Are you still talking to Father Heinz?"

"Yes, and your aunt. I'm really looking forward to living with her this summer."

"To her, you're like the little girl she gave up."

I didn't answer, but I liked the idea. To me, she was certainly like the mother I lost. E.A. rubbed the soles of her feet against mine. I thought about Paula and Susan. I could understand the physical comfort a woman could give, but I certainly wanted a man when it came to sex.

I looked at my friend on the sofa. She had her head thrown back, her blonde hair spilling out over the back of the sofa and her eyes closed, long lashes forming a dark semicircle on her creamy cheeks.

No matter what happened to Josh and me, I had gained one thing from this year in Texas. There was one person my age who knew everything there was to know about me and loved me fiercely. And I loved her.

The year in Texas gave me a lifelong best friend.

CHAPTER TWENTY-TWO

The summer in Dallas was healing. E.A. and I worked at Sanger's, she in the lingerie department and I sold cosmetics. Most of the money I made went to pay back E.A. I also sent checks to Josh when we corresponded. E.A. and I had a few casual dates with guys she had known in high school and spent a lot of time at the Hillcrest Country Club pool, baking in the sun on our days off and weekends.

By fall I was ready to go back to New York and fate, God or some higher power stepped into the middle of the fall semester. Whatever anger, resentment and hatred I held for my uncle was about to be cleansed. Aunt Grace, after telling me he had some "plumbing" trouble, called to tell me he had cancer. They had done one of those "open up and close back up" operations on him. For the next six months, I made trips back and forth to Brooklyn to help my aunt as her husband lost weight, was bedridden and finally moved to a hospital bed in the dining room, which was made into a complete sick room. With the permission of my professors, I cut classes most of the last week of his life to help Aunt Grace and the nurse see him through the last hours of agony.

At the visitation the night before the funeral, Mamie Hamilton and E.A. walked in.

I was standing against the wall, staring at the casket when I heard E.A. drawl. "Hi, honey. I'm so sorry."

I never thought I would cry over the man who violated me, but somehow this gesture of friendship let me grieve. Aunt Grace clung to Mamie and the four of us sobbed the way one only does over death.

After the funeral the next day, the four of us escaped to Manhattan for tea at the Plaza.

"Tell me about Miriam and Manny."

"She's pregnant, of course, but still going to school. She'll be goin' to class with one kid on her hip and another nursing away."

"Eleanor Ann!"

"She will, Aunt Mamie. She loves babies and she loves school. One day she'll teach.

"What's Paula doing?"

"She and Susan broke up. So she's decided to transfer somewhere they have a combined BS, nursing degree, where she can get out of school in five years."

The two older women stared at each other. "Oh, the times they are a changin'," said Mamie.

Finally, I asked about Josh.

"Haven't you heard from him?"

"He wrote all the time at first, but it's been a while." I didn't know how I felt, resigned, angry, resentful?

"When I see Miriam, she says he's doing great and they love him at the writing program. She says he gets published in these little magazines. I don't even know the names.

"That's great. It's what he always wanted."

I clenched my teeth and we talked about other things until time for the women to catch a taxi to the airport.

I did hear about Josh from time to time. As he had stories published, I scoured the magazines so I wouldn't miss them. Also, his friends Anita and Walter had married. Anita took a job at the Avery Library at Columbia. We began to have coffee and forged a real friendship of our own. At first, all I wanted was news of Josh, but she was a steady and thoughtful friend.

After I graduated, I moved all my things back to Aunt Grace's. Now that she was alone, she had begun to volunteer at a day care center, and we kept ourselves busy. My first job was at a magazine doing grunt work, but learning the direct mail business. I started to take courses at the New School in fund-raising and went on to work for a small not-for-profit.

One noon I went uptown to meet Anita for lunch and as I was walking across the Columbia quad I heard, "Sheila!" I didn't have to turn around to know who it was.

"We're going to have to stop meeting like this, in the middle of college campuses!" He threw his arms around me and kissed me as though we had parted last Friday. I went stiff.

He let me go. "Am I going to have to grovel?" He tossed the yellow pad he was carrying with a ball point pen stuck to it on the ground, and fell to his knees. He was actually kneeling on the pad, which I knew held his precious writing, and I couldn't help but laugh. It was a very small laugh, but enough to bring him to his feet. "C'mon. Anita's waiting."

I should have turned on my heel, but the piper was piping his lovely tune.

The casual coffee dates morphed into dinner, often with Walter and Anita, then I moved in with him into a crappy one-room apartment not far from our friends in the Village. We became the legendary hippies, Josh with a beard and me with long skirts, no makeup. We had about seven years of weeds and beads and Sundays with Aunt Grace, who not so subtlely wondered when we would get married. The few times the Coopers visited, it was the same. Gradually, nothing mattered to either of us but Josh's writing. There was always work on the magnum opus, which he superstitiously called "George" so as not to mention any working title. I gradually worked my way up from filing to a better paying middle management job with a series of nonprofit agencies, where I could simultaneously believe I was doing good while putting bread on the table.

We loved each other, or I thought we did. We certainly got along, but only later did I realize one reason was we always did what was important to Josh. But I was complicit. Josh was all that was important to me.

Our sex life was great, then comfortable and always safe, so far as I was concerned, since the invention of the little pills I picked up each quarter at Planned Parenthood.

Economically, things did improve. Josh brought in some money editing copy for various publishers and mentoring a few young writers. The Iowa degree was worth that much.

Then he began to sell some stories and finally, as the sixties wore down, he began to be published in magazines like the *New Yorker*. We moved to a small, rent-controlled midtown apartment. I began to look for a better job and we actually dumped the castoff furniture we had picked up on street corners and bought some new things. We also began to spend a little money going to the theater and attending functions. One evening at a gallery opening on Fifth Avenue, I noticed Josh in earnest conversation with a woman. She looked like every other impossibly thin and chic New York matron who went to such things; faux blonde and boney.

He beckoned to me and introduced me. "Sheila, this Estella Raphael. Estella, my friend Sheila O'Connor."

Her handshake was firm and her voice carried a distinct flavor of a native New Yorker. "So very nice to meet you. I've read some of Josh's stories and he's telling me about his book."

I laughed and said, "Oh, about George."

"What?" She looked confused.

"Sorry," I said. "Around the apartment, we refer to the novel as George. Josh thinks even a working title is a name that should not be mentioned."

She gave me a calculating look. I knew she hadn't missed the reference to "we" and "apartment." After all, I was more than a friend.

Her counter was one I couldn't match. She called the book by one of the many names Josh was considering and told me about connections she had at Knopf and several other publishers. She didn't mention her other connection with cocaine.

By this time, "George" was nearly finished, or at least its first iteration. Walter and I were Josh's primary readers. We would have discussions of plot, setting and character, but only after the weeks or months of writing Josh did alone at the desk in the corner of the living room. This book had taken a long time, being created in fits and starts between Josh's other work, the short stores and the publication of a slender novel he had written mostly when he was at Iowa. It had garnered some critical recognition and we hoped the longer book would earn a look from publishers who had at least heard of the author. Still, query letters and even first chapter submissions were routinely turned down.

To give Estella credit, she did get a reading from a major publisher, but they wanted substantial rewrites. She became Josh's chief reader and he began to spend more and more time at her apartment.

The inevitable scene was vintage Josh. I came home from work at five and found him sitting on the couch, surrounded by suitcases. They held his clothes. Evidently he had packed and transported to her place all his personal items. There were bare spaces on the walls and the shelves where he had displayed things he cared about. The Natkin painting was leaning against the bags.

He had the grace to look sheepish. "Sheila, I'm moving to Estella's."

"What a surprise," I said

"I should have told you earlier …"

"Stop right there, Josh. You certainly should have. You should also have told me earlier that you were going to Iowa, that you didn't intend ever to marry me and that you were sleeping with Estella. But typical Josh, you just put it off and put it off until push came to shove."

"Sheila …"

"No, don't say anything. Take your things and go. And Josh, don't call, don't come by and don't try to see me? Clear?"

"Yes."

"One more thing. I'm hanging the Natkin back on the wall. Estella has loads of art and I paid for most of that, as you very well know."

"Sheila …"

"Shut up, asshole." I said it and held the door open for him. That, I thought was the end.

And it was, until November 1970. I was both proud and angry when he won the Pulitzer the year before. I gagged every time I saw his picture in the society section of the paper, always dressed beautifully, always with fashionable Estella.

I took more courses at the New School and landed my present job, which paid me enough to meet the rent and have a little for some long-delayed luxuries.

Walter and Anita kept in touch, even though they were living in Queens with their two adopted children. Walter was a drug counselor and he would every once in a while tell me that Josh was supposedly working on a new book, but Walter wondered how much coke he was doing along with the writing. No drafts of the work seemed to have surfaced.

But the proverbial penny finally turned up. I got a call from Josh. It was on Saturday and Halloween, of all times. He sounded desperate.

"Sheila, it's Josh."

"Stop right there Josh. I can tell you're loaded and that's not my problem."

"For God's sake, I think I'm dying."

"Then get to a hospital, or the detox, from the sound of you."

"That's it?"

"That's it."

"I was there for you once, remember?"

He hung up and I did have a pang of guilt. Helping him if he was sick was different from a real rescue.

On Monday when I got home from work, he was sitting on the floor outside the apartment. For a moment I thought he really was dead.

"Josh. Josh!" I started to shake him. His eyes were glazed. I opened the door to the apartment and literally dragged him inside, hauling on his jacket to make him slide across the floor. I called Walter.

"I'll be right there, just keep him warm."

Walter came from work somewhere in lower Manhattan, so it didn't take him as long as I feared. Between the two of us, we got him into a taxi and to Bellevue. Walter knew how to get him admitted and took care of all the details. I felt like I was along for the ride, until we went back to the apartment for a cup of coffee and I made sandwiches.

"They'll only keep him a few days. Sheila, then he'll need some place to stay." He gave me a long look.

"Oh, shit."

"Not forever. Just until he can get into rehab or back with Estella. Rehab would be better, but I'm not sure he'll do that. We've talked about it before. Anyway, if he'll go, I think I can get him in by Thanksgiving."

"I guess Estella tossed him out."

"That's what he told me. Said they had a fight."

"Okay, Walter. I give up."

After all, it would only be temporary and then Josh Cooper would be out of my life again. And he was right. There was a time in our lives we would have done anything for each other.

So, back he came to the apartment, but this time with only a plastic bag with a few toiletries. I bought him some underwear and pajamas, put them down before him and said "That's it. When you leav,e all this goes with you and we're back to no contact. Capiche?"

He nodded.

For the next ten days, once he stopped shaking and I got some food into him, he was his old self. While I was at work, he even spent the days at the desk in the corner writing on yellow pads. We found ourselves sitting on the couch after dinner laughing at the same thing and railing together at whatever report of the Nixon administration was on TV. Then he would tell me about the new book and it did sound exciting. He slept on the couch and I was in the bedroom.

On Wednesday before Thanksgiving, he told me he was leaving the next day.

"Did Walter talk you into going to rehab?"

"I think he's found a place for me." He didn't commit to going where Walter recommended. "Sheila, all I can say is thank you. I didn't know where else to go. The last time this happened Walter said he wouldn't help me again. I'm more grateful – to both of you – than I can say. I nearly died."

I felt unwanted tears, but could only stare at him.

He didn't say anything more, but he did reach over and kiss me. And I let it happen. We were back in the bedroom, "Just once for old time's sake, I told myself."

The next day he left. What I didn't know was that he went back to Estella's.

The most peculiar thing was he left sheets of paper he had been working on. Curious, I read them and they made no sense. What was he doing? I was used to Josh's fluid prose, poetic but clear. This was some sort of experiment, perhaps, but it wasn't quite the magical realism of Gabriel Garcia Marquez or the meta-fiction of Pynchon.

It was just incomprehensible. I started to throw them away and then tucked them under the blotter.

From then until New Years, I was franticly busy with end of the year solicitations, trying to milk the last pre-tax dime out of our donors. Finally, by mid-January, I knew I didn't feel well. It was time for my annual visit to Planned Parenthood for the usual Pap smear and breast exam, and I thought I was going through early menopause. I didn't let myself consider any other possibility.

Peggy, the nurse practitioner, examined me and said I looked fine, but she wanted to do a CBC to be sure I wasn't anemic. "From the looks of your cervix – do you think you might be pregnant?"

"Shit, I hope not," I burst out.

"Let's test the rabbit, just to be sure," she said. We'll let you know the middle of the week."

"Peggy, what do people do about abortions, now that it's legal in New York State?"

"Put your clothes on, and we'll talk about it."

In her tiny office, she looked at me across a desk with neat piles of papers and folders.

"About termination, we refer out to doctors we know are reliable and safe. We don't do them here, although I can see the time coming when we will have to. But I want you to think about this. It's a surprise, isn't it?"

"Yes."

"Ninety percent of the women who call or come in with questions about terminations have already made up their mind and nothing I say is going to change that. But with you, I want you to know we help with adoption, if you want to do that, and we refer for prenatal care. After delivery, we go right back to taking care of you for birth control. You've been off the pill quite a while, haven't you?" She was looking at my chart.

"My relationship ended and I haven't dated much since, so I quit taking them."

"Sheila, if you decide for termination, it's a decision you can't undo. Some women really grieve that loss. Others don't or are just relieved."

I hadn't talked about my experience to anyone for years, but told her the whole story: my relief, my guilt, my working through all of it, or ignoring it during my years with Josh.

"This is different, so be sure. If you still want to go through with it, call and we'll make and appointment for you."

CHAPTER TWENTY-THREE

Thursday, January 21, 1971

January snow had been intermittent all day. It was a little after four. I had left work at three to go to the Planned Parenthood Clinic where Peggy confirmed my pregnancy. I had every intention of having them make an appointment for an abortion, then left without having made one. I just left and walked home.

I walked through new snow that made the city look clean and untouched. A baby. My baby. I began to list to myself all the reasons why having a child was not a good idea. I thought about the adjustments I would have to make. Every time I thought about a baby, though, I found myself smiling. When Peggy confirmed the pregnancy, I was delighted. On the day before Valentine's Day, I broke the news to Aunt Grace during my Sunday visit. At first, Aunt Grace thought it was terrible news but before I knew it she had started making plans from layette to where this baby ought to go to school. We would have continued planning for college if she hadn't suddenly interrupted herself.

"Sheila, where's Josh?

"I don't know and I don't care."

"Well, I do."

"I don't want him to have anything to do with this baby. It was a fluke that I let him back in my life, and I don't think I want to make that mistake again."

"It's his child and his responsibility, and in addition I want to tell him what a bastard he is. You find out where he is, or I will. Either way, I'm going to have my say. He's treated you like dirt all these years and I sat back and let him because I thought you loved him and in his half-assed way he loved you. I was glad when he cleared out."

I think this was the first time I ever saw my dear aunt completely furious.

"Okay, Okay. You're probably right. He should know. I'll tell him, but Auntie Grace, if he's not in rehab, he'll be too strung out to know what I'm saying. I might as well save my breath."

I put off looking for Josh for the next ten days. Then one day after work, I called Estella's apartment. Her butler was cool when I asked for Josh.

"Whom may I say is calling?"

"Just tell him Sheila. He'll know who it is."

"Is there a message?"

"Excuse me, but is Mr. Cooper there?"

"I couldn't say, madam."

"Couldn't say, won't say, don't know?"

"I couldn't say, madam."

"Then, if you are not going to let me speak to him, if he is there, yes, there's a message. Tell him I'm pregnant. And, sir, if you don't know where he is, I'm sure an attorney with a subpoena can find him, if it's necessary."

I slammed the phone down in the guy's ear. I didn't bother to tell him, so far as I was concerned, the attorney would never be necessary. I just thought I might get some sort of answer from Josh or even from Estella or Mr. Whoever, the butler.

The response was swifter than I had expected. Twenty minutes later, there was a thunderous knock on the door. "Sheila! Open up. It's me."

The tone reminded me of "Open up, it's the police."

Here we go, I thought. Josh burst through the door when I got the locks undone and turned the handle.

"What the fuck's going on?"

"I guess you got the message, I'm pregnant."

"You did this on purpose."

"I beg your pardon?"

"What did you do? Get someone to knock you up and blame it on me?"

"Do you mean you don't remember we had sex, right here, the night before you left. That was day before Thanksgiving, and I seem to be about three months pregnant. That makes it yours."

"You can't be serious. Estella's furious."

"Somehow I don't think she has anything to do with this."

"You'll have to get rid of it."

"It's a baby, it's mine and I wouldn't think of it."

"You certainly didn't waste any time the last time."

"Josh, you son of a bitch, you know that was different. And this time it's yours too. You're a bastard to throw that in my face. You know how painful it was for me. Miriam was always right about you. You're a hateful, spoiled brat. And you and your books are the only thing in the world that means anything to you. That and your drugs, which have made a lousy writer out of you."

The sound of the crack of his hand across my face brought us both back to painful reality.

"Don't think I'll ever acknowledge this child. You get exactly nothing from me. I have my career to think about and you're right. My writing is the most important thing to me."

"And don't you come near me or this child again, ever. I don't want a hop-head father anyplace close to my baby. I consider it mine, not yours."

"I'll make you repeat that in court if you every try to involve me."

"Don't worry. Just get out of here. And take this pile of crap with you." I picked up the yellow papers and handed them to him.

He grabbed them and swung out of the door, slamming it behind him. I stood there in a moment of terrible sadness. Gone was the handsome, affable, even affectionate boy. Gone was the young man with talent enough to be recognized by the literary world. Gone was my love. Cocaine had turned Josh Cooper inside out like a dirty sock.

I watched from the second story window of my apartment, through blurring snow. I clearly remember the back of his head, the luxurious hair just beginning to be tinged with silver, the broad shoulders oscillating ever so slightly as he strode away clothed not only in a full length black cashmere coat, but in his own anger. I watched him swing his tall frame down 77th Street until he disappeared from sight after cutting across the street toward Lexington Avenue and the subway. If his stride announced that he was frustrated and furious, I was simply excruciatingly tired.

I turned on the television, lay down on the sofa, pulled an afghan over me and fell asleep. Either my drowsiness or the traffic noise or the muffling snow kept me from hearing the sirens.

The first thing the six o'clock local news told me when I awakened was that Josh Cooper was out of all of our lives for one last time. The camera crew had pictures of a gurney with a body covered by a bright blue blanket. I noticed scattered in the snow were yellow pages with writing on them.

CHAPTER TWENTY-FOUR

Dallas, Texas
Thursday, May 17, 1985

The cabbie was looking over the back seat. We were stopped, in front of Neiman-Marcus. I paid him and made my way into the store, gratified to see that, although remodeled, it still had that old-fashioned department store look I learned to love at Macy's when I was a child. I hoped the Zodiac room hadn't changed much. I anticipated the taste of the rich chicken broth they brought before the meal in white demitasse cups. Chicken soup. How healthful. Better tasting and better smelling than cigarettes. I gave Josh Cooper one last thought. If he hadn't gotten run over by that damned bus, he would probably have died from lung cancer by now—or an overdose of cocaine.

I was relieved to have business behind me and indulge in good food and girl talk.

The Zodiac room was as light and airy as I remembered. The other three were already seated at a table for four. "Great timing," E.A. said. "We just got here. Haven't even ordered drinks." The waitress appeared as the women finished settling their purses under their chairs and beside their feet.

"What can I get you to drink?"

"Vodka martini with a twist for me," E.A. was the first to respond. She looked around the table like a conductor checking to see if the orchestra was ready to perform.

"Just Perrier and lime for me," said Miriam.

I considered a moment. "I think I'll have a martini too, regular straight up with an olive."

"Good girl," said E.A.

"You may have to carry me out of here. I usually stick to wine," I said.

"Paula?" E.A. asked as her eyebrows rose.

"What do you have on tap?" Paula asked. The waitress ran down a list of domestic beer. "Bring me the Bud."

"You sure? All you want is beer?" asked E.A.

"It's the beer I really miss. American beer." The waitress had already moved away from the table. "You know we can really get anything we want in Calcutta; it's just good, fresh, American beer on tap, or even domestically bottled, that I miss."

During the time drinks were served and food ordered, followed by the wonderful demitasse of rich, aromatic chicken broth, Paula answered a round of questions about India, her work, her friends there and her impressions of the country. At one point, she said something about her house and said our house.

E.A. was quick to interrupt. "Who's the 'our' in our house?"

Paula seemed surprised at her own slip of the tongue and E.A.'s rapid notice of it. "Parvati, my roommate."

"I thought you said you owned your house?'

"I do. But I have a roommate." Paula said. There was an edge of irritation in her voice at E.A.'s inquisition.

"Parvati," I said. "Is she as beautiful as I always imagined Parvati to be in the Indian myths?" I smiled at Paula.

Paula smiled too, and I thought I saw a look of possessiveness on her face. "She's a pretty girl," she temporized. "With two children."

All of us pounced on that revelation and I realized that regardless of having to endure Elise's teenage rebellion, my life would be bereft without her. Unconsciously, I had pitied Paula, not her lifestyle or her love, but her lack of motherhood; and here she was mothering two children.

Paula filled us in on Ajay, who was twelve, and Sita, a lively ten-year-old. Their mother was Hindu and their father Muslim. He died young and Parvati became afraid of his family since she was something of an alien and a widow in their midst. She had fled to the sanctuary of the hospital.

"Okay," said E.A. "We haven't done the picture bit. You've all seen my chick in the flesh. Let's get out the photographs, y'all."

We dutifully rummaged in our purses, Miriam coming up with a picture from last Thanksgiving of her three and Paula pulling out snapshots of the two in her house. I found Elise's school picture rather formal, but showing off her beautiful face with its striking blue eyes. Paula took it and murmured approvingly as I looked at Miriam's three boys. The older two resembled their father but the wayward Andy was handsome, taller that the others and had his mother's good looks. As I looked at Paula's two darkly pretty children, I heard Miriam gasp. She was holding Elise's picture and staring at me with her mouth agape, a look of total surprise on her face.

She closed her mouth and said, "Excuse me. I've got to go to the ladies room."

I took my purse and followed her into the lounge. She was sitting on a tufted.

stool staring at her reflection in the mirror over a long counter provided for women to freshen their makeup. I could see tears at the corner of her eyes.

"My God, Sheila. It's Deborah."

"Deborah who?"

"Deborah Cooper. Didn't Josh ever tell you he had a sister?"

"No." I went cold and sat down on the other stool.

The tears began to fall in earnest now and her breath caught in a sob. "She was my best friend. She died of leukemia when we were fourteen."

CHAPTER TWENTY-FIVE

Miriam and I ignored the curious glances of our two friends when we returned to the table. Although the food we ordered was excellent, the conversation was stilted, laced with unspoken questions. The Caesar salad I ordered tasted like cardboard. I decided to indulge in some crème caramel to see if I could stimulate my palate. It tasted flat.

When the four of us reached the sanctuary of our suite, we kicked off our shoes and flopped on the beds and couch in Miriam's and Paula's room.

"So what's going on?" E.A. was the first to speak.

"Hang on a minute," Miriam said. She reached for the phone, ordered two bottles of Merlot and four glasses. I preferred white wine, but at the moment the thought of any alcohol sounded good. I would hazard a headache, which was better than the pain of memory that had torn at me since my conversation with Miriam.

She flipped on the television, and we watched some mindless game show until the waiter brought the wine. No one spoke, as though we had made a secret pact.

After Miriam uncorked the first bottle, she filled the glasses and passed them around. The wine had a sharp, fruity odor, but the taste was decidedly smooth. I let the liquid run down my throat, barely soothing the turmoil in my stomach, but doing marginal good. I both dreaded and looked forward to telling the story they were all waiting to hear, but Miriam, assuming the role of moderator, had other ideas.

"You first, E.A. It's time you talked about Harold."

"Oh shit." E.A. ran a hand through her hair and took a deep breath.

I reached over and gave her a loose hug. I looked E.A. straight in the face and said, "OK, old girl. Let's have it."

Miriam sat down next to her on the other side. E.A. took her hands like a drowning woman, and broke into a flood of tears, making drowning a real possibility. Finally, E.A.'s crying turned to wracking hiccups, her heavy bosom jerking with each spasm. She pulled her hands away and reached for the small package of tissue on the night table. Her cheeks were streaked with mascara.

Miriam put her hand on her friend's shoulders. E.A. looked down as though it would be easier to tell the whole humiliating story without looking directly into anyone's face.

"We adopted Harold in 1960, three years before we adopted Edwina. He was a terror as a kid, but we didn't think a thing about it. You know, the 'boys will be boys' thing. Or at least Jim Ed didn't. I've got to say it drove me crazy at times, especially in the late afternoons when I had put up with him all day. I know that's an awful thing to say about your child."

"Every mother gets worn down by four in the afternoon, E.A.," Miriam said.

"I know, but anyway, we really did think he was a fairly normal kid until he got into grade school. Then he started getting into fights, he didn't seem to have many friends, and I did think his father was awfully hard on him. First kid, you know, first son. Harold had to do it all just so, to please Jim Ed. My dad adored him, namesake and all, and I thought spoiled him." E.A. hesitated.

"Go on," Paula encouraged.

E.A. digressed, "God, I miss my Dad. He died about four years ago. At least he never saw Harold arrested and sent to prison."

"And your mom?" I asked.

"Oh, wouldn't you know, she's still alive and kicking—mostly me. It's all my fault."

"Not so," Miriam encouraged, and added with emphasis as she rubbed E.A.'s back, "Never was."

E.A. shrugged. "Anyway, long story short, Harold was really okay, I think, until he got to seventh grade. Then he just went nuts. In fights, stealing things; from me, money mostly; from his dad, some tools and stuff. Even from his grandfather. We knew it, but never told Dad. Finally, the police picked him up. We got a good lawyer and got him off on a misdemeanor. He straightened up for a while. But then he left home at eighteen. He had no desire to go to college. He never was much of a student, but did like fooling with the horses on the ranch. Hated the cattle. Anyway, he went to Houston and worked construction for awhile, then moved to San Antonio. They arrested him there last October and he was sent to Palestine. There's a minimum security facility there."

"Drug charges," Paula said.

"Yep."

"Did he refuse any treatment or rehab?"

"He wouldn't hear of it, and neither would Jim Ed. And he didn't want anybody to know. Especially Manny and Miriam. He was so embarrassed."

"Honey, we love you both. You could have talked to us about anything."

"Jim Ed wouldn't hear of it. He made me promise. Edwina's been our salvation. And I do talk to her, too. She keeps telling me there's not a damn thing

I can do." The tears started again and E.A. jabbed at her eyes with the tissue.

"So what was the telephone conversation last night?" Miriam asked.

"Oh, Lordy."

"Come on, E.A., what's going on?"

"He escaped last week. They still haven't caught him. Wouldn't you know the damn kid would pull a stunt like this right before his sister has her big graduation do? He always was jealous of her."

"Is that what the call was about? You were talking to Jim Ed?"

"Yep. Nothing." She sighed. The tears started again. "Damn, Miriam, if they just don't shoot him." She began to sob in earnest again.

Miriam tightened her grip on E.A.'s shoulders and gave her a kiss on the wet cheek.

"How terrifying," she said.

"Even if he is such a bastard. He's my baby, for God's sake."

"I guess babies grow up, E.A. and just have to take their own consequences. There's not much you can do about it," Paula said.

"I know. I just feel so guilty."

"Why? What did you ever do but try your very best."

"I should have let Jim Ed discipline him more, and then there's the fact that he's adopted."

"Now, honestly, E.A., do you think beating the child any more would have made a difference?"

"Probably not."

"And look at it from his view. You and Jim Ed took that child in and made him a part of your home. It was probably the best moment of his life," said Miriam.

"I know. I just can't help thinking if he had been really ours, not somebody else's, none of this would have happened. If only my plumbing had worked."

"Oh," I said, sounding rather distant to my own ears. "I don't know. They all seem to come with their own set of instructions. Elise drives me nuts. She's not like anyone I know in the family. She's an iceberg, at least to me. I can't even get a decent conversation out of her."

"How old is she now? Fourteen?"

I looked at Miriam. Yes, Elise was just the age Deborah had been when she died.

"All girls are nuts at that age. Crazy hormones or something. She'll come around," E.A. said.

"Was Edwina like that?"

"Actually, she wasn't. She had another way of ignoring us. She was always busy. Always away from home. She was a cheerleader; she was on the girl's basketball team. She was always at some club or class meeting."

Miriam turned to me and I was terrified. "So, Sheila, tell us about Elise."

I got up and refilled my glass, silently offering more to the others. E.A and Paula held out their glasses. Miriam shook her head.

I sat down again. E.A. had begun at the beginning and so would I.

"After I graduated and was working, Josh moved to New York. We had mutual friends and sort of ran into each other. We started dating casually and then moved in together for ten long years, from '54 to '64. It seems incredible now. Anyway, he was still working sporadically on his Ph.D. and writing. I had a job with a small nonprofit to keep food on the table and he worked part-time at Walden Books. We didn't have a car, didn't need one." That was a stupid detail, I thought. "He finally graduated, taught one class, taking the Long Island Railroad and the bus to Hofstra, and started in earnest on the book. We had a nickname for it. George."

Paula looked curious.

"He was superstitious about using its title before it was published. Most of that time, we had a blast. It was hippiedom in the Village. He grew a beard and I didn't wear makeup and pulled my hair back in a ponytail. Beads and weed."

I took a long sip of wine and wished I hadn't quit smoking. "And then he met Estella. Rich Estella. Doyenne of the literati. And bound and determined to have Josh. He would sneak off to see her for a while, but it was really the cocaine he couldn't resist. Or so I told myself."

Miriam gave a little groan and reached for her wine glass.

"He moved out; I got a better job and didn't see him for three years. Finally, he came back one day, saying he was going nuts not being able to finish the book. Like an idiot, I took him back while he wrote. He wrote night and day and did manage to get the first draft done. Then he disappeared again for five years."

"And you're Nora in the book, aren't you?" said Paula, "I always thought so."

Lord, was it that obvious? "Characters are some of a lot of people. Anyway, he went straight back to Estella again."

"Mother always referred to her as Mrs. Gotrocks. Al Cooper has a more unflattering name for her," Miriam said.

"Most of the rest of it you know. The book was a runaway success and he moved in with Estella. I cried a lot. Swore a lot and went back to work. One night he came by, stoned and crying. I was really afraid he was going to die on my doorstep. His friend Walter and I managed to get him to detox and Walter talked me into letting him come back to the apartment for a few days before going to rehab. And I got pregnant. When I was three months along, I called him and told him. I had talked to Aunt Grace and thought I should. I guess maybe I even hoped he would decide to come back, clean up his act and settle down to writing. No such luck."

I hadn't cried about this since the day he died, but now I couldn't go on. Paula came over and sat on the arm of the couch and put her arms around me the way Miriam had held E.A.

"That was the last thing he wanted, and he didn't want some kid, especially some bastard kid messing up his image. It seems he had told Estella and she was furious. He demanded I get an abortion. I had done it once; I could do it again. It was then I realized how much I wanted this baby and what the drugs had done to Josh Cooper.

I finally gave way completely to the tears and Miriam went to the bathroom, dampened a washcloth and brought it to me.

"Anyway, I refused and he stormed out of the apartment. I saw him walk down the street and turn the corner and then heard on the evening news he had been run over by a New York City Transit bus."

We were all quiet for a while. The tears were gone. The fear was gone and only deep remnants of the grief remained.

"My aunt saw me through the pregnancy and doted on Elise. One day I had her on the Promenade in Brooklyn Heights in her stroller. I was reading and this nice looking man came up to me in shorts and running shoes. It was love at first sight for him, but not with me. With Elise." I smiled in spite of myself, remembering Hugh and how completely he ignored me while talking to a two-year-old. "We married and he adopted Elise."

"Sheila, is your uncle still living?" asked Paula.

"No, he died horribly of cancer my sophomore year. It was all the punishment I could wish on the old guy. Then Aunt Grace died two years ago, so there are just the three of us."

"Sheila, you've got to do something," Miriam said.

"What?"

"You've got to tell the Coopers. Al was so devastated that he put away all Deborah's pictures when she died. He won't let anyone talk about her. I think Adele is still grieving over both the children and she has practically adopted my kids as surrogate grandchildren. She has to know. You've just got to do this for her."

I had a moment of real chagrin. In all the years, I had never thought of the Coopers. How selfish of me. Perhaps my upbringing had left me with some shame that single mothers in the eighties didn't seem to feel.

I got up to reach for the phone, changed my reservations.

Later that evening, Jim Ed called E.A. to say Harold had been captured without incident, but his stay in prison would be lengthened.

I had to call home and hoped I would get Hugh. Elise answered. "Hi, sweet."

"Hi, Mom." She sounded subdued. "Are you having a good time?"

"Yes. Are you guys doing okay?"

"Yes."

"Is Dad home?"

"Yes, but can I talk to you first?"

"Sure,"

"Mom, I'm sorry I was such a jerk to you."

"Apology accepted. I was a jerk, too."

"Mom?"

"Yes?"

"Can I ask you a question?"

"Anything."

She took a long time responding. "Did you love my father? Not Dad, but my ... first father?" I had forgotten that romance was the dominant thing in every girl that age. And she had hesitated over the "biological" or "real" decision and come up with her own solution.

"Very, very much, my dear. I'll be home day after tomorrow and I promise to tell you all about it."

"Love ya'," and she turned away to call Hugh to the phone. I explained about not returning until Monday and asked him to call my office and tell them I wouldn't be in. After all, I had gotten the Behneke donation and I deserved a day off. I also asked him to be sure Elise would be home right after school on Monday.

On Sunday, I drove to Fort Worth with Miriam. We called on the Coopers and I went over the whole thing. When Alfred Cooper saw Elise's picture, he got up without a word, went to the library and took a portrait from the bottom drawer of the desk. He brought it back to the living room and put it on the piano. Miriam was right. Elise looked just like her aunt.

"We always thought he should have married you," he said, and my eyes filled with tears of gratitude.

Adele was quieter, staring out the window, but I thought that haunted look had left her eyes.

"Sheila. Would it be all right with you if I talk to my granddaughter, if she wants to talk on the phone?"

"Talking on the phone is her greatest pleasure. I'm sure she would love to talk to you."

"Could we make it soon?"

"What about late tomorrow afternoon?"

"Now, only if she wants to. I insist."

I agreed

"And Miriam, Andy's in New York. They should meet."

"Oh my God, Sheila, she's matchmaking already. And Aunt Adele, I wouldn't wish Andy on anyone's daughter, especially a friend."

"He's a wonderful boy."

"He's a mess and way too old for her."

"Fourteen and twenty-two, of course. Twenty and twenty-eight? Perfect."

Alfred and Miriam got up in tandem putting an end to this conversation. I kissed Adele on the cheek. "Tomorrow," I said.

The plane ride home was subdued, but I was immeasurably glad to get out of the taxi and have the door of my own apartment close behind me. Hugh was waiting in the door of his study.

When Elise came in at four-thirty, her father asked her to put her books away and come into the kitchen. I had made a pot of tea, and over the distinctive smell of hot Earl Grey I asked her if she was ready to know about her father.

"Yes," she said. "I've always wondered about my real parents."

"The bad news is I am your real mother. The good news is your birth father won the Pulitzer Prize." Then I told her the whole story or at least the parts appropriate to a teenager.

She was pensive for a while. "So am I Jewish?"

"Not technically," Hugh said. "Jews – except Reform Jews – consider you Jewish if your mother is. But you know, sweetie, you could always make that choice."

She was quiet a moment. "And I have a grandmother and a grandfather?"

I nodded. "In Fort Worth, Texas."

"Tiffany calls her grandmother Bubbe. I think that's a cute name." She drew circles in a spilled bit of sugar on the table. "Could I talk to her? My grandmother?"

"I suspect she's waiting by the phone," I said.

We got up from the table and made our way down the narrow hall to her bedroom. I took the Princess phone she spent so much time on and dialed the number I knew from long ago. The phone connected and rang. I handed it to her.

As I left the room I heard her say, "Hello? Mrs. Cooper? Bubbe? Uh … I'm Elise."

This was one conversation neither parent was going to interrupt. I walked down to Hugh's study where he was sitting on the sofa. He had brought our teacups to the study, freshly filled and mine laced with milk and sugar. He had his feet up on the coffee table, a road atlas open on his thighs. I sat down beside him and pressed against his body as he put his arm around my shoulders.

"What are you doing with the atlas?"

"Planning a trip."

"Where are we going?"

"I've always wanted to see the Old South and Texas. Elise will be out of school in a couple of weeks and you have vacation time coming. It's about time Elise met her grandparents and I got to meet the Kilgore Rangerette in the flesh."

I chuckled, drinking in the serenity of the quiet room along with the sweet taste of the tea. I sighed involuntarily. This would be a different trip to Texas, one unburdened of everything but curiosity, and I realized that for the first time in thirty-four years, I had no secrets to pack along with the clothes.

The End

ABOUT THE AUTHOR

Photo by Drake Sorey

Janet Taliaferro lives in Virginia but has been a summer resident of Wisconsin since she was eight years old. She is a graduate of Southern Methodist University and holds a Master's Degree in Creative Studies from the University of Central Oklahoma, where she received the Geoffrey Bocca Memorial Award for graduate writing. She is a member of Washington Independent Writers and Wisconsin Fellowship of Poets.

Her novel, A Sky for Arcadia, was a finalist in the 2002 Oklahoma Center for the Book Award. She has published short stories and poems in The Northern Virginia Review, New Plaines Review, Deep Fork Anthology, Dream Quarterly International, Tight Fearless Books' "Touching," and electronically on blogs by Robin Chapman and Atticus Books.

Also by Janet Taliaferro:
Wakonta Calendar
Breaking the Surface Poems: 2007–2009
CityScapes
A Sky for Arcadia

Visit her web site at janetmtaliaferro.com

www.ingramcontent.com/pod-product-compliance
Lightning Source LLC
Chambersburg PA
CBHW051822170626
46807CB00003B/988